DO YOU HEAR WHAT I HEAR?

CLAIRE HAMILTON

This is a work of fiction. Names, characters, places, incidents, and plays are all products of the author's imagination or are used fictitiously. Any resemblance to actual persons, living or dead, business establishments, events, dramatic productions, or locales, is entirely fictitious or coincidental.

Do You Hear What I Hear?: A Paranormal Love Story

COPYRIGHT © 2021 by Claire Hamilton

All rights reserved. No part of this book may be used or reproduced in any means whatsoever without the written permission of the author or Fleur de Lys Books, LLC, except for brief quotations embedded in reviews or critical articles.

Contact information: ClaireHamiltonUSA@gmail.com

Publishing history:

First edition, 2021

Print ISBN: 978-0-578-31881-3

Digital ISBN: B09HJGXCMJ

Published in the United States of America

All quotations from F. Scott Fitzgerald (*The Beautiful and the Damned*, first published March 1922, *The Great Gatsby*, first published April 10, 1925, and "The Sensible Thing" first published July 15, 1924) are in the public domain.

All quotations from "The Skye Boat Song" as written by Robert Louis Stevenson, first published in 1892, are in the public domain.

Quotation from *'Twas the Night before Christmas: A Visit from St. Nicholas* by Clement C. Moore, first published December 23, 1823, is in the public domain.

Quotation from *A Christmas Carol. In Prose. Being a Ghost Story of Christmas* by Charles Dickens, first published December 19, 1843, is in the public domain.

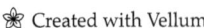 Created with Vellum

To my dearest husband, Jim:

"Two souls are sometimes created together and—and in love before they're born."

~F. Scott Fitzgerald.

CONTENTS

Prologue	1
1. Where Is Home?	3
2. Listen to Your Heart	12
3. A Matter of Trust	23
4. Ties that Bind	39
5. Head & Heart	48
6. How Dare You?	61
7. Mysterious Ways	75
8. Can't Help Falling in Love	85
9. I'm Not Famous	100
10. Like Real People Do	116
11. Arsonist's Lullaby	125
12. Ordinaryish People	139
13. Zero Tolerance	152
14. Mad about You	169
15. The Skye Boat Song	187
16. Under Pressure	197
17. Glorious	205
Epilogue	216
Acknowledgments	225
Volume	227

PROLOGUE

There are still truths only relayed to modern ears in whispers, forced to masquerade as myths.

Magic.

Atlantis.

Soul mates.

Hidden within these truths are often secrets: abilities, once common, that are now dismissed as impossible...talents appearing as gifts on the surface, but are often curses as well: the ability to hear the thoughts of others. Telepathic speech not bounded or limited by distance. The ability to touch objects, or people, and know of events that swirled about them...

Although these facts are not public knowledge, they are real. Scientists and skeptics may scoff at their leisure. It matters not. Those who know, know what has not been lost. We do not feel any obligation to history, or to prove our claims. We simply wish to live in peace, enjoying the blessings we have even as we seek a surcease of our pains.

While there are those who sneer, it matters little to those who labor under these burdens, for burdens they often are. Romantic fools blather over what they believe soul mates are, but with no concept of the price the bond exacts. No one sees the heavy shadows accompanying the abilities and legacies that frequently skip generations, in turn preventing proper tutelage, to explain what is carried within infinitely tiny DNA twists and turns...

Therefore, I am requested—nay, firmly instructed—by my mate, and others like ourselves, to set the following down, so our offspring may have a record of what happened.

They must know. Knowledge should never be lost.

1

WHERE IS HOME?

"On behalf of all the flight crew on Flight 211, we would like to welcome you to JFK Airport, New York City…"

Henry Rhys had already tuned the flight attendant's speech out, having heard so many he could deliver one half-asleep. In multiple languages. The flight from London's Heathrow airport to New York was not onerous, but he was already restless, eager to stretch his long legs. Being two inches over six feet meant he was never comfortable in any airplane for long, no matter how lush the onboard accommodations.

The privilege of having seats in the first class cabin meant he had every comfort and advantage at his fingertips, which included priority deplaning and luggage off-loading. His profession and celebrity status granted him additional perks: he was met as soon as he stepped off the jetway, avoiding the dreaded Immigration/Passport Control queue. Instead, he was escorted to a private area, answered a friendly, swift set of questions, and was sent on his way. Beside him was his friend, and long-suffering public relations manager, Greg Knight.

"Bet you can't wait to get home, eh?" Greg's grin was playful, knowing from long experience how antsy Henry could get after a flight.

"Wherever it is this time," Henry replied, his tone morose even as he had his public face nailed on, his expression pleasant. "Another hotel suite for months, with no personal effects. But I suppose I can't complain."

Greg stifled a sigh. "Here we go," he thought, "one of those moods, and we just landed…?" Aloud he cajoled his friend and client, "If you like, you can go straight to the car, and I'll arrange for our bags to be sent…"

"No, don't be absurd. I'm not so up myself I cannot collect my own bags," Henry answered, his smile automatic as the flashes began, his eyes remote.

The men were loosely flanked by security to keep paparazzi a decent distance away from them. This was necessary as Henry's star continued its dizzying ascent into the heavens. Although Henry was in New York for his first tour on Broadway, he cut an extremely recognizable figure as not just a star on stage, but also blockbuster films, and a model splashed across magazines and billboards occasionally if he could not avoid it. Only Greg and his agent, Beatrice Fowler, knew how violently Henry fought those contracts, saying he always felt as though he had been turned into a commodity himself by the end of those shoots. It took all of Greg's considerable diplomacy to not only convince Henry the endorsements would enhance his image, but be relaxed enough not to ruin it. Henry enjoyed the reputation of being a consummate gentleman. Greg worked hard to make sure his client continued to hold onto it.

In the early years of his career, Henry went through his days with smiles that were contagious, giving all around him the right words at the perfect time. He instinctively knew how to lift the mood of the most tense sets, gently lifting sagging spirits with his inimitable baritone voice that encouraged or consoled as needed.

But in their last few trips around the sun, Henry was subjected to increasingly sad and bitter moments that seemed to be coming closer and closer together. He would pace, endlessly lost in thought, his expression never one of looking forward to the next project, or even the next day with any real happiness or contentment. His eyes would constantly dart from one area to another, as though they were hoping to alight upon something…or someone…but never doing so.

And hopes delayed…hopes denied…were draining the spirit from his soul.

As Henry made his way to baggage claim, his eyes rested on another traveler making her way past the carousels from the opposite direction, pulling her luggage behind her. She was just like any other passenger, but for some reason, she tugged at Henry's attention.

Perhaps she reminded him of his sisters for a moment. Like them, she had rich auburn hair, a thick curly mass she had pulled back as it spilled carelessly past her shoulders. Henry ran his fingers through his own dark hair as he watched her pass through the corner of his blue eyes. Unlike many around her sporting discreet earbuds, she had a giant pair of headphones covering each ear. Evidently she was enjoying her music, because she had a spring in her step that was almost a dance, a skip as she headed for the doors leading out where cabs were in wait for their next fare. A bright smile adorned her face as her head kept time with a beat Henry could not hear…her joie de vivre coaxed a grin to his face.

"Why the smile?" Greg tipped his head to one side, moving his lips carefully. One never knew when a reporter lay in wait.

"That woman…I mean…those headphones, reminded me of the hairstyle Princess Leia wore. The pastries on each side of her head…? Like cinnamon rolls. Did I ever tell you about the time I met Carrie Fisher?"

"Only a million times. Give or take."

Not hearing Greg's answer, Henry continued, watching as their bags were brought to them. "I'll never forget it. What an amazing woman she was…and her dog, what a wonderful pair…Greg…"

"Henry, you know why you don't have a dog." Greg sought to forestall a familiar argument.

"Why?" Henry's voice was perilously close to a whine. "Other people travel with their dogs all the time…"

"We've been over this, Henry. The issue isn't travel as much as it is you don't have the time to take care of the poor beast," Greg continued, patience personified. "You would need to train the dog. Feed it. Walk it. Spend time with it, bond with it…Henry, there are days you are barely home long enough to shower, fall into bed, and do it all over again. It wouldn't be fair, you know this…Things tend to come your way fairly easily, but you would have a responsibility to your pet. It's a living creature, not simply a possession to amuse yourself with when the mood strikes you."

Henry was crestfallen. "I know…but sometimes…" He trailed off as Greg continued to shepherd him towards the vehicle waiting for them outside. The heat of late August was a shock after the air conditioned terminal.

They walked out just in time to witness the woman of the headphones let out a surprised cry of pure, unmitigated joy further down the sidewalk. She was leaping into the arms of a laughing, dark-skinned man who caught her up in his arms, pulling her up until her legs were wrapped around his waist. They could hear both of them, the man chortling as he spun her in a circle and she cried out in glee, "Peter…! Oh Peter, you darling!"

Henry's eyes were soft, and so sad as he watched the pair

get into a cab. He wondered when was the last time he had felt so much happiness about…anything, really.

Greg sighed as their driver loaded their luggage into an SUV. Henry was quick to jump into the backseat with privacy tinted windows before anyone recognized him.

It was going to be a long trip to their lodgings.

AUBREY STAFFORD TURNED to Peter Rivera with shining eyes. "Peter, you never said you were going to meet me, you tricky tree trunk …! What if my flight was delayed, what if…"

Peter guffawed. "Oh, please, give me some credit. I was tracking your sleigh, Elf. And I haven't seen you since Santa was skinny…I didn't want to wait another moment. How many places have you been this time? Five? Ten? How many presents did you bring me? Presents…presents..!" he chanted, pretending to grab her backpack, making her laugh. "If there are no tacky souvenirs, I am tossing you from the cab right this second…"

The driver caught her eye in the rear view mirror. "Hey lady, do I need to slow down so you can tuck and roll?"

Aubrey was still giggling. "A lot of help you are! No, I'm safe, he has his ticky-tacky souvenirs…"

Peter wrapped a long arm around Aubrey, teeth gleaming in his broad smile, complete with one gold-capped tooth on the side, giving him a piratical look of which he was immensely proud. "Aw, honey, I'd let you slide. This once… Missed you too much. You were gone six whole weeks! That's just too long. Don't ever be gone that long again…"

The cabbie whistled. "Six weeks? What do you do for a living?"

Peter crowed, "You're lookin' at the best travel writer since Kerouac, my good man…any time you get a travel book, chances are Elf wrote a piece in it. Where were you this time?"

Aubrey shoved Peter even as he tucked her protectively into his side. "Thailand, Cambodia, Vietnam, Singapore, Indonesia, and the Philippines."

"Oh, is that all?" Peter sniffed, pretending to be bored.

"Six countries in six weeks, I'm exhausted," she protested. "I was everywhere, wrote my fingers off, photos everywhere, reviewed more places I care to think about…the worst part is, after awhile I don't think I remember any of it. It's so much at once…I see it, write about it, and move on to the next destination. It isn't restful or a vacation, you know."

"Cry me a river," the cabbie grunted. "Anything better than being stuck in this car day in and day out…"

Aubrey's eyes became sympathetic. Reaching into her backpack, she retrieved a small plastic bag. "I hear you. Take this." She dropped it over the seat.

"Aw, no, lady, I didn't mean…"

"Don't fight her," Peter advised, a glint in his eyes. "The red hair on this woman is no lie. Stubborn? You have no idea…"

The driver opened the bag at the next light, and found a soft Merlion keychain. "Merlions are the official mascot of Singapore," Aubrey explained cheerfully, and chattered about her visit there for the rest of the ride to her building.

"But…"

"Enjoy it, with my best wishes. It's just a little thing…I always have things like this in my bag for crying kids. That one glows if you squeeze it. It's like a stress ball, and if anyone could use a stress reliever, it's a New York City cabbie! Stay safe," she insisted, paying the fare as well giving him a healthy tip. Peter scowled at her, but she waved him off, muttering about a business expense. With a smile and a wave, the man drove away, already squeezing the souvenir in his hand.

"That was a kind thing you did," Peter hugged his friend in the lift that had not gotten any faster in her absence.

Do You Hear What I Hear?

She shrugged, self-conscious. "I always have little trinkets, you know that...in case there are fussy babies. Don't worry, I have another one for you, friendo."

"I don't doubt it...you're the best ever, sister-from-another-mister..."

"Brother-from-another-mother," she returned, her affection sincere. Soon after she opened her door, her jaw and shoulders dropped as she realized Peter had more than made good his promise from when she left: not only had he aired out her corner loft, but also stocked her refrigerator and pantry with staples, knowing she would be exhausted from the transit from Southeast Asia to New York.

"Oh, Peter..." Tears thickened her throat.

"I told you, I missed you...e-mails and video calls are fine and good, but not enough," he replied, gruff and uncomfortable. "My bitch-from-another-ditch..."

Aubrey beat him with a sofa pillow. "You want your presents, or not...?"

Peter had met Aubrey when she first moved to New York. They both worked for Voyager Publications, Aubrey as a writer and Peter in the graphics division. Soon Peter decided he wanted a another direction in his life, but the two remained close, especially when Peter learned how alone Aubrey was: no brothers or sisters, her father died when she was a child, and her mother two years ago. Peter's father was highly critical of what he deemed his son's "deviant lifestyle" and relations were extremely strained; Peter's mother was not one to speak against her husband. While his siblings were completely accepting of his open homosexuality, they were spread across the country, from Los Angeles to New Orleans to Miami.

The two became the most unlikely family imaginable, the petite redhead Peter mockingly called "demented elf", "diet Sprite" and "Santa's workshop runaway" among other things, and the massive man of color Aubrey referred to as a "talking redwood", "walking tree trunk" and one night, "Rainbow Ent" which Peter made her swear under threat of burning all of her Tolkien books and *Lord of the Rings* (extended edition, no less) DVDs to never call him again.

"Then. Stop. Picking. Me. Up."

"Okay...redheaded Hobbit..."

After Peter had left for the night, sternly reminding his best friend to get some rest, Aubrey sat in the darkness along the windows of her loft to better see the lights of the city reflected in the river below her. She was exhausted, to the core of her aching and unsettled soul.

She was glad to be home. Traveling was exhilarating and she adored many aspects of it, but the pace set was brutal. At heart, she was an explorer. A voyager. But all explorers, all voyagers needed a home port, didn't they?

But now she was here, the bottoms of her feet felt tight. Itchy.

She chuckled as she recognized the sensation emanated from her psyche, and wasn't yet another traveler's "souvenir" requiring a trip to the pharmacy. The humor faded when she realized the joke was still on her.

Aubrey sank every penny she had into this apartment, using the small life insurance policy she had inherited when her mother passed, the sale of the tiny property she grew up on, as well as royalties Peter was unaware of, and mortgaged herself to the hilt. It was small, but boasted floor to ceiling windows. For reasons she was never able to understand, the only thing that seemed to bring her peace at times like these was being close to water. Landlocked, she became agitated, unable to relax or rest. Sleep would become sporadic; after awhile she could barely sit still. Aubrey learned to accept this as one of the many quirks in her makeup. Her tiny home was worth every cent, for all she was seldom in it.

She wanted...needed...to have a port to return to where she could drop anchor. A safe harbor. Yet now she was here,

Do You Hear What I Hear?

she was already beginning to wonder about her next voyage out into the unknown.

Was this, then, truly her home?

Disconsolate with that thought, she sighed, and went to bed.

2

LISTEN TO YOUR HEART

Henry poked at his scallops nestled on a bed of risotto, listless. All around him, Beatrice, Greg, and three others animatedly discussed projects for him to become involved with once the curtain came down on *Gatsby*, his current show. He had been so enthusiastic about the opportunity to star in this adaptation of F. Scott Fitzgerald's *The Great Gatsby*, and had pounced upon it when he heard about the production the previous year. He didn't feel anything remotely close to that level of excitement now.

"'Gatsby believed in the green light, the orgastic future that year by year recedes before us...but that's no matter—tomorrow, we will run faster, stretch out our arms farther...'" he murmured, brooding over how he had felt such a close connection to Jay Gatsby, a man who remade himself, longing constantly for the woman he could not have, searching for an elusive contentment, and never finding either. Forever reaching back into the past to recreate it in the present, and drag it into the future…

Henry could not see his future, at present.

"What's that, Henry?" Greg prompted. He felt he'd been

swimming upstream for months, coordinating with Christine Abbot, Henry's personal assistant, ensuring Henry got from meetings to interviews, to rehearsals, to photo shoots, all on time, always bearing his famed trademark smile. Henry's moods were becoming as unpredictable as the weather. At times he was still the man Greg began working with over a decade ago, a walking ray of sunshine and enthusiasm, in love with his craft, awed he had made it as far as Broadway, which was a dream come true.

Greg knew he could rely on Henry's rockbed dedication to giving his best work on a daily basis. He knew—and used—everyone's name. No one was beneath his notice; he was gentle and courteous with everyone. His oft-repeated line of, "We are a company," showed his commitment to working together as a unit.

And yet…

Michael Thomas, the actor portraying Nick Carraway, had pulled Greg aside recently to inquire, lines of worry scoring his forehead, "Is everything all right with Henry?"

"What do you mean, Michael?" Greg deflected with a genial smile, even as his heart sunk. He had arrived at the theatre to collect his friend and all but frogmarch him to another high profile event. Henry was dreading this one in particular, hence the need for Greg's presence. Otherwise, Henry might escape at the first possible opportunity.

"Henry's great, don't misunderstand me…no one works harder, did you know he was the first off-book?" Michael, a Broadway veteran, was clearly impressed. "No matter what technical issues we have to endure, or what goes wrong, he handles it like a pro. Nothing seems to rattle him…but sometimes he goes to a place that seems…bleak," Michael confessed. "I went into his dressing room today, and I found him looking out the window, almost in tears. He damned near took my head off, as he should have, the door was closed for a reason. But the look on his face, Greg…"

Greg maintained a neutral expression as he listened. "Did he give an explanation?"

"He brushed it off as being in character, thinking about Jay and how he was fixated on that damned green light...but Gatsby was never that low. He wouldn't allow it, he was forever searching and scheming. He couldn't comprehend failure. When I challenged Henry with that, he shook his head, whispering, 'We can't know what Gatsby was thinking in the early hours of the morning, staring at that fucking light, Michael...it must have felt as though he was on the edge of an abyss.' Then he apologized for being so rude when I barged in, and was himself again. But damn, Greg, if you could have seen him...It was as though his dog had died right after he'd learned there was no Santa Claus."

Greg lifted a shoulder with a smile. "There's no Santa Claus...?! Besides, he doesn't have a dog."

Michael's face hardened. "You're supposed to be his friend, Greg. I thought you'd take this more seriously. I see I was mistaken." He turned to leave, but Greg stopped him.

"I apologize, Michael. I didn't mean to offend you. All I can offer is I've seen Henry mine deeply into characters through the years, deeper than I will ever understand. He climbs back out, without fail. I am with him almost every day, and yes, there are moments he visits dark places where he seems lost, but I promise you, he invariably comes back out in one piece."

Michael looked at Greg carefully, taking Greg's measure before he replied, "I'm holding you to that. I just met Henry, and you've known him for years, as you've said...but he's done this for too long to get lost in the Method. I'd hate to see him trapped by depression and not get help."

Greg nodded. "Thanks for letting me know. You're a good man for telling me. But I assure you, Henry's fine. It's because of moments like these I'm grateful he's never taken a role in

Hamlet or the Scottish play. If he did, I think I might have to take a sabbatical!"

The pair parted amicably, but Greg began to watch Henry even closer, and requested Christine do the same, expressing his concern that perhaps Henry was homesick. The plucky young woman did her best to keep the mercurial actor's spirits up, but reported back to the PR manager Henry's moods were like a yo-yo, and it was becoming difficult to conceal this from his colleagues. While he was never rude or unprepared, his smile was less bright, his eyes less warm.

Back at the luncheon, Henry simply shook his head. "Just a passing thought," he mumbled. "I might want a break from work after this production wraps."

There was a stunned silence. Henry's work ethic was renowned in the industry. For him to voluntarily take a moratorium was unthinkable.

Beatrice looked at her client. "Henry, obviously you will have the holidays…and then the first two weeks of January," she said slowly, as though she was speaking to a child. "We always leave the first two weeks of January for your hols…"

Henry nodded again, poking at the scallops, then the lemon asparagus risotto it was paired with. "I know," he agreed robotically.

The restaurant manager stopped by the table, and saw Henry's mostly untouched plate. "Mr. Rhys…did your lunch not suit you?"

Henry smiled automatically. "The food is lovely. My mind is elsewhere. Business matters, you understand…it's distracting."

"I understand…that makes my request awkward." The man paused, his face reddening. "I wished to ask for your autograph, you see…" He had a playbill for *Gatsby* in his hands, and shifted his feet. "Forgive me."

"Not at all!" Henry's public smile was intact, much to

Greg's relief. Henry had yet to show his darker mood to a fan, and this would be a terrible place for the façade to begin to slip. With a flourish, Henry penned his name with a marker Greg always kept in his breast pocket for just this purpose. "Ah, Greg, I thank you," Henry murmured in genuine appreciation.

The restaurant manager left with unfeigned pleasure, and Henry looked down at his plate with renewed, hidden frustration.

Henry felt he had barely kept himself afloat the past few weeks. His grandmother had warned him, but he hadn't listened, she had counseled him of the dangers of drowning in a morass of hiraeth, of longing for someone that he could neither name nor find. He had thought playing Jay Gatsby would be good for him, a way to explore the sensation of reaching for the unattainable. Exploring the character fully would serve as an exorcism of sorts, and he would be able to overcome these desires.

He could not have been more wrong. Plumbing the depths of Gatsby had made his soul even more dissatisfied and frantic, and he was afraid he might drown in bitterness and despair.

"What does it matter," he thought resentfully. "None of this matters!"

Then he heard a feminine voice in his head ask him, as clearly as if she was sitting alongside him:

Henry Rhys, why are you so angry?

AUBREY WAS FINISHING her lunch with Joelle Rogers, her editor. The scallops with risotto had been delicious, but she could only eat a few mouthfuls before her throat became tight once more, making it impossible for her to swallow. The waves of distress, irritation, and overwhelming restlessness battering her for weeks closed in again.

"Aubrey, are you listening?"

Do You Hear What I Hear?

"The revised manuscript is due is two weeks, the final edits should be done right before Christmas. Release date still set for March," Aubrey repeated, a parrot in neat business clothes that still did not feel natural on her body. It was late October in New York City, the most beautiful time of year in her opinion, and yet she was sitting inside this stuffy see-and-be-scene establishment. She was battling a strong urge to drop everything and run...but from what, or to whom, she couldn't say.

"Well." Joelle was slightly mollified. "You aren't eating again. I insist you package your lunch and eat it at home before you turn into all hair and eyes. I want an author photo for the jacket, and I won't take no for an answer this time."

"Joelle, no."

"Aubrey, yes. Why are you fighting me? You won't agree to hardly any publicity, it's like you want your book to fail! This is your work, and it has so much potential, I've gotten so much buzz for this! You're already using a nom de plume..."

"No."

Aubrey looked up as a man walked past them, almost quivering with excitement. He had something clutched in his hand as he walked to the reception podium. "I wonder what has him so happy," she mused, her body losing a bit of rigidity as she followed him with her eyes. Their waitress overheard Aubrey's remark as she came with the dessert menu, and she speculated in an excited whisper, "That's the daytime manager. He must have been able to get Mr. Rhys' autograph. He's quite the fan."

Joelle's eyes became as large as her plate. "Henry Rhys is here? Where?"

"The private dining area. We'll never see him, I'm sure. They used the private entrance," the young woman sighed, her face regretful.

Aubrey shook her head. "Henry Rhys...I don't think I

17

know him. The name sounds familiar, but I can't place the face."

The waitress was shocked. "Of course you know who he is, everyone does. Come with me..." Without giving Aubrey a chance to demur, she beckoned the amused writer to the podium to see the playbill. "I don't care how unprofessional this is. You need to see his picture."

Aubrey looked at the pamphlet cover, a man and woman on the foreground facing each other, with a green background. The man was gazing at the woman with hope and longing, the woman looking past him with a bright, oblivious smile. Aubrey leaned closer, trying to see the man's face better. As she did, her fingers brushed the edge of the booklet, and a gush of feelings, thoughts, and images flooded over her.

"Oh, Henry Rhys," she thought in confusion. "Why are you so angry?"

She thanked the waitress, murmuring her understanding and was returning to her table when a deluge reoccurred, unsolicited.

Without invitation, without request.

Because I am tired of being a commodity. I am tired of being invisible except for everyone's entertainment. Is that good enough for you? May I be left alone now?

The waves were overflowing with despondency; oversaturated with discouragement. Aubrey stumbled, catching herself with the end of the table. Joelle looked at her with concern. "Hey, Aubrey? Are you all right?" Aubrey was usually so graceful, one of those individuals you saw dancing at the corner waiting for the light to change, bobbing her head in time with the music swirling in her head through those ridiculously giant headphones on her ears...twirling aimlessly around the poles in the subway cars. It was her way. She hadn't had any alcohol with lunch...

Do You Hear What I Hear?

"Yeah." Her eyes were unfocused. "Sorry, had something on my mind."

"Star struck?" Joelle teased.

"Oh. Um, no." Aubrey sat, and shivered. She retrieved her jacket from the back of her chair. Her smart blouse wasn't warm enough any longer.

Henry was used to hearing people think about him. Or around him.

He had been able to hear the thoughts of those around him his entire life, it seemed.

His grandmother had been the one to explain to him what was going on, why the world was such a noisy, confusing place. How to manage it. Why he was the way he was. Why he could hear, but never speak…unless…But no, there was no point going down that path, hope was a very heavy burden.

Then, the soft voice spoke again.

That is a very sad thing, Henry Rhys, and I am sorry. I wish you well, and hope you find the peace you seek.

He sat bolt upright. The voice was gentle, compassionate, and still so close the speaker could have been right next to him…and yet completely new to him.

The voice…answered him, somehow. Which meant *she* heard *him. And was able to answer.*

Aubrey was just beginning to relax from her little hiccup, smiling at Joelle, when she was smacked with another wave.

Wait, wait…you can hear me? Where are you? **Who** *are you?*

Aubrey paled. Oh, this was not good. So not good…

She was used to the Voices. She knew how to handle her auditory hallucinations. They were annoying, sometimes intrusive, but they couldn't hurt her. And they could never respond to anything she said, or did.

As long as that held true, she was okay.

They could not talk back.

A memory from a trusted mentor surfaced, wrapping her in a warm blanket of safety, reminding Aubrey it was impossible for hallucinations to hurt her...but if they escalated, she should call him. Immediately. There were medications, safe places she could go...

"Joelle, I don't feel well," she whispered. "Migraine. Going home."

"You look like shit," Joelle agreed, aghast at how all the color had washed away from Aubrey's face. Even her freckles were barely visible. "Let me call you a cab."

"No. Fresh air. Gonna walk."

Wait, don't leave, where are you? Please don't leave, answer me, I know you must be close by, I...

HENRY WAS LOOKING around him wildly. The private dining room he and his team were ensconced in looked over the public area. They had the privilege of mirrored glass, so they could see without being seen.

Greg had noticed Henry's change in mien. "Henry, what's up, man?" He kept his voice low, trying not to call anyone else's attention to the way the actor was looking down at the patrons below.

"Excuse me, everyone, I...need fresh air," Henry announced. "Greg, have Christine...reschedule..." His voice trailed off, his keen eyes rapidly bouncing around until they fastened on a pair of women as one stood abruptly, to the obvious distress of her lunching companion.

"Henry, you know damned well I am flying back to London day after tomorrow!" Beatrice's eyes were a kaleidoscope of exasperation and bewilderment. "What is wrong with you? Greg...?"

Henry did not reply other than a vague, "Sorry," as he grabbed his jacket, and vanished.

Her voice in his head was just as clear even as it begged:

Please, don't talk to me anymore. You wanted peace, remember?

Do You Hear What I Hear?

I'm giving it to you, leave me alone, you aren't supposed to be able to hear me! You can't hear me, you can't...

The lunch crowd was treated to quite the scene as Henry Rhys bolted publicly through the dining area, his eyes locked on the figure of a slight young woman who had fled through the revolving glass door, and was becoming lost in the tide of pedestrians.

No! No, I can't lose you! Please listen to me!

IF THERE WAS one thing Aubrey Stafford knew how to do, it was shut the Voices out. She dug into her oversized shoulder bag, retrieving her headphones even as she was walking so rapidly she was almost running. Her feet would send her hate mail later that night, but she would worry about it later. A playlist blasting in her ears, Aubrey retrieved a pair of thin leather gloves and donned those as well.

"Almost home almost home," she was mentally chanting to drown out the Voice's pleas that she simply *Stop, I beg you! Listen to me!*

As she was forced to wait at a red light, she began to relax. It was broad daylight. Mid-day. She was on the edge of the park she could see from her loft. She was safe.

A hand brushed her shoulder blade.

"Excuse me..?"

She heard a man over her music, his tone was cultivated, his voice somewhat breathless.

But she knew who it was, because she had heard him before, but not through her ears.

His voice washed over her even as she turned. Terrified, and yet somehow exhilarated.

"You're real," she breathed, looking up, and up, at the face of Henry Rhys. "You're really real..."

Henry smiled down at the face of the young woman he had

seen dancing in the airport, wearing massive earphones, but now seeing the one, the One he had been hoping and despairing to find for so many years. The One his grandmother had told him to watch for…The One he needed to be complete…

"It's you," he breathed in reverence. "After all this time… I've been waiting for you."

3

A MATTER OF TRUST

Aubrey may have been relieved to find "the Voice" was in fact tied to a real person, but she still looked remarkably like an animal caught in a trap, or one framed in headlights of an approaching vehicle. Henry took a step back, hands in a conciliatory gesture, hoping to show he meant her no harm.

"For someone with such short legs, you have a powerful stride," he jested lightly. "I worked up a sweat trying to catch up, but I would have done much more before I risked losing you. Why wouldn't you answer me? I just wanted to talk, I didn't think you would see the harm in that…"

The light had long since changed, and people were bumping into them as they passed, rushing to get on with their lives. Aubrey flinched with each contact, every touch. Henry was still confused, but all of his protective instincts were roaring. This woman was *his*, by all that was sacred and profane, and he would take care of her. He extended his hand slowly, so she would not be startled by any sudden movement.

"It's a lovely afternoon," he coaxed. "Would you come and sit in the park with me? Either in sunlight or shade. Can you trust me enough to do that? Don't you have any questions you want to ask me?"

Mute, eyes wide and pupils blown, she nodded. With caution that bespoke a high likelihood of bolting once more should she feel threatened, Aubrey reached out, accepting Henry's hand. Henry noticed at once the way his hand engulfed hers, and how she was wearing gloves, despite the mild temperatures.

"Are your hands that cold, milady?" Henry guided Aubrey to the park, holding her hand as carefully as if it was thin porcelain.

She remained silent. Aubrey chose not to give this tall, muscular man any information about her until she was ready, and at the moment she was not prepared to answer that question. He towered over her as badly as Peter did, although Peter was built like a wrestler, and Henry was more lean. Still, she had no illusions about his physique. She sensed the muscles through his clothing that was undoubtedly tailored to fit his form: his blazer hung open, revealing broad shoulders tapering down to a narrow waist and hips, but the shirt fabric strained across his chest. When she cast her eyes around, she could not help but notice the way his pants also were snug around his thighs and rear. Her mind was disjointed but one runner recognized another, which meant even as he joked about her pace, she could never outrun him, especially with those long legs of his. And with his long arms that perfectly matched the rest of his frame, he could snag her easily…She swallowed, throat tight, mouth dry. The only thing keeping her from panicking and fleeing at that very moment was the amount of people everywhere, surely Henry Rhys, celebrity, would not do anything egregious in full view of the public.

"May I at least have your first name? I do not know how to address you…may I have that much? You have the advantage over me," Henry continued, leading her taut body down a path towards the water. Instinctively, he knew she would relax if she could sit on one of the benches facing the Hudson River.

"My name is Aubrey," she answered quietly. "I regret appearing rude, but I don't know you. It may be unkind of me, but I have learned to be careful with men I don't know. Women as well, but…"

"You don't have to explain. I have two sisters, one older, one younger. Neither of them are much taller than you, and trust me when I say I have lectured them long and loud about safety. For all they are smaller in stature, however, they take the privilege of family and frequently threatened me with grave bodily harm if I did not stop patronizing them with my overbearing ways. But then I set Dad on them, so I had my revenge in the end," he chuckled, waggling his thick dark eyebrows at her, hoping to make her laugh. He was rewarded with a slight smile, so he pressed on, "Do you have any annoying brothers? Sisters you are either fighting with or banding together against your mum and dad?"

The smile evaporated like fog as she shook her head. "No, I am afraid I don't. Dad died when I was quite young, and Mama passed a few years ago. I do have Peter, though. We adopted each other, you could say. I am very fortunate to have him in my life. He is like a big brother to me…emphasis on big." She slid her eyes to the side, hoping he would catch the idea she wasn't so alone in the world no one would miss her if she vanished.

Henry hid his smirk. He understood her very well. "Aubrey, I have a confession that might have you running from me, but I beg you hear me out before you sprint like a gazelle…I am fairly certain I've seen you before today. Did you fly into JFK about two months ago? Mid-week? I'm fairly confident I remember seeing you the day I flew in from Heathrow. I was at baggage claim and saw a woman very like you, wearing headphones just like yours…she wasn't walking as much as she was almost dancing, happy as could be, dragging her bags behind her. What caught my attention at first were those headphones, you see...they rather reminded me of Princess Leia's cinnamon buns." He leaned grinned, making a nod towards the headphones she had pulled off her ears and were now resting around her neck.

Aubrey was now looking at him with an air of astonishment, but no longer in fear, he was pleased to see. He rushed on, "I was traveling with my public relations manager and shadow, Greg Knight, but that's incidental...when we stepped out to get to our car, this same woman let out the most joyful shout I'd heard in some time and simply leapt into the arms of a tall man she called Peter...is that your Peter? Was that you?"

The transformation that took place beside him made his heart sing. Aubrey was laughing as she pulled her hand from his grasp to clap her hands as she all but sparkled with glee. "It was! I'd just returned from a six-week trip, and he surprised me completely. I had no idea he planned on meeting me at JFK. Such a Peter-like thing to do...he is so good to me, and I love him very much."

Henry gave an exaggerated shiver. "I shall endeavor to avoid upsetting you. I should not like for this Peter to have cause to search me out with reasons for adjusting my plane of existence." Then he paused, his heart beginning to pound. Aubrey said Peter was "like a brother" and perhaps that reflected her feelings for him, but what if Peter felt differently? "Peter sees you only as a sister?"

"Yep," Aubrey answered, distracted as they reached the gangway by the water.

"Are you certain about that," he inquired, his voice low and bashful.

Aubrey looked at him, confused. "Dead certain. I don't have the right equipment. May we sit down? I walked rather hard in these boots, and my feet are cross."

Do You Hear What I Hear?

Henry's lips twitched. "Ah. That does make the matter clear. And please, yes."

Sitting facing the water made things easier for him as well: there was less likelihood of his being spotted by paparazzi, and they wouldn't have to face each other as they talked, either.

Aubrey unzipped her fashionable footwear, completely unselfconscious as she took out her feet and stretched them out in the sunshine with a sigh. Then she flinched. "Am I being rude?"

"No!" Henry's laugh was hearty. "I love the way you are so unassuming."

She nodded. His deep voice, paired with his native British accent, was very soothing, brushing against her ears like music. Her heart was beating in a new rhythm, and she felt a comforting pull, urging her to set down her armor and shields. With a deep breath, she locked those urges up fast in her chest, and remained silent.

"Now, will you tell me why you would not speak to me? I could tell you weren't surprised to hear my voice, but you were dead set against answering me. Why? How did I upset you? Believe me, it was the last thing I wanted to do. You said, 'You're really real.' What did you mean?" Henry was eaten alive by curiosity, so when Aubrey wrapped her arms around herself and shook her head, almost violently, he was crushed.

"Fair enough," he scolded himself under his breath. "What a fool, asking for answers before I have given you any, I should know better. In fact, I do know better, and Grandma should box both my ears for treating you this way, when it's plain as the nose on my face you don't know."

Her voice was tight as she looked at him sideways. "What don't I know?" Tension radiated from her frame once more.

Henry was brought back to himself. "I am making a hash out of this!" He pulled on his hair with both hands in despair.

"Grandma never lifted a hand to me except to pull me by my ear when I desperately needed it as an idiot boy getting out of hand. I know you said you didn't have a brother, but I am sure you understand there are times young boys can be blockheads."

Ah, there was that fleeting grin again. Encouraged, he continued.

"My grandma Mairéad was…simply the best. I loved her with all my heart, until the day she died, and I do to this day." He turned to touch her with his eyes, searching, vividly blue and scoring her to her soul. "She would rescue me from my sisters, taking me to her farm out in Wales for summers as a boy. She was my dad's mum, and I would run as wild as a heathen. No tea parties, getting nagged into dresses, having my hair fussed (he shuddered)…just good clean…or more truthfully, filthy fun. It was a small holding, not a grand commercial setup. Grandpa Griffin had sheep, as who didn't…but that's neither here nor there. When I was a little boy, she often took us for walks.

"Grandma would tell me amazing stories…about island kingdoms, ancient and no more after having fallen into the sea…dragons flying over the skies…magicians who could make things move with the power of their minds alone… other magics that gave people the ability to recognize their best friends, the very moment they laid eyes on them…the rarest of all, those who could see possible futures yet to be…

"Being able to hear the thoughts of others. Being able to speak to another's mind.

"As I grew older, I knew the stories she was telling me were more than humble fairy tales, because she was communicating with me more and more without ever opening her mouth. The 'stories' she had reared me on were the oral traditions of the heritage we shared."

Henry stopped, still gazing intently into Aubrey's eyes. She had been listening, as enraptured as he himself had been as a child. Henry had a gift for storytelling. No hint of skepticism marred her expression.

"I say 'we shared' because it was something special to just the two of us. Not my father, nor my sisters had the gift...or the curse." His lips twisted.

Aubrey's eyebrows knitted. "I don't understand, Henry."

A reluctant grin crossed his face. "That's all you have to say thus far? 'You don't understand?' You aren't going to call me a liar, a madman, someone who is trying to trick you?"

Aubrey broke his gaze to look out over the water. "Not yet. For my own reasons, I am withholding judgment. What I don't understand is if she had telepathic abilities, and you did as well, why not the rest of her descendants? Why would you call it a curse? I think I can guess, but I would like to hear your thoughts first."

Privately, Aubrey thought this was easily one of the more bizarre afternoons she had spent in a very long time...but not the strangest. She wasn't as scared as she had been earlier, God knew she had been a lot more frightened in her life. She wanted to hear more of what this attractive, intense, and charismatic fellow with the charming accent had to say. Something inside of her was very drawn to both him and his tale alike.

Henry extended his hand, palm out in encouragement once again. Aubrey took it, and did not flinch when Henry sandwiched her tiny one between his. "Have your hands grown warm, with you sitting in the sun? Will you take your gloves off?"

"No."

Her flat refusal surprised him. Clearly, she wore them for more than warmth. But he continued his narrative.

"My grandmother and I have our abilities because our genetic soup allowed trace bits of our DNA to surface. We aren't like most people, you see. And even though my father, and my sisters carry the same trace of DNA coding, it remained dormant."

"What makes you different?" Aubrey asked calmly. "Are you...not quite human?"

Henry's laugh was boisterous. "No, we are completely Terran. We are just from a civilization that died out, many, many millennia ago...

"We are descendants from the lost continent, the lost Kingdom of Atlantis.

"What is more, I strongly suspect you are, as well. Which is why I was able to speak to you. I cannot speak to anyone, you see, unless...well, I will get to that later."

Aubrey's jaw opened, just a bit. Then she snapped it shut again.

"Here it comes," Henry sighed. "Go ahead. Tell me I'm insane."

She shook her head, not violently as before, but still perceptibly. "Henry, I am not...I would never...I simply cannot be."

"There's more, if you will let me tell it," he implored.

"Yes. Please."

"I can never offer you proof. There are no records. How can there be, when the very existence of Atlantis has been dismissed as an allegory? But I can tell you about how their descendants still walk on land today. Not many, it is true. Most perished when the island fell under the waves, for reasons no one knows...but we were a sea-going people. Voyagers, explorers, traders...and therefore, it stands to reason some of its sons and daughters escaped the Desolation, as those who survived came to call the utter and total destruction of their homeland. Now, those of us who are left could not even tell you where it lies...there are more myths than there are descendants, I fear. All that remains are the oral histories, passed down through the generations. It's a bitter pill. How much of the stories have been embellished? How many have been lost over the years? Who can say? All my grandmother knew, all I know, is what our hearts tell us is true: the People of the Waves had gifts that have died out over the centuries. Telepathy is but one of them, and I have no doubt my version is but a weak, bastardized version of what flourished back in the height of Atlantis's glory."

"Dragons?" Aubrey's voice held a wistful, hopeful note. Henry grinned even as he marveled over this being the first subject Aubrey latched onto…his curiosity grew even higher.

"Dragons I cannot vouch for personally," he laughed. "Neither could Mairéad, for all that she was much older than the grandmothers of all of my friends."

Henry took a deep breath and sobered as he went on with his tale. "The saddest part of this story is also the truest part: as each year goes by, there are fewer and fewer people aware they have descended from the People of the Waves…as genetic stars align and children are born, carrying the tridents in their souls…they simply don't know, as their parents didn't know, or their parents before them…the children are an anomaly…I was lucky. Mairéad watched her children closely, and then her grandchildren. I was the only one to show signs of our genetic heritage…as she was the only one of her generation—out of the five children her parents bore, and out of nineteen grandchildren! Her grandfather was the one to take her aside to tell her everything he knew, as his great-great-uncle had told him. She searched a long time to find another woman, someone who could share…um, ladylike secrets with, but never found a single one."

"She must have been very lonely," Aubrey commented, even as she still gazed out into the river, watching the seagulls swoop and soar in turn.

Henry was touched by her compassion. "I think she was lonely at times, but not always. Mairéad had an incredible capacity for taking life as it came. I think you will agree as I continue…

"I had inherited the ability to hear the thoughts of those around me. Some might call it a blessing. Others would call it a curse. Throughout my childhood and adolescence, I was a quick and motivated student of everything my grandmother had to teach me.

"It was hard, and frustrating. What people said was often not what they were thinking, and the noise was profoundly distracting.

"She taught me how to block out the unwanted, intrusive thoughts of those around me, and how to cope with the disappointment, and often pain of the inherent duplicity of the human race. You know the quote 'Everyone lies'? Well, it's not far off...but I learned to take the good with the bad.

"There were times the noise felt overwhelming; it would hurt my heart to 'overhear' cruel thoughts, or discover lies often before they were even uttered. But," his face brightened as his expression became smug, "I learned my lessons fast, and was never caught out by unscheduled quizzes or inspections. To this day I am rarely caught off guard by anyone."

Henry released Aubrey's hand to tug at his hair, then pull at the neck of his shirt, and rub his jaw. His phone chirped, but he silenced it without a glance. Slowly, he continued his narrative, leaning forward with his forearms on his thighs.

"I never took any, ah, flirtations beyond a date or two. I thought nothing of it. I felt there could be someone special in just the next room, and I was quite happy to keep looking for her."

He shifted, unaware that Aubrey had mirrored his position so she could look at him surreptitiously. His cheerful attitude was shifting, clouding his eyes.

"Before I left for university, Mairéad wanted to have one more talk with me. I am grateful she did, as she died my first term. If she hadn't...if I didn't know...I would think I was going mad today, in truth. But it is...was...the hardest thing of all to hear." He swallowed over the lump in his throat, and

Aubrey, who never touched anyone she wasn't very close to unless necessary, reached over to lightly stroke his knee.

"Easy, Henry. You don't have to share anything you have no wish to, or is too personal. I am sorry for your loss. I can hear how close you were, and that you loved her dearly."

Henry tensed, barely restraining his gasp when she touched his knee. Even though Aubrey was not addressing him directly, he could hear her, a stream of consciousness for a brief moment:

...so sorry, Henry, can't figure out how you think I'm involved, can't possibly be who you think I am but so sorry to see you so sad, this pain is real, this is true, not a lie not a trick, just love....never knew my grandparents...how lucky you were to have someone so hard to say goodbye to...

With great reluctance, he took her hand from his knee, and as he suspected, her mind closed to him. He had a fleeting image cross his imagination of a flower closing its petals, as one might at sunset... "Stay focused, man," he scolded himself. Somehow, she had to initiate contact for him to hear her. Aubrey did not know what she was doing. No one had taught her, yet she had this control. Amazing...how Mairéad would have loved meeting her! His throat closed completely, and he choked on a small gasp. Just for an instant. Mairéad had so longed for this moment, in so many ways. But he had to man up, and finish strong. He held her hand, and squeezed it.

"You are incredibly kind," he rasped, his much vaunted timbre lost as he spoke. "I want...I need to get to the end. You need to understand. All right?

"Mairéad was very frail by now. I told you, she was so much older than the grandmothers my friends had. I never thought anything of it. That evening I saw her, she was stumbling over words, she didn't know how to start, and she didn't want to try to communicate without them, either...

"At first, I thought it was something of a generational

joke, my very old grandmother telling me how she went on the internet, trying to find others like her, and failing spectacularly." He snickered. "Can you imagine? My ancient grandma...." he looked up at the sky, "Sorry, Grandma! Don't pull my ears!...trawling Reddit? Going to God knows where, searching for people who claimed to know about the Lost People of the Waves...but I didn't give her the credit she deserved. She was swift to cull the charlatans and the frauds. After a time, she was able to find a few...a very few, scattered over the globe. They were all hoping to learn something new, but what happened was they simply added to the chorus of what they already knew, instead..."

"Such as?" Aubrey's voice was soft. Respectful. Henry would never be able to honor her enough for that.

"Mairéad learned what she believed was a unique experience was...tied directly to her heritage." Henry stopped. "I'm not giving her story justice." He paused. Aubrey was quiet, patient as he collected his thoughts, and began again.

"I remember her and Grandpa, when they were together. Of course I was a boy, completely unobservant for the most part, but I could tell they loved each other. It was obvious, it was in the way they spoke to each other. Their actions. Little acts of love you don't notice until they're gone." He wiped his eyes, not even noticing the tears that collected. "Grandpa took ill one afternoon and died soon after. It was a blessing he didn't suffer long. Mairéad was the most loving and patient nurse you could ask for. She was devastated when he passed. I knew she loved my grandfather.

"But that last evening we were together, she explained to me why she was the oldest grandmother in my peer group... It was because just like I was experiencing, she too felt there was someone out there, just beyond her reach, someone she was desperately longing for. She yearned for a person she knew nothing about, and had never seen. So she waited, searched, hoped, and the years passed by until she simply snapped out of this, conviction, for lack of a better term, all at once. Mairéad felt she had, as she phrased it, 'wasted' years of her life reaching for something she couldn't have. She had to stop dreaming, and start living. She allowed herself—again, her words—to begin dating my grandfather. They wed, then she was having his babies. She was most agitated at this point, insistent I know she never regretted their marriage, you understand?"

Aubrey murmured, "You know love when you see it, Henry. I have no doubt their mutual devotion was genuine."

Henry turned to look at the woman sitting next to him, rather than be a coward and look out into the water. "Mairéad would have given much to have met you. I wish so much she could have...Believe me when I tell you this, if nothing else: she would have been overjoyed to sit with you as I am. You are so gentle, and have such a good heart, to listen to me ramble on and on..."

Aubrey flushed, her pale skin taking on a more normal hue as opposed to the pallor she had in the restaurant and then when Henry touched her at the corner. "Don't be so sure, I have the devil's own temper when pushed."

Henry's grin split his face, dimples appearing on each side. "Ah, and she would love you even more for it...but I have to go on...

"Mairéad told me when she spoke to the others, who were all men, they mentioned the exact same phenomenon...the feeling of...longing. Almost starving for someone...and almost to a one, each either felt like they 'settled' for a spouse rather than live alone any longer, or one day felt as though they 'woke up' and decided they needed to get on with life... except for four.

"Those four had their One. The One their souls cried out for...their soul mate."

Henry slewed his eyes sharply to Aubrey, waiting for her incredulity. Her disbelief.

This time, he was not disappointed.

While she said not a word, he could see the struggle in her expression. The way she was fighting to remain placid while not backing away from him. Rejecting his chronicle.

Rejecting *him*.

He raced on, terrified silence would widen the gulf he could see forming.

"For the first time ever, I didn't believe one of Grandma's stories, and I am somewhat embarrassed to admit that I thought, 'Oh, *bullshit*!' so loudly and clearly she heard me as if I spoke it aloud. She cuffed me for it, snapping, 'Manners, young man!' Remember how I told you I cannot speak telepathically? There are a few exceptions to that...and trust me, that was one of them...ow..." He rubbed his ear, looking at Aubrey with a little boy face.

Aubrey's lips twitched despite herself. "I think you survived your ancient grandmother's correction."

Pouting, he continued, "Sure, take her side...! Mairéad then told me this: my soul mate would always, *always* be able to hear me. Telepaths had that joy. Regardless of the miles that separated us. We would be able to speak as clearly as though we were sitting right next to each other.

"I challenged her. I asked if that was the case, how was it she was never able to find hers? The answer was simple: with all the voices in the world, how could she know whom to listen for? If she, my grandmother, my flesh and blood, tried to speak to me, but I had never met her, how would I recognize her voice?"

"You couldn't. That's an unfair scenario, unless there was some emotional tug, you could not know who she was," Aubrey's forehead wrinkled as she tried to figure out this puzzle where she only had a handful of pieces, and Henry felt himself even more drawn to her.

"Exactly. The only way she could ever hope to get my attention would be to say my name...and once again, if I did not know she was my grandmother, why would I even hear her out?"

Aubrey shifted, uneasiness rising within her inner core as she recognized the ring of truth in his words.

"I am always susceptible to hearing the thoughts of those around me. I know what my sensitivity levels are…touch makes it almost impossible to block out someone completely, while proximity and intimacy with people also play a part. Mairéad teased me if someone ever spoke to me when I was alone I was not to take the easy way out, assuming I was either mad, or being inconvenienced by some spirit, because when I was little I was afraid of ghosts. She urged me to answer, saying it may well by my soul mate, reaching out to me."

"Henry, if soul mates are meant to be your…missing part, as I understand it, what would cause someone to suddenly give up on the idea, as your grandmother did? It sounds like rather an abrupt rejection of a concept so important to her. Then she went ahead and had a happy life without him. So what is the point?"

He exhaled heavily. "I asked her that. The answer is…not pleasant.

"All of her group talked about this. They could only guess, you know. Who is to say if their mates were of a compatible age? What if the reason they suddenly no longer felt tied to their One was because…they passed on? There was speculation they married another. But most of them came to realize marriage to another would not sever the ties that bound them. It could only be on some level, souls recognized the One they were yearning for simply was no longer on the same plane of existence they were. It didn't stop the longing, but the sharpness of the pain…dulled, somewhat."

Henry's smile became bitter as he added, "That's when I dashed for the loo to vomit."

Aubrey reached out and touched him again, gingerly. "Why?"

"It was hard to face that moment of truth. I recognized it for what it was...realization of the betrayal of the belief I was in control of my heart."

He turned and looked out over the water again.

4

TIES THAT BIND

Like quicksilver fish, her thoughts flitted through his:
He truly believes what he is telling me...even with my gloves on I can tell that much...but surely there must be some mistake. I'm nobody, from nowhere...maybe...

I can hear you, Aubrey. Henry spoke without moving his lips. *When you touch me, I hear you. When you aren't, I don't. You should know this...And you aren't 'nobody.'*

Aubrey jerked away from him as though she had been stung. He sighed. "I had to tell you, it wasn't polite otherwise. I also would like to say you cannot know how peaceful, yet uncanny and thrilling, it is to be alongside someone and *not* hear what they are thinking. Quite a novel experience. Grandma knew how to shield her thoughts from me, but she was the only one." He paused. "What do your gloves have to do with anything?"

Aubrey's pupils dilated again. "I don't want to talk about my gloves."

"Please tell me this much. Do your hands hurt you in any way?" Henry hoped this was not the case, because he had very few resources he could pull from if she was suffering. But he would try.

Clearing her throat, Aubrey focused on a seagull. "No... not as such. No pain."

After a moment, she spoke again. "Is there anything more to your story? Not that I am saying what you have told me isn't quite enough to digest...and I thank you for your courtesy."

Aubrey was glad she was sitting down. Having Henry not only speak inside her mind again, but addressing thoughts she just had, was a shock. He could have taken advantage of her so easily, but chose not to. It spoke volumes about the kind of man he was, his intentions, and his sincerity. She refused to acknowledge that the more she sat and listened to him, something in her heart warmed and stretched towards him, like a greening vine reaching for the sun.

Her jaded, cynical self, with its antenna always listening for signs of danger, warned her perhaps his demeanor was a front, meant to lure her into a state of relaxation before he sprang a trap, but her sense of logic warred with it. He was... Him. Why would he go through this elaborate charade? It seemed a ridiculous waste of time...no, that was taking even her paranoia a bit far.

"You are staring holes into that poor bird," Henry commented mildly. "May I ask you what is going on in your mind? Or will you not speak to me at all? I have bared my soul to you, told you things no one knows. And I mean that sincerely. My sisters do not even know what I have shared with you today, let alone my few friends. It isn't something you bandy about in idle conversation, 'Oh, hello, I can hear your every thought, my forebearers spring from the lost continent of Atlantis, but those of us who remain prefer to refer to it as the Lost Kingdom of the Waves. So, what films have you seen lately? Read any good books? Lovely weather we're having...'" He trailed off.

"Can you tell me about those who found their soul mates?

How did they find them? How did their relationships work out?"

He took her hand again, without asking this time. "Each one was a different situation. Mairéad only spoke briefly about each, but the way her eyes shone as she did!...One couple literally grew up together. It was difficult to know where one ended and the other began, she said, they were like two trees twining around another—each keeping their own identity, but supporting the other in everything they did." He paused before adding, "She said it was the most beautiful thing she had ever seen, and I could see envy in her eyes...Another pair literally bumped into each other in a train station. They did not even speak the same language, but agreed when their skin touched, it was if the magnetic poles shifted. Their entire world upended, and nothing was the same again. Nor did they wish it to be. They knew, instantly, that everything was going to be different. They missed their trains. They found a place to stay in Ghent, Belgium, and spent a week there learning each other's tongue...in more ways than one," he laughed.

Aubrey blushed, looking down at her feet. Seeing this, Henry pushed on.

"The next story is more extraordinary. This fellow was in a thrift store. He picked up a book, and when he did he knew, simply by touch, his soul mate had held it recently. You see, he was gifted with psychometry. That means sometimes when he touched things, he would have a flash of knowing who had held it last, or something about the person who had touched it...am I making sense?" Henry made it a point not to look at Aubrey directly, but was keenly aware how she had become very still, and how worn her gloves were.

"I hear you," was all she would say.

Disappointed and vindicated by her nonresponse, he continued, "The man was almost demented, going from shopper to shopper, asking them if they had been interested in the book. He almost got tossed from the store for harassment. But he was completely focused on finding the person who had, in the words he told Mairéad, not only held the book, but caressed the cover before setting it down."

"Did he find her?"

"Him!" Henry replied triumphantly. "He did. As it turned out, his mistake was asking the customers…it was an employee who had set the book out. The employee didn't want to sell the book, you see, he was so reluctant to put it on the floor. But the rules were ironclad, employees were not allowed to keep donated merchandise for themselves, and he could not afford to purchase it. Of course, the first thing our fellow did was buy the book. The second was take his soul mate to lunch…and the rest, as they say, is 'they lived happily ever after'…"

Aubrey remained quiet, but a small grin played around the corner of her lips.

"I saved this story for last, because it is not as happy as the others, but it still needs to be told," Henry's face twisted with conflicting emotions. "This final man found his mate in an unusual setting. He worked as a nurse in a hospice unit in Paris. Many found his profession depressing, but he was committed to giving the best care he could to those in the final stages of life."

"No," breathed Aubrey, tears in her eyes, her voice shaking. "I don't want to hear this…"

Henry dared lift her chin, and look into her eyes. "He says they were the best four months of his life, Aubrey. Would you deny him that? Either of them? She was alone, in pain, and he gave her unquestioning love. She gave him purpose and the answer he had given up hope of finding. When she slipped away, it was peaceful and in his arms. Afterwards…at least he knew. He wasn't left wondering."

Aubrey shook her head in denial, drawing herself up into a ball on the bench. "But…"

Do You Hear What I Hear?

Henry wrapped his arms around her, amazed at how easily she fit into his embrace, and she did not flinch or fight him off. "What a perfect fit she is, I could almost slip her into my pocket," he thought in a haze of euphoria, so staggered he was to be holding the prize he had searched and hunted for after so many years, his One… "Recognize in her case, she didn't know why she was so uncomfortable, feeling as though she had gone through life longing for something she had never found. She thought she was going to die without having solved a puzzle that plagued her, waking and sleeping. Not only was he able to give her the solution to that puzzle, he was able to give her love, joy…surcease of pain. It wasn't for long, but in the end, it was everything. That was what Mairéad was desperate to instill in my thick skull: that no matter what I attained, no achievement, no gain in life would mean more than ashes if I turned my back on my soul mate should I find her, or she tripped over my thick self…

Mairéad would often chuckle, saying she suspected the Welsh were largely descendants of the People of the Waves. No other culture could have come up with the word 'hiraeth' that so encapsulates what we carry in our hearts…"

"Hiraeth?"

Aubrey turned her head, breathing in his scent, finding it soothed the ache his retelling of the last pair of lovers had caused.

"Hiraeth is a uniquely Welsh concept. It's a combination of ardent yearning, a regretful longing or an intense desire for the Wales of the past…and to a soul, everyone who carries the trident in their soul has the same feeling. It's restlessness. Feeling unsettled. Looking for home, but never quite finding it, because it doesn't exist. Have you ever felt the same, tiny Aubrey? Unsure of where you belong? Perhaps the only place to grant you peace for any stretch of time is the seaside? It's no coincidence if that is the case…remember, the only reason there are any descendants of the Lost Kingdom of the Sea at all is they were explorers. Adventurers, all of them carrying that wanderlust in their hearts. Those original travelers expected to return home at some point, I'm sure. But their homeland vanished, and they were never even granted the closure of knowing why."

Aubrey pulled herself away from Henry completely. His words were hewing too closely to the quick, and she was afraid he was going to see through her at any moment. It had taken years to build her defenses, and he was demolishing them with his words and the traitorous feelings they evoked. In less than an afternoon…!

"Aubrey?" She was jerking her boots on, biting her lips.

"Henry…I can't…my mind is too full, I…"

"Tell me where I went wrong. Tell me what I said that didn't ring true," he pleaded. She couldn't be walking away from him!

"That's just it. I need to process everything. Don't you see…If what you are telling me is true, I will need to recalibrate the entire way I look at my life!"

"But do you?" He moved quickly for a man so large, she thought unhappily, because now he was actually kneeling in front of her as she finished fastening her boots. "Do you feel unsettled if you are in one place for a long time?"

Aubrey's face was set with great reluctance as she answered, "Yes…I also can't stand being landlocked for a long period of time. My feet become itchy, I am unbearable. I need to leave and find a body of water, or a river…anywhere I can hear a current, or waves."

Henry's expression was tender and his voice soft as he asked, "What do you do for a living, Aubrey? You mentioned you were returning after being away for six weeks when I saw you at the airport. That is a very long time…"

"I'm a travel writer…" she admitted, knowing everything she said was giving strength to his speculations. His cocky grin only made her lean back into the bench.

Do You Hear What I Hear?

"Ah, I see...and tell me, do you have any, um, talents that you do not speak about? Talents that might be linked to your wearing gloves when it isn't remotely cold?"

Her lips mashed together. Clearly this was not a topic for discussion. Henry dropped his head. "All right, milady. We don't have to talk about that if you do not wish to...but if you need some time to think about everything, I beg of you, don't leave me without a way to speak with you again. I have no doubt you are walking through life as strong as the sea, but you are walking blind, Aubrey...I know the emptiness you are hiding in your heart, because it is in mine as well. You sit at night, wondering what will quiet the pain, don't you?" He reached up and caressed her cheek, brushing the hair away from her face. "There is an invisible cord, connecting our souls together. We don't need each other to survive, obviously, as we've managed just fine so far. In fact, many would say we are prospering. I have this great career. I think you must have one as well...but are we thriving, Aubrey? We can run away, we can deny it, but we cannot break the tie that binds us. In fact...I have been looking for you my entire adult life.

"Have you been looking for someone? Perhaps...looking for me? Not this mug, not the foolishness that is attached to who I am, but...just maybe?"

Aubrey stopped looking past Henry, once she heard the raw, hopeful need in his voice. She couldn't ignore it, or him. It would be too cruel.

"I don't know," she answered honestly. "If I wanted to search, as you say, I would not have allowed myself to, because it would be too dangerous. I don't...didn't...want any attachments in my life, any real intimacy. It's easier to be alone, to travel light. No one would want my baggage."

"Baggage? Because you have such, how did you put it, itchy feet? How much baggage can a precious heart like yours have? Are you killing people and stuffing them in your luggage?"

Her smile was enigmatic as she dug in her shoulder bag. "Now that would be telling...judging things by their appearance is always a mistake. You say your sisters are not tall, would you make the error of determining how much trouble they can get into by their height?"

Once again, she surprised Henry into a belly-laugh. "Good God, no, and please never tell them I made such an egregious blunder! They'd have me cut down to size before I could think to beg for mercy, not that there would be any..."

Aubrey handed Henry her cell phone. "Here. Call whatever number you wish me to have access to, and that way you will have my number. For reasons that escape all logic, every rule I live by...I am not running away. But I need to think about everything, Henry. You've turned my world on its head, and I don't know what to do, or where to go. I don't even know what you want from me!"

Eagerly he accepted her phone, and entered his personal cell number. He returned her phone, and looked at his with reluctance, only to wince. Greg was almost apoplectic, demanding to know where he was, if he was all right, what in the devil was he about by not responding, and so forth. His agent Beatrice had only sent two texts, although hers were more forceful, insisting he contact her at once. Christine was more deferential in tone but just as persistent, informing him Greg was having fits and would he please do her the favor of getting back to him, as Greg was now driving *everyone* crazy? He was shaking his head when a text arrived from an unknown number:

"Hello from Aubrey Stafford. I like the sound of water, staring at birds, and listening to stories."

His good humor and excitement restored, he texted back:

"Greetings from Henry Rhys. I carry a trident in my soul, and I also like the sound of water. I particularly like petite redheads who wear large earphones resembling Princess Leia's cinnamon rolls. I will be listening for you, however you wish to speak to me."

He stood, stepping back so she could rise for their walk out of the park.

"Remember," he said quietly before they parted ways at the stoplight where he caught up with her, "*You* don't need the cell phone to speak with me. Just think my name, and speak. I will hear you. Try it now, as you are heading home…I will always hear you."

Aubrey bit her lip, and nodded.

"May I call you a cab? I feel bad, I frightened you so…you were almost running," he added, remorse in his face and voice.

She shook her head. *I will be fine.*

A huge grin filled his face. "You didn't even have to call me by my name…" He took her hand and placed a small kiss on the back. "Be careful, and please, reach out to me. I know you need your space, but it is so hard to just let you walk away…God, that sounds terrible when I say it out loud! Forgive me, please."

Aubrey reached up and patted his cheek. She felt all of his sincerity. There was nothing dark or sinister in this man. There was nothing but his fear she would disappear. Henry did not catch any of her thoughts, just her concern he give her time, and, as she was aware of the undercurrent of stress from stacked up text messages, that he have some peace.

"Whoever they are, Henry, your life is your own. They don't own you…you deserved an hour with a repressed woman on the banks of the river," she teased him, then waved as she walked away.

He watched her for a few moments, then forced himself to turn, and hail a cab.

He had his own music to face.

5

HEAD & HEART

Peter Rivera had had enough, to put it mildly.

To be blunt, he was pissed off with one Aubrey Stafford.

His sister had become smoke. Impossible to pin down for over a week, and he had a bellyful of it. He had done everything short of filing a missing person's alert for her cracked ass, he fumed as he made his way to her door. He'd called and left messages. All he got in reply were brief texts, assuring him she was "fine" but "had a lot on her mind." She promised she would call him "as soon as she had her head on straight."

"Wouldn't hold my breath on that, Sis," he'd grumbled. "Christmas will be here first...what in the hell is going on, Elf..." It was a Thursday evening, and as soon as Peter left work, he headed straight for their favorite Korean barbecue restaurant and placed a massive order for takeout.

He was going to stake out Aubrey's door if he had to, and proceed to hogtie and force-feed her while she talked about what the hell caused her to go to ground. He had a strong suspicion if she was ducking his calls and not hanging out with him, she was either working herself into a shadow and

Do You Hear What I Hear?

not eating, stressing herself into a shadow over something (and not eating), or else sick to death…and not eating.

"Damned woman, making me jump at shadows, watch, she's found herself a man at last and is lying in bed with him rolling between the sheets and I am gonna be stuck with a week's worth of chow and looking like an ass in the bargain," he grumbled, hoping that was the case as he pounded on her door.

"Aubrey Stafford! You open this door right now, you redheaded Hobbit! I have a ton of Korean in my arms and it ain't gonna eat itself!"

Aubrey flung the door open, and Peter was not happy to see he had not been jumping at shadows, after all.

"Sis, you look like absolute shit. Let me in, and gimmie a plate, a fork, and some of that beer I left the last time I was here. Then you better tell me who I'm gonna have to kill for making you look like this. Nobody makes my little sis look this stressed…Then I'm gonna kill you myself for not talking to me about it. What have I told you about hiding from me, diet Sprite? You've lost what, ten pounds?"

"Stop yelling, Peter, you sound like a fishwife," Aubrey answered, her voice flat and tired. "And you need your eyes checked. I haven't lost any weight, and you know where everything is, as you invited yourself over. I love you dearly. But I am very tired, I am behind on this deadline, my head is splitting, and I can barely string two words together."

Her dispirited rejoinder had Peter even more upset. Aubrey's usual responses were usually either to apologize profusely for upsetting him, or to tell him to kiss her ass, after he had just used such language. If she had been drinking, she would have said worse.

"Aw, honey." Peter set the bags down, and walked over to her. "Permission to hug, or will you threaten to punch me in the junk?"

Aubrey chuckled, and wrapped her arms around Peter's

waist. "You irritating Ent. I love you, but you shouldn't be here. I am the worst company imaginable, no one would want to be next to or near me..." She was interrupted by her phone chirping, and she sighed. "God. How does he...I'm sorry, Peter, excuse me. I need to answer this text."

Peter watched as Aubrey's tongue slid out of the corner of her mouth while she punched the screen firmly. "Anyway. As I was saying, I'm wretched to be around at the moment. I'm struggling with..."

"Who is that?"

Aubrey looked at Peter as if he had suddenly sprouted two extra heads. "What?"

"I asked you who was that, just now...Who's texting you?"

Her eyes narrowed to slits. "I beg your pardon? Are you suddenly my keeper?"

"No, I'm your big brother...the big brother who is getting ready to kick the ass of whoever is giving you that headache because he's stalking my little sister!" Peter folded his arms and glared back. "You were mad the jerk texted. You said, 'How does he...' How does this dirtbag what, Aubrey?"

"He's not a dirtbag and there will not be any ass-kicking, you ass!"

"Not a dirtbag, huh? Then why're you lookin' so tired with those dark circles under your eyes and your hair lookin' like you been stickin' your finger in the sockets? You are never behind on deadlines, and what's more, the day you can't hitch words together and make 'em sound like music I'm checkin' for your pulse!" Peter was becoming so enraged he was losing his polished diction in favor of the patois he grew up speaking.

"Get your beer, Peter, before I throw it at you!" One of Aubrey's shortest fuses was Peter taking cheap shots at her hair, and he knew it.

"Who is it, Aubrey!"

"None of your fucking business!" Aubrey exploded.

"Oh, she's mad now," Peter thought. "No alcohol on board and the cussin' has seriously begun…" Then he demanded, "How long has he been bothering you?"

"He's not bothering me, Peter…! I don't…he's…oh, shit!" Her face crumpled. "I feel so wretched because I can't make up my mind, and I can't bear the thought of leaving him hanging, that's not like me…!"

Peter softened at the sign of her distress. "If you aren't sure, that's it, then. If he can't take it, too bad for him, and while I understand no one would like to see you slip away, he has to respect 'no means no,' or else I'll drop a brick on him."

"I'll drop a brick on *you*!" Aubrey flared. "I'm the one with the problem! Not him!"

Peter rolled his eyes. "Yeah, this conversation definitely needs a beer. Now I'm the one with the headache and I'm beginning to see what you meant about not being able to string words together. I've no idea what in the hell you are saying, Elf. I'll plate mine and some for you as well. If you'd get the beer and something for yourself, that should be fair, huh?" He was being crafty. This way, he'd make sure he put a good portion in front of her. He didn't care what she told him…Peter was too familiar with Aubrey's habits. He didn't think she had an eating disorder, he just knew when she became upset, she…shut down. That was scary enough, and he was grimly determined to feed his sis before he left.

Even if it meant he had to resort to drastic measures. A devilish gleam came to his eye.

"Hey, Santa's Little Helper…? You want to picnic on the floor by the windows?"

"Take that back right now, Rainbow Ent!"

He grinned, and put more food onto her plate instead.

As they sat, Peter noticed Aubrey picking at her jeyuk bibimbap that he swore she ordered just because she giggled every time she said the name. "Spill it," he ordered her.

"What's giving you so much trouble? Who is he, and why has he got your drawers in such a twist? I've never seen you like this about anyone, you keep everyone at arm's reach. Seriously, if he's penetrated your armor this far, he must be pretty damn persistent. Do I know him?"

Aubrey snorted. "I don't think so. His name is Henry, and he's Persistence, personified. I told him he'd laid a lot on me and I need to seriously think about having any kind of relationship with him...I can't get my head and heart to agree! I find myself feeling things I've never felt before, my head tells me to stop, but my heart, Peter..." she looked at her best friend, and her helpless expression caught him by his own heartstrings.

Aubrey had cared for him through more affairs than he could count. For all that she had never been in and out of relationships, Aubrey knew how to love, without measure or limits. He knew this well. When Peter asked her why she never "put herself out there," her replies were usually vague and unsatisfying. The one night he got her drunk enough to lose partial control over her tongue, she admitted she hated holding still very long, which destroyed the one serious relationship she had. She came back from a month-long trip early, ecstatic at the prospect of surprising Paul, her boyfriend of three months. She was the one surprised, as she found him balls-deep in someone she considered a friend.

Aubrey was incredibly slow to trust as it was. After that, she decided not to risk her heart, to anyone.

"What is it about this Henry that has you thinking about him," Peter asked, his curiosity piqued. "And eat your yuk."

He was pleased to hear her snicker as she had a bite. "It's hard to pin it down, I wish I could just say, 'it's his smile', or 'we have things in common', or 'I like the way he thinks'... but I can't. It's more than that. There's something I can't define, and it's making me crazy! He haunts me. Not literally," she added anxiously.

"Do you wanna bang him?"

Aubrey sprayed out the mouthful of water she'd just taken. "Jesus, Peter!"

"Nope, just Peter." His grin was wide and devilish. "So, do you? I think I should meet this guy. Size him up. Let him know if he hurts you, I'm gonna hurt *him*…and he better have good medical benefits. Dental too, come to that…"

Aubrey threw him a dirty look as she grabbed a napkin to wipe down the window she'd just drenched. "You're such a massive jerk. What's more, not only does he want to meet you, he's already seen you. How's that for an eye-opener?"

"You showed him a photo? Did you make sure you chose one that highlighted my good side?" Peter preened.

Aubrey related how Henry saw their encounter at the airport, and he was both stunned and pleasantly shocked. "Wow, I guess someone really is always looking when you least expect it. Crazy…Eat more yuk, Elf…"

She shook her head. "Anyway, I told him how close we are, and I think he got nervous that maybe you and I were an item. I said you were my brother-from-another-mother. He asked if I was sure all you felt was…filial affection."

Peter choked on his dumpling. "Um. That would be a definite…"

"I just looked at him and said I had the wrong tackle."

Peter roared. "Succinct and to the point. That's my sister-from-another-mister!"

"Yep."

They were quiet for a little while before Peter pushed harder. "So, what's the problem? I haven't heard a problem yet."

Aubrey hunched her shoulders, and her best friend watched with dismay as she went into her "trying-to-disappear" mode. "I don't think he and I will mesh very well in the long run…"

"Why the hell not? He in the mob or something? You run

someone over and he's a cop? With the way you drive, it's no wonder Santa never gave you the reins…"

She hunched further. "Stop it. No."

"You know I'm not gonna stop. Tell me."

"It's his…lifestyle. I don't think…"

Peter sat up straight, fire flaring from his eyes. Just as teasing Aubrey about her hair was a short fuse for her, intolerance of someone's lifestyle was a hot button for him. "Oh girl, you did *not*. You did not just shut a man down because of…? You said his 'lifestyle'…what the hell did you mean by that? Is he a drag queen? A stripper? You, who have never shown any kind of bias against me or my friends, and even I will admit I have some pretty fucked-up friends…"

"Henry? A drag queen? A *stripper*? Oh my God!" Aubrey doubled over laughing, howling until tears were streaming down her face. "No! Nothing like that…oh, shit, I am just going to have to tell you. You've probably heard of him. His name is Henry Rhys."

Peter became very still. "Henry…Rhys."

"Uh huh," Aubrey stopped giggling, and managed to drink some water and have a bite of supper.

"The actor, Henry Rhys."

"How many Henry Rhyses do you know? Yep. That's him. I guess you know of him then? I…"

Peter scrabbled to pull up a photo on his phone. "This guy. This Henry Rhys."

Aubrey looked at the picture. "Uh huh. That's not what he looks like right now, though, his hair is darker, and shorter… did you know he's doing a play right now? On Broadway and everything…"

Peter let out a sound both dolphins and dogs could hear. "*Henry Rhys*. Henry Rhys, from the *Nebulae Chronicles* is calling you and you're giving him the *brush off*?"

Aubrey's expression suddenly became stony. "And your reaction is exactly why I don't know if any relationship with

Do You Hear What I Hear?

him could ever work. How could I ever...be...with him, and not be noticed? I don't want anyone taking my photo, I don't want the world to know where I am, I want to be happily invisible. Anonymous. If I should...be...with him, everyone will stare." She tucked her chin to her chest.

Peter shook his head. "Honey, who, or what, are you hiding from? I know you said you left the podunk town you grew up in, and you said you never wanted to go back. I get it. You don't see me going back to my ancestral homelands either...but what could a Hobbit like you be running from? And I would bet my tooth Henry has enough PR people on staff cover up, scrub up, and clean up whatever it is, leaving you smelling like the rose you are, even if you did grow up on a dung heap...did you?"

"Did I what?"

"Grow up on a dung heap. You never told me shit."

"I see what you did there," she deflected as she stood and brought her plate of food to the counter to box the leftovers.

"Aubrey, if you don't want to tell me, I ain't gonna push. Tonight, anyway. But I will tell you this, and it's not because you're dating tall, dark, and Welshman sexy...if you keep hiding from whatever it is in your past, you are letting the bastards win. And they do not deserve your future. You are giving them your present as it is. You're stronger than this, Sis." He followed her to the kitchen, and scowled. "Not that you're gonna stay strong if you don't eat!"

"Quit nagging, you walking redwood!"

"I'm gonna do worse than nag if you don't straighten up. I'm not even joking. I will move in and force-feed your ass. You think last Christmas was bad? You haven't seen anything."

Aubrey gave him a sidelong glare. The previous Christmas she had been so tied in knots over finishing her manuscript that the real world did not exist. Peter finally unlocked her door to find her with her headphones on, and a few paltry takeout containers in her bin. He'd picked her up, threw the headphones on the sofa, and tossed her into the shower, clothes and all. She hadn't showered in days, and not eaten a decent meal in a week. Livid, Peter was like Velcro for the rest of the holiday, physically dragging outside once a day. It didn't matter if Aubrey wanted to go or not.

"I love you, Sis. You're all I've got in this city, and I will be damned if I'm gonna let you get sick over this, or anything else," he added quietly. "Remember how many times you've held me together when my world got flaky around the edges? It works both ways."

She looked up into Peter's eyes, dropping her usual attitude. "Peter…I feel like I'm frozen even as I want to run to him."

He wrapped her in his arms. "You need to set yourself free, my darling. You're locked yourself in a cage. Whatever it was, back there, you escaped…but then you locked *yourself* up. Why you wanna do that? You don't need to be scared anymore. I will beat the crap out of anyone that comes near you, and this Henry guy, if you and he are meant for each other…he'll take care of you, as you take care of him. But you gotta let yourself out of the cage. I know when you do, you're gonna be a tiger. I want to be there to see it."

She huffed.

"Yeah, you make that noise now. Just think about it. And I don't care how big of a star he is, he hurts you, I will still mess up his pretty boy face."

"He knows that," she said, her words muffled against his chest as he hugged her tight. "He said so the first day."

"Good-looking, talented, and smart. Some guys have everything," Peter whined, then pulled Aubrey's ponytail. "It's getting late, Hobbit, and I need to be at the office early tomorrow. I have presentations coming together and I need to make sure they'll be ready to fly."

"I am sure they'll be amazing. *You're* amazing. Good-looking, talented, and smart." Aubrey's words were earnest as she hugged him. "You are the best thing that's ever happened to me, Peter Rivera, and I don't know how I got so lucky to have you in my life. But I'm so thankful."

"Ah, stop it, you're making me blush…" Peter tugged her hair again. "Now I am leaving all of this food here because I'm coming back and we're gonna finish it. This weekend. Got it? Don't even think about ghosting me because you know I have a key and you know I'll use it if you force me. I won't like doing it but I will if you try vanishing on me."

"No ghosting, even though it's the week for it."

HENRY FOUND REMAINING LOCKED in his role that night one of the biggest challenges he had ever encountered.

Without fail, once he donned his costume, he slipped into the mindset of his character. It was as simple as that. Nothing could remove him.

But tonight, in the middle of his heartfelt line, "I knew my mind would no longer be free to romp like the mind of God, that falling in love would change my destiny forever," he could not help but overhear Aubrey's laughter, rich and as clear as all the bells in the world. It filled his heart—and then he "overheard":

Henry? A drag queen? A stripper? Oh my God!

It was impossible not to lose his rhythm with that. He hesitated a fraction of a second, but was able to continue. It was only due to thousands of hours of practice and training he was able to retain his composure at all! Still, he was gripped with an insatiable need to know to whom she was speaking, and how this topic had arisen…

The fact she was thinking of him lifted his spirits faster than bolting a shot of the finest scotch on the planet. He had already texted her right before he'd stepped onto the stage to let her know his play was beginning, and that as ever he was thinking of her. As he did, he sensed her disquiet, and catching a fragment of her thought *I am the worst company imaginable, no one would want to be next to or near me...* He ended his text with, "I will always wish to be with you, even in your worst mood. Your Henry."

A text popped back up before he could power it off:

> Break a leg, Henry, I know you will shine. I think of you often as well. So grateful and humbled by your patience.
> Aubrey.

When the curtain dropped that evening, Michael found him as he was preparing to go out and greet fans at the stage door. "Hey, don't think I didn't catch your little bobble there...what happened, man, you okay? Not like you, I was afraid you were stifling a sneeze! I was ready for anything... remember when Alicia had allergies and was holding back sneezes the entire show? Late September caught all of us hard."

"Will you stop harping over that?" Alicia Stephens, the actress cast as Daisy Buchanan, appeared from behind Michael. "At least the nasal quality of my stuffy nose made my upper-class drawl sound authentic. Just wait, Michael, karma is a bitch! Maybe you'll have incurable farts...!"

Henry rolled his eyes at the two's playful bickering. "Then we'll be the ones to suffer. Let's go, you lunatics, our public awaits..." He was grateful Alicia sidetracked Michael so he was free to cast his mind out like a net, hoping to catch any elusive thoughts from Aubrey before he had to block out the deluge of screaming thoughts and words from outside the theater. He was desperate, longing for anything, but all he heard was the rushing sound of his blood between his ears.

And a tsunami, threatening to drown his sanity...

He smiled, answered questions politely, signed his name repeatedly, blocked questions he did not wish to answer with long-standing practice. His heart felt like it was pulsing, beating, searching for Aubrey's. It wanted to beat in time with hers, if not the exact rhythm at least in harmony...

Never before had he felt such stress where his head was telling him to stop while his heart was telling him to run! Henry knew he needed to give Aubrey time. Instinctively, he knew if he advanced too aggressively, she would retreat so far and fast he would lose the battle and the war. He still didn't understand her reluctance to be with him after their talk in the park. It had been *so long*...why could she not talk to him beyond her brief, admittedly sweet texts?

The day Henry finally got to lay his eyes on his One, the theater was dark. Otherwise he wouldn't have had the time to follow her, or else (and more likely) he would have been forced to call in his understudy (and wouldn't *that* have caused a ruckus, both Greg and Beatrice would have deep-fried his arse). But the following day, Henry gave the performance of a lifetime...he *was* Jay Gatsby in a way he never knew possible. His performance was filled with so much gusto, even his costars were amazed, and complimented him afterwards.

"Damn, Rhys, what the hell?" Michael asked him afterwards. "I don't know what inspiration you were drawing from, but we all want in on it!"

He simply shrugged, looking down at his feet with a modest grin. "Everything came together, on the inside. I found my green light," he deflected.

Henry couldn't, wouldn't, explain he had found it when he saw Aubrey's eyes...not green, not exactly. Hers were more of a kaleidoscope, where he saw all the colors of the sea washing together, and he drew the power of his Gatsby from that, crashing over and through him.

Henry wanted to send her flowers. An entire shop's worth. Gloves, any kind she wanted. A new shoulder bag, the one she was carrying looked heavier than it needed to be...

whatever women liked these days...He wanted to meet Peter, and promise he would treasure this woman like no one had ever been cherished since the beginning of time.

Finally, Henry was bundled off into his waiting vehicle, and he pulled out his phone. He was about to beg Aubrey to allow him to see her again. He couldn't bear being so close to having his One in his life, but not allowed access to her. She was what he needed. If he wasn't actively performing, she was all he thought about, even as he was forced to adhere to his packed calendar of meetings, interviews, publicity events, and more meetings. Greg was constantly running interference for his inattentiveness, and Christine was working miracles as he constantly forgot little bits and pieces of himself everywhere.

Powering on his phone, Henry bolted upright from his exhausted slouch in the rear seat when he read the following:

> Henry, you have been so considerate, not being impatient or frustrated as I have tried to process and understand everything you told me (with both my head & heart). I still am struggling, to be honest, but I am tired of fighting what my heart wants, which is to get to know you better. I know you are always in demand, so your time is precious. When could we get together? I would love to see you again. Sincerely, Aubrey.

6

HOW DARE YOU?

As much as it almost drove Henry crazy, he realized he would to wait until Sunday to meet with Aubrey, as he had not one show but two on Saturday, the matinee as well as the evening event. This did not prevent him from sending her a flurry of texts beginning the instant he saw she had reached out to him at last, even though it was quite early Friday morning.

```
Aubrey? Are you awake?

…Oh God, I just saw the time. So
sorry! I hope I didn't wake you up. If
so, please go back to sleep!
```

> Henry, I'm a writer. It almost guarantees I'm a night owl.
> How was tonight?

> It went fine, except I almost lost my
> rhythm when I caught you mentioning my
> name, "drag queen," and "stripper" all
> in the same breath. Dare I ask? Are
> you trying to find a new profession
> for me?

> Oh God. You weren't supposed to hear that! In fact, why and HOW did you hear that?! I wasn't trying to get your attention, I am so sorry! *hides face* *hides under bed*

THE IMAGERY of Aubrey diving under a bed, scarlet with embarrassment, was too much for the exhausted man, already high with elation over Aubrey's desire to see him coupled with the usual post-performance buzz.

> I am laughing so hard the driver must
> think I am punch-drunk with exhaus-
> tion. Don't fret, but you have to tell
> me. You really do. It's only fair!

> This is not something I can explain over text...!

LIKE A WAVE OF WARM WATER, Henry felt Aubrey's mind reach his. Henry's laughter in volume as she shared her memory of Peter's sharp scolding.

Do You Hear What I Hear?

. . .

JONATHAN RIKER HAD BEEN DRIVING Henry around since his arrival, and their rapport was such the chauffeur sighed, "Sir, this isn't fair. Can you let me in on the joke, or is it too personal? If it is, I'm backing off...but it's late, and I've never heard you bust a gut like this before."

Henry's chest almost burst from the confines of its shirt, he was so proud to reply, "It's my...this woman I'm...you can't say anything, Jon!"

"Oh, come on, sir, I signed my name to so many nondisclosure agreements I don't even think my own mother knows what I do anymore. You gotta give me something...!"

Henry was laughing so hard as he tried to recount the small scene, it took almost the rest of his trip home before Jon understood the gist of the story. Then both men were howling.

"Sir, that's it...you gotta show up to meet this Peter with a feather boa."

Henry wiped his eyes. "That's genius, Jon. Make it so, Number One..."

As usual, Henry eschewed having his driver open his door for him. Groaning at Henry's jest and behavior, Jon shook his head. "Goodnight, sir. See you tomorrow, bright and early."

"AUBREY?" Henry was still texting her as he walked into the express elevator to his suite.

                                            Yes, Henry?

```
Would you and Peter like to come to
the play Sunday night? I can promise
you some seats, as my guests, of
course...afterwards, once I've scraped
off the face paint and changed, we
could go out somewhere. Anywhere you
like. The three of us. So Peter may
interrogate me at his leisure.
```

Henry, you don't have to do that...although if Peter finds out you offered and I declined, he may dangle me over the side of my balcony until I cry...I'm afraid he's more than a bit of a fan of your movies. The *Nimbus Chronicles*?

IT DID NOT BOTHER Henry one bit Aubrey was oblivious to the series of films that catapulted him to international fame. He loved the work, and the original followers of the series were genuinely appreciative of his efforts to remain true to the character in the novels he portrayed.

Before he met Aubrey, his ego would have been bruised. Not badly, but enough to sting. He put so much of himself in everything he did, always stretching to perfect his craft.

Now? It meant nothing at all.

```
It would be my utmost pleasure to host
my One and her adoptive brother...I
suppose you have not explained to
Peter anything about the intricacies
of our relationship?
```

> Oh God, no. He knows nothing about me and my…
> quirks. And I am going to keep it that way.

```
I understand.
```

HENRY DID UNDERSTAND. Greg had no idea how Henry could hear everything Greg thought, right down to how his friend suffered from lactose intolerance after eating ice cream, so refused it with a smile when in public, but indulged when he was alone.

```
I hate to say goodnight, but I need
sleep…
```

> Get some rest, Henry. I will talk to you tomorrow. And I
> promise not to think anything about you and new
> professions. Especially when I know you are engaged in
> your current livelihood. *giggle*

```
Thank you, Aubrey, your sacrifice is much
appreciated.
```

Henry quickly fell into a blissful slumber, he was not only exhausted but his emotions had been violently tossed up and down in the past twenty-four hours. He was ripe for a crash.

If he was aware of how close Aubrey was—only a few city blocks—it might not have been so easy for him to succumb to the lures of Morpheus. Aubrey herself was struggling with waves of her own emotions. She couldn't even lock herself away in the world she had created without his gentle assault on the walls of her defenses. How *very* dare he scramble her head and heart so?

She eked out another hour on the manuscript before giving up. "Sorry, Joelle," she muttered as she crashed into her own bed.

Peter was indeed overjoyed at the notion of attending *Gatsby* on Sunday and he was annoying as a mosquito while planning his wardrobe. "Peter, I don't know where we are sitting," Aubrey whined as Peter perused her closet. "I don't know what the appropriate dress code is. I will ask Henry…"

Speaking my name, dear one? I am thankful I am not onstage!

Aubrey's eyes glazed for a moment. Henry's voice purring in her head caught her very much off guard, even if it did not throw him off stride…

Peter is driving me mad, wondering what to wear tomorrow. I told him I would ask you where we were sitting, as I am sure that will affect the dress code. And please, the cheap seats are just fine. Honestly, they are…

I will have my assistant, Christine Abbot, contact you for clarity. She is very kind and patient. She has to be. Look at whom she has to put up with…! I need to rush, though, we're prepping to warm up for the evening show. I will be thinking of you…you are my green light. Give my best regards to Peter, I am looking forward to meeting him tomorrow…

"…damn it, Aubrey, where do you go in that head of

Do You Hear What I Hear?

yours, have you heard me at all?" Peter was pounding his fist on her open closet door. "Are you all right?"

Aubrey scowled. "Do you know how to do anything to a door besides bang on it? I was trying to think, I knew I had forgotten something, and besides, I…need to pee," she improvised, trying to escape his penetrating gaze.

"Pull the other one, Elf, it's got bells on it," Peter shot back. "I reheated Thursday's takeout, and you're gonna eat…"

His reply was a saucy raspberry and an extended middle finger as she fled for the sanctuary of her bathroom…slamming the door for emphasis.

Henry was true to his word. About an hour and a half later, Aubrey's phone rang.

"Hello, Ms. Stafford? Hi, I'm Christine Abbot, Henry Rhys's personal assistant. He asked I call you about tomorrow evening, he said that you had some questions. How may I help you?"

Aubrey could not help but smile at the friendly voice. "It is so kind of you to call on a Saturday evening…"

"Think nothing of it, I do whatever the man asks, and he was most insistent I phone you as soon as possible…" Christine proceeded to describe the tickets available for Aubrey and Peter. "There are a pair of seats on the Orchestra level, center, third row from the stage, or a box on the right… however, I am going to be indiscreet and volunteer the box seats, for all the cachet, will not give you the viewing experience the Orchestra seats will. I have been up and down the different seats in the house to get a feel for the best lines of sight."

"Oh," Aubrey stammered. "You sound like an incredibly busy woman…when did you find the time?"

Christine was amused, hearing how a task of twenty minutes (and was a bit of a break from dealing with Henry's mercurial temperament) had created such a favorable impression with the woman on the line. Was she getting a better understanding of why Henry's jock was in a knot…? But no, she had been given the strictest of instructions to secure the best seats for one Aubrey Stafford and Peter Rivera. So maybe not…

"Honestly? Just this morning," she laughed.

"Look, Ms…"

"Just Christine, Ms. Stafford."

"Then you must call me Aubrey. I told Henry repeatedly, I don't want to tie up expensive seats. I am just as happy with less…"

"Oh, no you don't," Christine interrupted, laughing again. "I was given a very specific set of orders. You wouldn't want to get me in trouble now, would you?"

"No, of course not!" Aubrey floundered. "Which would you recommend, then?"

Christine smoothly persuaded Aubrey to accept the Orchestra level seats. When Aubrey pleaded for guidance on appropriate clothing, however, the PA wasn't nearly as decisive.

"The important thing is to be comfortable," she advised. "Dress for the weather and your plans following the show. I've seen people come in jeans! Today's theater world is past 'black tie optional'!"

"Christine, I can't thank you enough for your help with selecting our tickets…but for dress code advice, you've been no help, whatsoever."

Aubrey's dry remark elicited more laughter. "I aim to please…when you arrive tomorrow, simply go to the box office at the 'will call' line and give your name. You will be taken care of from that point."

Sitting in the cramped office away from the public, Christine swiftly blocked off the seats as Henry instructed, thinking, "Aubrey, I don't know who you are, but oh my God, you sure will be taken care of, you don't know the half of it yet…"

Do You Hear What I Hear?

Christine was not attached to Mr. Rhys's personal staff, but the theater company. As such she had worked with actors from all over the world. Some were polite, others were such divas she would swear every night it would be her last production, she would rather work with toddlers needing naps and diaper changes than deal with pseudo-adults, ever again.

Mr. Rhys was a joy to work for, even if somewhat manic-depressive, obsessive-compulsive, and had the attention span of a gnat at times. He was always considerate and well-mannered, even when the vein in his temple began pulsing and the muscles in his square jaw tensed. She could usually soothe his temper and keep him on track (although she warned him she would never again cross the city because he'd left something behind. She didn't care how special it was, it would need to be couriered, he would have to purchase another, or he would have to do without. Enough already...! But he had been so sad...those puppy dog eyes...!).

"Face it, Chris, he played you like a fiddle," she muttered, making certain the staff knew Mr. Rhys's VIPs would be attending the following evening's performance, and all that entailed.

Back in Aubrey's small loft, Aubrey was left staring at her phone. "Well, Peter, I guess we can wear...whatever we want?"

Peter whooped, "You know what this means, don't you, Sister-Mine?"

"It means dressing up, with heels, and your Strutting-It Suit, doesn't it?" Her voice was much put-upon, even as her smile was tolerant.

"Get them out. Right now. I won't hear anything about not being ready tomorrow!"

· · ·

Henry was tapped out by the time the curtain came down on Saturday, but he still managed to spend some time at the stage door. So far, he had not missed a single one unless it was announced at the close of the show. Those times were invariably due to some publicity event or scheduled schmoozing.

Greg would always make sure he was present at said affairs. Henry could only be depended to smile and behave for so long after a demanding production, and it was written into his contract there never be any such events on Saturday evenings. Greg had seen what could happen when Henry's famed bright smile and customary polite demeanor turned more feral…it was just this side of terrifying. Having witnessed it once, Greg wanted to make certain it never happened again. True, the woman Henry turned on was intruding on his personal space, seeming to think her donation to the particular cause also purchased a part of his time and person, and she was generally an unpleasant, narcissistic individual…but Henry's few innocuous words flayed her to the core. All while his amused facial expression (corners of his mouth turned up, front teeth exposed) had the hallmarks of a smile…if one could ignore the manner his teeth looked more like he was baring them in a challenge as his blue eyes promised no mercy.

Tonight, however, Henry simply smiled, made inconsequential chatter with his fans, and signed as many autographs as he could in the short period of time allowed before he said goodnight.

"I'm so tired, sweet Aubrey. Are you even awake?" Henry's fingers fumbled so badly, he was grateful for autocorrect.

> Of course I am. Sleep? Bah, humbug. I have a deadline.

Do You Hear What I Hear?

> My One could never be mistaken for
> Scrooge…You are made of strong stuff,
> but I am not surprised at all, you are
> so focused on your craft.

HENRY STRUGGLED to become more coherent.

> Everything ready for tomorrow? Chris-
> tine sent me a message, you have your
> seats reserved, Orchestra seat center
> third row…You are happy, yes? Chris-
> tine promised you were…

> Considering how I said I would be just as pleased to have seats in the gods, yes, Henry, I am overwhelmed. I've been to a few plays before, but never a Broadway production, and never this close to the stage. I am very excited. Peter is VIBRATING! We bickered over what to wear like an old married couple. Of course, he had the final say.

HENRY GRUNTED as he read that last, now wide awake. He didn't care for the mental image of Peter getting a fashion show from his Aubrey, much less the "married couple" simile.

> Why does he have the final say?

Henry. Peter is a gay man who is a very talented graphics designer. He has more fashion sense in his little finger than I have in my entire body. I hate to fall back on what sounds like a blatant stereotype, but in this case it is completely true.

```
Will you be comfortable? There is no
point in wearing anything if you
aren't happy. I know…! It's bad enough
when I have to wear something I really
despise for an afternoon of ridiculous
photo shoots, but in my downtime? No!
I would never ask that of you. Please,
wear whatever you want!
```

Relax. I don't have any clothes I didn't choose on my own. Nothing was forced on me by Peter or anyone else…I'm wearing a sweater dress with leggings. Nothing grand. Now Peter…HE will look amazing. He has his Strutting-It Suit and he's cracking it out from the dry-cleaner's bag.

HENRY SMIRKED AT THE IDEA. He could imagine the pair of them already.

```
Be thinking about what to do after-
```

> wards. I don't care where, as long as
> there will be an opportunity to get
> something to drink, and we can talk.

I repeat: relax. Go to sleep, Henry. Sweet dreams. See you tomorrow!

HENRY'S SMIRK softened into a gentle smile.

> You have the tenderest heart. I hear,
> and obey, my One. Perhaps I will see
> you as I dream, teasing about the
> periphery of my senses. I will sleep
> all the sweeter if I do. I can't wait
> to see you again.

AUBREY'S FINGERS traced over her screen as she read his words. She was completely at a loss. Never had she been the recipient of such devoted wooing and her head was being turned just by his words. She shook her head, perversely vexed. Constantly being at war with herself was exhausting.

No one would understand her reluctance, her need to remain anonymous. There was a reason she had fled to the largest city she could find, damn it!

Scrooge couldn't be the only one ever haunted by ghosts of his past, she groused, crawling into bed...How very *dare* Henry come into her life, just when she was so damned certain she had locked every part of her life into place? Now she felt she was looking at the ruin of all her walls, her defenses in disarray. She might as well be on the run all over again...! Aubrey could no longer lie to herself: she was truly charmed by his words, his turn of phrase...she...liked him.

She punched her pillow, then turned over with a huff.

Sitting on the other side of the bed was Aubrey's security object. She reached for it, drawing it to her breasts. It was the one thing in the world that held her ultimate, complete trust: she knew when she touched it, she would be inundated with pleasant Scenes, loving Voices.

It was her dragon, a gift from Peter. She always heard his voice, saw his smile. It never failed to bring her comfort when she was stressed, angry, feeling frantic, as she was now.

Henry's words followed her as her eyes closed, as he continued to haunt her heart.

She fell asleep at last, dreaming of Peter...and Henry.

7

MYSTERIOUS WAYS

Aubrey was more than a little nervous when she went to pick up the tickets at the box office. The playhouse was teeming with people, a shoal of chattering theater-goers seemingly swimming at random from one area to the next. Peter's solid presence behind her restored her courage.

"Hello, my name is Aubrey Stafford, and I should have a pair of tickets waiting for me, please? For myself and Peter Rivera." She offered her driver's license for identification.

There was a slight flutter of activity in the small area behind the glass. "Thank you, Ms. Stafford. If you would just step to the side, someone will assist you in just a few moments."

Aubrey turned to look at Peter anxiously as she took his hand in hers. Even here, she was wearing her signature pair of gloves. Tonight they were black, matching her boots. Peter was dressed as nattily as if he was going to his own wedding: a slim plaid suit, complete with waistcoat, paired with a hunter green turtleneck that matched her own sweater dress almost perfectly. Combined with his ebony hair and warm cinnamon bark colored skin, he looked as though he could be a shareholder in the historic building.

Aubrey looked at her outfit doubtfully as she watched a woman in a cocktail dress sail by, and bit her lip. She needed to pull herself together. In her loft, she was perfectly content with her mockneck green sweater dress with its lantern sleeves. It was supposed to stop at her upper thigh, but she was so petite it came lower. Paired with sleek black leggings and heeled boots that came almost to her knees, one sweater became a dress Peter assured her was the "epitome of chic" and she just had to trust him. She had let her hair stay curly for a change rather than fussing with the flat iron, and between herself and Peter pulled it into a elaborate braid. She felt herself in the outfit, the sweater complimenting her feminine curves without clinging to her so snugly she felt self-conscious. She would never be happy feeling like a toothpaste tube, being squeezed in the middle, she confided artlessly to Peter one evening while they were talking about women's fashion, and he laughed until he fell off the sofa.

"Stop it," Peter said without moving his lips. "You are my beautiful Santa's Little Helper, you look sexy as hell, and if you eat that lipstick off I will tell Henry how you can't sleep without the plush dragon I gave you several years ago..."

"Do it," she growled, "and I will..."

"Hello, Ms. Stafford? Mr. Rivera? If you would step this way, please?" A woman dressed in a sharply tailored suit greeted them as she stepped from a door marked "Strictly no entrance."

Peter looked nonchalant, as though entering restricted areas was a commonplace activity for him, and kept a firm grip on Aubrey's elbow, forcing her to walk alongside him. Once they were separated from the public, the woman grinned at them. "Hi, Aubrey, I'm Christine. I will release you back into the wild in a moment. I simply wanted to take the opportunity to introduce myself to you, and Mr. Rivera, in person."

He gave Christine a happy smile in return. "Just Peter! Mr.

Rivera is undoubtedly sleeping it off after watching the Patriots lose in the fourth quarter..."

Christine laughed, the same carefree burble Aubrey remembered from the day before. "There's always next week...Aubrey, Peter, here are your tickets for the usher..." She also handed them each a bag stuffed with souvenirs, insisting they were standard for VIP guests. There were a variety of items, from t-shirts to stickers to magnets, but Peter's eyes widened at the sight of a poster autographed by the cast and director.

"Aubrey," he breathed. "It's like they knew I was coming...!"

She shook her head in dismay, but before she could protest, Christine easily forestalled her arguments. "If I may be indiscreet, Henry has hardly enjoyed any personal guests. Michael Thomas, who plays Nick Carraway, has had easily three times as many. It's to be expected, I suppose, with Henry's friends and family living in the UK. It would give him great pleasure to give you the entire VIP experience." She looked at them both shrewdly.

Just as she anticipated, Aubrey's expression visibly softened. "I didn't even think of it that way...how isolated he must feel sometimes," she murmured, fingering a postcard bearing the same image as the photo on the playbill.

Christine's inner radar was definitely sounding. Aubrey and Peter gave every appearance of being a couple, down to the way they dressed, and yet...

"As a part of your evening, please help yourself to the bar." She placed bands around both their wrists. "I know, they clash with your lovely outfits, but as soon as the curtain comes down, you can take them off. Henry requested that once the show has concluded, please remain in your general seating area. Someone will come to escort you to his dressing room. I know he is quite excited to go out with you after the show. He is even cutting out his usual stage door appearance."

Before Aubrey could object, Peter ran over her by saying, "Christine, this is wonderful, and thank you for meeting us. We don't want to keep you, if Mr. Rhys is looking for you..."

She smiled, and shook her head. "Trust me, right before the curtain goes up, he isn't looking for anyone. He is locked in his dressing room, deep inside his head. In fact, I don't think I could even find Henry Rhys right now...just Jay Gatsby." She thought for a moment. "If you like, I could take your bags, and leave them in his dressing room so you won't to have them around your feet. The theater is a beautiful piece of architecture, but there isn't a lot of room for bags. It's hell during the winter, we have a coat room, but it's never big enough...!"

Aubrey frowned. "I wouldn't want to disturb him while he's preparing..." She was very careful not to say, or even think Henry's name, aware of the distraction it might be for him.

Christine's radar ping went up an octave. "That's very considerate, but trust me, I will wait until he has left. I value my hide too greatly."

Peter cocked his head to the side. "Crabby fellow, is he?"

Christine snorted. "It isn't so much what he says, as how he says it...the fire from those eyes, yikes! No thank you..."

Peter and Aubrey relinquished their bags, and she returned them to the lobby. Peter then propelled Aubrey straight to the bar, where he got her a glass of wine along with a small plate of canapés for them to share. He didn't know if he would finish his old fashioned, and he didn't care. He wanted to get some food into his Hobbit, and hope the alcohol would get her to relax and enjoy herself. He kept her at ease while she was doing her hair and makeup, but when they were getting in their cab, he could see the skin around her eyes and mouth begin to tighten.

Do You Hear What I Hear?

"Drink it, Hobbit...or the dragon is gonna fly and tell all..."

THERE WAS someone shut away in Henry Rhys's dressing room, but it was not Jay Gatsby.

In fact, the man looking in the mirror wasn't even sure he was Henry Rhys.

This man was a shambling, nervous wreck. What had he been thinking, inviting Aubrey and Peter? Why hadn't he simply invited them to meet him somewhere after the show?

"Pull yourself together," he fiercely ordered himself.

He could not speak to Aubrey without her reaching out to him first...he could not text her, certain she had turned her cell phone off, being such a conscientious person...

To hell with it. Henry picked up his phone. He had been texting her before every performance since he met her, why should this one be any different?

```
Aubrey, I know you are out there,
somewhere in the house...perhaps I will
be able to see you. Most likely not,
the way lights are situated, it is
difficult to see into the audience. It
is probably better this way. If I was
to look out and see you sitting there,
I might forget everything I have
learned. I might even forget my name.
Because the only thing I will know,
beyond a shadow of a doubt, is I have
finally, FINALLY been so blessed as to
find my soul mate, through sheer dumb
luck...and she is Sitting. Right. There…

…Along with Peter, who will never let
```

> me live it down if I cannot deliver,
> so I must pull myself together, and
> assume the person of Jay, who did not
> realize his 'dream must have seemed so
> close that he could hardly fail to
> grasp it. He did not know that it was
> already behind him'…Mine is right
> before me!
>
> The waves, the tides have finally
> turned and brought you to me. My boat
> is no longer beating against the
> current, and my God, such sweet
> relief! I can look to a future now.
>
> Looking forward to whatever it is you
> wish to do once the curtain closes.
> All I need to do is shed Jay, and
> become your One, once more.
>
> Soon, Aubrey. Look for me.

He mashed the send button with his thumb, and powered the device off.

In the bar area, Aubrey was slowly draining her wine glass when her phone let out a discreet vibration. "Damn," she muttered. "Forgot to turn it off…"

"Who's texting you on a Sunday night?" Peter lifted an eyebrow. "If it's Joelle, tell her, 'Get lost…' and turn off your phone, Hobbit. Or am I gonna have to start calling you 'Philistine'?"

Aubrey saw Henry's number, and flushed. Was he telling her he changed his mind? He had gotten everything all wrong? Maybe he had better things to do this evening, maybe…she viciously locked her heart up, and opened his message.

Peter was watching her reactions intently, and when he saw her flush, and then go pale as her eyes became glassy, he yanked the phone from her. If the bastard was gonna back out on her, now, Peter was going to be civilized. He was going to take care of his darling little sister. And then he was gonna beat the ever-loving shit out of the man...no one makes his sister cry, not ever. Especially not when she was just beginning to come out of her shell!

But reading Henry's words touched Peter's secretly romantic heart. God *damn*, but the man had a way with words. If Henry Rhys had been sending his little sister texts like these, no wonder he was managing to pry open the cage she had locked herself into...

"Give that *back*!" Aubrey hissed. "Do you have any manners *at all*, were you raised in a *barn*? Peter, the older you get, the more impossible you get!"

"Girl, has he been writing poetry like this to you all along?" Peter gave the phone back, but knew he wouldn't forget what he read.

Peter watched a documentary once when he couldn't sleep, thinking it would bore him to snoring. It didn't work. He somehow became interested, God alone knew why. What stuck with him was a quote, something about a riddle wrapped in a mystery, inside an enigma. And damned it that wasn't his Aubrey...Aubrey who was more like a riddle wrapped in a wad of gum, inside a headache.

Aubrey was well spoken. Intelligent. She hated doing math, she struggled with splitting checks and figuring out tips. She would wear gloves almost all year long. When Peter nagged her about it, she shrugged it off but wouldn't discuss it, and refused to take them off.

Here was a ridiculously handsome man, who was all but panting after her with words like these, yet why wasn't she flying out of her self-imposed prison to get to know him, at least?

Peter shook his head as the lights dimmed once, warning patrons it was time to take their seats. He wished Henry luck. Aubrey was certainly a mystery walking, and could knock a man to his knees trying to figure her out.

Henry was...brilliant.

Aubrey was entranced by the entire production, the ensemble was so talented, they interacted seamlessly, like choreographed dancers. The sets were elaborate, perfectly detailed for the Gilded Age, but never so overpowering they distracted from the actors. The music selections playing in the background were exquisite, further enhancing the mood of the scene and the dialogue.

But above all, Henry simply shone.

He never dominated the stage in a manner that stole attention from his colleagues. No, he was too much of a professional for that...and yet, Aubrey could not tear her eyes from him. She wasn't entranced by his handsome form, clad in bespoke suits, or his hair, gelled into waves and curls.

It was the power of Jay's expressive face...the naked emotion Jay would allow to escape when he thought no one was watching. Aubrey was familiar with the story, but watching it unfold in front of her pinned to her seat, enthralled.

She and Peter had a perfect, unobstructed view. They had a clear vista of the entire stage, and the unfolding tragedy.

When Jay stared longingly at Daisy, something in her heart rolled over. The genuine hunger he felt for her, the yearning...Aubrey had to catch her breath. Anger roiled in her breast as she watched the spoiled heiress float though the disasters she created, and waited for Jay to clean up, even to his destruction. When the final gunshot sounded, she jerked

Do You Hear What I Hear?

violently, cramming a fist in her mouth as she moaned. Jay's murder took place offstage, thank God. Peter's face was stoic, but he wrapped his arm around Aubrey, who was shaking.

The final act of the play, the ultimate and final repudiation of Gatsby by everyone save Nick Carraway, left Aubrey feeling dizzy, and ill. She kept reminding herself it was just a play, that everyone (again, so careful not to use anyone's name) was truly well, including Myrtle and Wilson. Yet she was so enraged on Jay's behalf, Aubrey would have found immense satisfaction in making practical use of the self-defense classes she had taken faithfully since she began living on her own...Daisy and Tom would learn, to their sorrow, that *some* people would stand up for those they loved...!

Henry's part in the drama was over.

He knew where his Aubrey was sitting.

Of course he did, he knew it the moment his foot crossed onto the stage. He did not have to see her (such a lie, of course he did) because he could sense her. Her excitement, agitation. All of it grew as the play progressed, and her responses fed him. It was the most heavenly feedback loop he'd ever had, a sacramental experience. She was blessing, consecrating his work, and exorcising all his past demons. He could feel her, and he could continue to give Jay life.

Once he was offstage, he peeped through the lighting booth so he could witness her reactions for the rest of the play. Her violent reaction to the gunshot was unexpected. He wished he could be next to her, hold her, reassure her he was fine, it was simply smoke, mirrors, and noise... ("Darling, has something happened in your life involving gunfire? You're all but clinging from the rafters...") His mind twisted around what he did not know or understand, but he longed to touch and heal whatever hurts she carried behind her eyes. He knew he could, if she would allow him...

Then, it was over. Curtain call, encores, and he could look upon her face, and smile. Of course, he could not fixate upon her, but he could still smile and have their eyes meet, "alone in space" as the novel said.

He dashed off, eager to clean Jay's end from him so his night, his life, could begin.

8

CAN'T HELP FALLING IN LOVE

A fterwards, Peter and Aubrey sat and looked at each other.

"That was...intense," Peter offered.

"Yep," Aubrey agreed. Her voice was still a bit shaky, although she had recovered after seeing Henry's eyes find her, and smile warmly.

"Where do you want to go? You know he's going to defer to you," Peter prodded.

Aubrey's expression became thoughtful. "He wasn't particular," she mused aloud. He assumed you would wish to interrogate him at leisure. Those are his words, not mine...," she chuckled. "For myself, I want to take him anywhere he can get something warm to drink!"

"After that performance, I can imagine he needs to coat the throat! There's any number of places to grab something to eat if he's hungry...do you think he's hungry?"

"Like a bear," came Christine's amused voice. "Sorry, I didn't mean to eavesdrop, but I couldn't help overhearing. Usually he has something waiting in his dressing room, and he all but inhales it. As he didn't ask for anything this evening, it's a safe bet he's ready to devour anything right now. Come on, let me take you backstage."

She guided them through a warren of narrow halls, with the pair doing their best not to gawk and stare.

The door wasn't flashy with a star or placard, and Aubrey laughed quietly. "So, not *The Muppet Show* decor?"

Christine laughed. "You'd be surprised how often we get that question!" She knocked on the door obnoxiously, leading Peter to snicker, waggling his eyebrows. "Special delivery," she sang, and the door flew open, revealing Henry's beaming countenance...and sporting a feather boa.

Peter was stunned into silence for all of two seconds, before he was howling with laughter. Aubrey was covering her face with her hands, and Christine was confused, but not shocked. She'd seen worse.

Henry tossed the pink scarf aside with a hearty laugh. "Please, come in! It's very small, so we won't stay long, but I have your bags...and at least you can say you saw where I take Jay on and off six days out of seven."

Peter was interested examining the environs. Aubrey only had eyes for Henry, who was smartly turned out in trousers, a rolled neck pullover and blazer.

Henry was just as captivated, drinking in Aubrey for the first time. It was one thing to see her face in a sea of others, but quite another to see her within arm's reach. "You look divine," he breathed, bending to kiss the back of her hand, not commenting on the gloves.

Christine prudently departed. "Bingo," she told herself smugly. It did not matter how much Peter and Aubrey appeared to be a couple. She knew Henry would never be so crass to show such blatant fascination with another man's partner. She made up her mind to waylay Greg, ASAP. If anyone knew the scoop, he did.

Aubrey blushed. "You look amazing...you were fabulous tonight. I was transported. I knew you were talented, but to see you in person...I was mesmerized by you...I mean, your performance," she stumbled.

"I could see you, but I didn't dare look," he admitted bashfully. "I needed to maintain my focus."

Peter looked up, and Aubrey scolded herself. "Where are my manners? Peter, be pleased to meet Henry Rhys. Henry, this is my family, my brother in all but blood, Peter Rivera."

Both men gave the other strong handshakes that did not strive for dominance. Seeing this made Aubrey smile.

Gathering everyone's bags, Henry said, "My driver is around back, ready to take us anywhere you would like to go. Please allow me this, so we can slip away without being noticed." More than anything, Henry wanted to ensure they could leave without being asked for autographs, selfies, or the like.

Neither Aubrey nor Peter were intimately familiar with restaurants in the theater district, but Aubrey knew places close to her loft building, which was not far away. Soon they were at a rooftop bar, and Henry was sighing as he guzzled glass after glass of water, chased with a warm old fashioned. This immediately caught Peter's interest, and it wasn't long before the trio was talking and laughing as though they were old friends by the time their food was brought to them. The conversation was lighthearted, Henry regaling them with tales of other productions where things had gone disastrously wrong on-stage and how he and his co-stars ad libbed, trying to keep the scene going. Peter joked about having to deal with everything from fashionistas to photographers to magazine publishers, whereas he was "just a lowly graphics designer looking for the WiFi password" to upload files, trying to remain calm when everyone else was having a meltdown. Aubrey grinned and recounted having to use a combination of Google translate, pidgin languages, and in one memorable case, draw stick figures when she lost her translator due to a stomach bug.

"I still have those sketches somewhere," she reflected as Henry looked at her with awe and utter delight. "Nothing quite like trying to create a stick figure theater just to ask how many bathrooms a place has...or come to it, where the closest hospital is. Just in case, you understand."

"I need to see those stick figures," Henry declared eagerly, but Peter snorted, "You really don't. I love my Hobbit, but she can't draw for beans."

"I can draw and quarter you," she replied sweetly.

"You wound me, Elf. You've hurt me to my heart." he clasped his chest as she stood to use the ladies' room. Aubrey rubbed her knuckles into his skull lightly, answering, "You have no heart, you talking tree trunk..." With a wink, she disappeared.

As soon as she was out of earshot, Henry leaned forward. "Quickly. Man-to-man. Not breaking any confidences, what can you tell me about Aubrey that you think I should know? I'm asking for anything."

Peter leaned back, eyeing Henry with a grin. "Let's see... Aubrey...she hates math. I mean hates it. She gets tense splitting the check and figuring out her portion of the tip, so her solution is to just leap on it like it's a grenade, taking the blast."

Henry shook his head. "That won't be an issue."

Peter shook his head. "Now see, that right there is gonna get you in trouble," he warned the man sitting across from him. So far, Peter was picking up a good vibe from the Welshman. What won Peter over was the way Henry listened to her. He was genuinely interested in what she had to say, all the while looking at her as though he could not believe his luck at having her seated across from him.

Henry sat up and looked affronted. "My mum, dad, and grandma all taught me better than that, I'm no bounder," he protested.

Do You Hear What I Hear?

"Not saying you are, but that one is as stubborn and independent as they come. She's taken care of herself for so many years, it's not only all she knows, it's her comfort zone. Keep that in mind," Peter answered soberly. "Let her pick up the little things now and again. It will keep her much more content..." Then his expression lightened once more. "Our Aubrey loves to sing. She's got quite a set of pipes on her. But God, she can't dance. At all. She's dangerous, in fact. The arms start moving, those legs start jumping...She's a menace. She has rhythm, but no idea what to do with herself. Best to leave her a wide buffer."

"No!" Henry objected in dismay. "I saw her walking in the airport, she seemed so...light on her feet!"

"Yeah, well get her on the dance floor and you'll see another Aubrey," Peter grinned, his teeth gleaming in the darkness. "In fact," he checked his watch, "how tired are you? Ready to move on? I know you had a busy weekend, and you really poured it on tonight. I thought I was gonna have to sit on Aubrey a few times to keep her from flying onto the stage and taking a whack at Tom and Daisy. She's got quite the temper, that red hair of hers is no lie, so don't say no one warned you..."

Henry's return grin was just as bright. "I am off all day tomorrow. The night is young, and they don't roll up the sidewalks here until four o'clock in the morning, even on a Monday..."

Peter rubbed his hands together. "Get ready. I know just the place to take you. I can't stay all night, but I can't wait for you to see what she can get up to... I know you've seen her nervy, and that's because she's been burned. You need to see her having fun. Oh, and by the way? She *adores* it when you call her 'Santa's Little Helper.' Whisper that into her ear and she's an instant softie..."

Henry's eyes narrowed. "Now, why do I get the feeling you're taking the piss?"

Peter just gave him a shark-like stretch of the lips. "Try it, and see...oh, and here she comes now."

Henry immediately stood, and Peter gave him more brownie points for it. Maybe he shouldn't have teased him... nah. He's a big man. He'll figure it out.

Peter told Aubrey, "Finish up, Sis. We're going to Acoustics."

Acoustics was a small music club set in a basement a few blocks from the Manhattan School of Music. Throughout the week, it featured live music from a variety of groups all vying for exposure, as well as karaoke nights. Acoustics could boast knowing at least a dozen current popular indie groups who had played there at one point, and had personalized tour posters to prove it.

Peter had friends there from way back, and when he met Aubrey, he took her hoping she would enjoy herself. He did not know how much she loved to sing, or flail madly about the dance floor, but he was quickly schooled. His friends quickly became hers, and they would go as frequently as her schedule would allow.

Sunday nights gave students priority: anyone attempting to get feedback for current projects was allowed stage time. The music spanned the range from classical to hip hop. The genre didn't matter, it was the performance. If no one was game, it was a casual karaoke night, or even the bartender playing DJ. The club had a modest dance floor, allowing Aubrey and anyone else to cut loose.

Peter assured Henry no one would hound him at Acoustics; no one ever knew who might walk through the door. If the staff felt someone was giving a celebrity too much attention, the star-struck patron would receive a friendly reminder to give the poor slob a break. If the request wasn't honored, the fan would be ejected.

Acoustics was about music.

Do You Hear What I Hear?

Peter was greeted with boisterous enthusiasm, but when Aubrey was spied behind him, the cacophony grew.

"Elf! Elf! Elf!" The chant rose, to Henry's amusement.

"Oh, shit," she laughed, embarrassed. "It hasn't been that long, give me a break."

Lucy Walker leapt over the bar in one smooth motion. "Oh my God…! Look what the cat dragged in! It's been what? At least two months, I haven't seen you since mid-August at least…! Where the hell have you been?"

"The question is more, where haven't I been," Aubrey responded dryly. "Lucy, this is my friend Henry. Henry, this business tycoon and music aficionado is Lucy…anything Henry wants, please put it on my tab for this evening…"

Henry opened his mouth as he pulled back, looking at Aubrey with eyes opened wide in dissent. It was then Peter's thoughts slammed into him with all the finesse of a bucking ram in breeding season: *Don't do it, man, don't go there, you picked up the check for supper and that chapped her butt because she was the one who picked the place out…*

"Thank you, Aubrey," he replied, quietly gracious. Peter gave him a discreet wink.

Lucy was nodding. "You got it, Aubrey."

There was a small group working on a Celtic piece, and as Henry ordered an Irish coffee (his throat still feeling strained) he saw what Peter meant. Aubrey was joyously moving to the beat and he was…appalled.

"Oh, dear…" he trailed off.

Peter sipped his half-and-half. "Told ya," he smirked, the glass covering his laughter.

"Christ, she looks like one of the kids from *A Charlie Brown Christmas*," Henry moaned.

Peter snorted, almost choking. "She does! Oh, she totally does…! I am so gonna go home and watch that now, so I can figure out which one she is…!"

A pianist was next. As he played, Aubrey did not dance,

although she was bouncing on the balls of her feet, clearly caught up in the music. "Watch this," Peter whispered. "That's Dan Fielding. They've been doing this almost since her first night here…"

Aubrey leapt up onto the small stage, keen to savor Dan's playful, if unorthodox cover of a popular Beethoven score. She lightly rested her one hand on his back, the other on the piano, her eyes closed, still moving to his playing, enthralled by the magic he was creating.

Peter smiled at her. "My Hobbit. She often does this when he plays, saying she wants to feel the music, as well as hear it…She wants to feel it in her feet, too, when she's home and the neighbors are at work…In the car, she wants to feel it in her damn sternum. Pity your eardrums…"

"She works from home often then?"

"When she isn't off globetrotting," Peter answered, looking down at his glass. *I wonder when she will tell him about the novel?* Henry's interest piqued. His One was a novelist as well?

Aubrey leaned forward once Dan finished. As he asked her a question, she laughed, and he began another piece. Now her hand moved to rest on his shoulder and he began a passionate adaptation of a Beethoven sonata, with a driven, demanding rhythm. Soon, her head was bobbing (*Oh God, Henry, she's gonna start head banging in a second…*).

Henry did not think Beethoven translated into "head banging," but he found out he was wrong…

"When are you gonna sing, Elf?" Lucy prompted, and Aubrey rolled her eyes.

"I'm not warmed up," she objected.

"Then pick something easy…you must start somewhere," Henry answered lazily.

Peter gave Henry an enthusiastic high five, and Aubrey sniffed. She called the Celtic group back and this time accompanied them, giving spirited renditions of popular favorites.

Peter stood, stretched. "Well, that's enough for me. She'll be here until you say you're tired, or you're tossed out. I didn't realize how much she needed this. Look at her. She's on fire."

Henry's face hurt from smiling. Aubrey was a different woman from the scared creature he more or less chased for ten blocks. If he squinted, he would almost think she was illuminated, or her clothes were being stirred by a breeze that existed nowhere else.

Perhaps they were.

Henry slipped Peter his number. "If you ever need anything…if you think she needs anything. Please text, day or night. If I can't reply because I'm otherwise occupied, my assistant Christine will see, and either respond to you directly, or grab me if it's an emergency. I know she has you, and you are more than enough…but…"

"I get it, Henry. I think you two might be really good for each other. I've caught her looking at you in ways I've never thought possible. But I still gotta say it. You hurt her, I am gonna sincerely fuck you up."

"Peter…" Henry turned to look him directly in the face, so Peter could see him as clearly as possible in the dim lighting, "If I ever hurt her, I am already sincerely fucked. But yeah. I won't fight back."

Peter gave Aubrey a kiss on the cheek, and whispered something in her ear that earned him a smack in the ribs with a half-laugh, half-scowl.

Henry ambled over. "Are you always beating on your brother? I'm just curious. God knows my sisters don't hesitate to haul off and let me have it if the notion strikes them…but unlike Peter, I strike back. I pick them up and hold them over my shoulder. And spin. That usually gets my point across…"

"Ugh, Henry…" Aubrey wrinkled her nose. "If Peter did that to me, I think I'd puke…"

"That's the general idea," he tapped the tip of her nose.

The music continued, and sometimes Aubrey was a part of it. Other times she was happy to…Henry didn't know if he could call it dancing, but it brought her so much joy, he just stood back watched with a tolerant, happy expression.

But finally, he could bear it no longer. He walked up to Aubrey and murmured, "Dance with me?"

She looked up at him, stumbling mid-step. "Henry, I… well, you've seen…"

"It's all in the leading. If you trust me, I think we'll be okay," he assured her, hope in his eyes.

By now her hair had escaped the coiffure she had spent so much time creating, and he brushed tendrils from her face. She bit her lip, and nodded.

Her gloves had remained on her hands throughout the night…but as she looked into his eyes, she hesitated, and took them off.

Henry had already tipped Lucy, and with a huge grin, Henry positioned both of them for a waltz as Elvis began to croon "Can't Help Falling in Love."

Aubrey was stiff at first. She felt clumsy, and stupid. Henry persisted with gentleness, and it wasn't long before they were gliding across the floor, Henry resisting the urge to lift and twirl Aubrey even as his heart had lifted off and taken flight the moment she removed her gloves, allowing him unfettered access to her mind.

He felt her awkwardness, her acute sense of inadequacy. She had been excited and free before, undisciplined and wild with her joy. A waltz was the antithesis of that…and yet, now she was thrilled to be in his arms, listening to the music, feeling his strength and the depths of his affection for her. His sincere desire to take her into his life, cherish and protect her.

I know it's fast, his mind flowed over hers, a silken rush of warm current. *And I know we still need to talk about so many things…call me a fool, I couldn't care less. We are meant for each other, you and I. Do you feel this, at all? Being soul mates doesn't mean love at first sight, not exactly...but you are my One, sweet Aubrey. Do you sense this, even a little?*

Aubrey's head was spinning. *I can't explain how or what I feel. I don't have words for it...all I know is whatever it is, I want it...I want you in my life, if we can make it work. I need...my privacy, I can't stand in front of the world without any armor. I would prefer to live in shadows, with quiet...but I don't want to walk away from you, Henry. You bring my heart a sense of... standing on solid ground.*

The music ended, and he looked at her. *It's so late, but I don't wish for tonight to end, nor do I wish to push us into anything we aren't ready for. I think I should bring you home.*

She wrapped her arms around his waist, and the contact had him closing his eyes with bliss.

Yes, Henry, take me home...but perhaps...you could stay? I have space for you, and even some clothes for you to change into... but if you'd rather not, I understand...

Henry kissed the top of her head. *I will stay as long as you will have me, however you will have me.*

Aubrey was shaking her head at herself, she could not believe she was actually allowing someone—anyone—a *man!* —see where she lived. It had taken her over a month before she let her guard down enough to have Peter come to her loft.

"It might not seem like much to you, but it's mine," she spoke, partly apologetic, partly defiant as she opened the door and turned on the lights. Aubrey could only imagine what Henry was used to, and her tiny apartment still cost an obscene amount of money, by anyone's standards.

Henry shook his head, dismayed. "No. Please don't think, don't ever feel that way. Do you believe I'm an idiot? That I don't know what New York City real estate prices are? Granted, I'm not in the market to purchase anything, but having worked with the theater company and listened to others talk about prices per square foot when costing out storage prices...This view alone commands a hefty price tag...you must be in high demand as a travel writer, Ms. Stafford."

Aubrey's face was blank as she sat on the sofa to remove her boots and her gloves. "I couldn't afford this on a travel writer's salary, Henry. When Mama died, she left me a small life insurance policy. Between that, and a few other...sources of income, I was able to make a sizable down payment. Let me show you where Peter keeps some spare clothes for when he crashes here. The fit should be close enough..." She went to the smaller bedroom, her mind drifting to how Henry felt when she held him, his body, Henry was sculpted like something in a museum, she was certain of it, with lean, well defined muscles...she shook her head, embarrassed, trying to dispel those thoughts. Henry caught only a vague shadow of where her mind was, and ducked his head down. He was pleased his One found him attractive. He had spent countless hours in his younger days in wasted attempts to "bulk up." It was swimming against the tide: his DNA simply didn't allow for it. Sometimes he still felt inferior to men who looked as though they could rip tree trunks apart with their bare hands...He followed her covertly from under his eyelashes as she returned. She was carrying soft sleep pants paired with a huge t-shirt that had an outline of a tree, urging the reader, "Keep Calm and Don't Be Hasty." Henry's breath caught as he took up the shirt in reverence.

"Aubrey...! This is...where did you find this...?!"

Her entire expression brightened. "You really like it? You understand the reference?"

Henry rolled his eyes, "Of course I get the reference, who wouldn't? It's only Treebeard, the star of *The Twin Towers*, in my humble opinion..."

Aubrey squealed, jumping in place. "Yes! Do you know how long it's been since I heard someone else say 'Treebeard'...?"

Henry hugged Aubrey, still holding the shirt.

Go change, Elf.

Aubrey stuck her tongue out at him, but ran the few steps to her room, laughing with elation. "Another *Lord of the Rings* fan! I win!"

Henry looked at one of her bookcases. An entire shelf was devoted to the works of J. R. R. Tolkien. Henry did not know how to express the overpowering sensation of correctness, of *rightness* that was flooding through his soul, as another puzzle piece slid into place in his soul, with a resounding "click."

"Aubrey, you aren't a runaway from Santa's workshop. Nor are you a Hobbit…but you are an Elf, straight from your beloved novels, complete with the sea-longing Tolkien imbued in them…and why should you not be? Any man who wrote with such passion and clarity about a race harboring nostalgia for their homes, married with such unquenchable yearning for the sea, undoubtedly carried the trident in his soul," he breathed, eyes shining. "Of course you are drawn to his works…like calls to like, after all."

Aubrey emerged, her face glowing from the ruthless scrubbing she gave it to remove any traces of makeup, coppery hair cracking from a similar brushing, a nimbus floating about her. "I'm sorry, Henry, I couldn't hear you. What were you saying?"

Henry had not realized how long her hair was, as both times he saw her before she had pulled it up in a ruthlessly tight chignon or braided updo. In bare feet and her own pajama pants and t-shirt (proclaiming "Though she be but little, she is fierce!") she was radiant in his eyes.

*As beautiful as you looked in your finery…now, you are Titania, queen of all the faeries…*Henry stuttered. He wanted to scoop her up, kiss her senseless, and take her to his bed. Her bed. Simply take her…because now, she looked real, to him. Someone he wanted to come home to, every night. Someone to make a family, a life with, snuggle when it was cold and stormy, have breakfast, dinner, and tea with...and...

Aubrey, do you have the extended editions of the Tolkien films...? Henry stroked her face. Aubrey leaned into him, soaking up his warmth. It was colder than she enjoyed, now that October was over and they were in the early hours of the morning.

Her mental voice was unbearably smug. *In ultra HD Blu-ray, thank you very much, Mr. Rhys. I am no philistine.*

She felt, as well as heard his groan. *That's it, I'm moving in. One movie marathon, please...*

Sunrise found both of them stretched across Aubrey's bed, innocent and haphazard as havoc played out on the television set on the wall. Henry's snores were deep and rhythmic as he starfished across the mattress, clasping Aubrey with one arm, her plush dragon with the other. Aubrey was cuddled up against him, his chest serving as a pillow, sound asleep.

Meanwhile, Peter was standing miserably outside Aubrey's door, feeling like the worst friend, worst brother, and biggest asshole of the universe. He had texted her multiple times, begging her to let him in, as he had left his regular wallet in the spare room the night before. It was bulky, and he felt it ruined the line of his clothing. But now, he was in a jam. It contained a business card with a contact he desperately needed. He had an incredible amount of work to do today, and he was kicking himself.

The fact she wasn't responding led to all sorts of interesting possibilities...and he was happy for her.

But he *needed* Seung Tam Moreno's personal contact information. And the business card was the only place he would get it. The up-and-coming designer from LA had handwritten the information on the back, Peter knew he wouldn't find it anywhere else. Seung was an undiscovered genius in Peter's eyes, and he was obsessed with a quest to release the young man's energy and talent upon the world.

Do You Hear What I Hear?

Knowing he would rather have a root canal done (nasty, terrible things, even if his had netted him a flashy gold crown, and he loved it so), he cautiously unlocked Aubrey's door.

He could hear her television playing...oh, no. He could hear the unmistakable drawl of those damned Ents...! Well, her bedroom door was open, and there wasn't a sound to be heard, other than those stupid trees nattering on (and was that a saw he heard? He didn't remember a saw...), so he made his way to the room, walking on the outsides of his feet. She must be zonked...he wondered what time she rolled in last night.

He didn't mean to look into her room after he grabbed his wallet. But the door was wide open, the room was right next to the spare, and what *was* that buzzing sound, anyway?

The sight that met his eyes gripped his heart and squeezed with such intensity, tears flooded his eyes, even as he had to battle to refrain from snorting. He whipped out his phone, snapped a few photos in case blackmail was required over his Hobbit at any point in the future (never let it be said Felicia Rivera's son let opportunities pass him by—he made his own luck) and hightailed his ass out of that loft as fast as his size eleven shoes could carry him, locking the door securely behind him.

And laughed himself sick, all the way down the street to the subway.

9

I'M NOT FAMOUS

Hours later, oblivious of their early morning visitor, Aubrey and Henry sat on the sofa. Henry was grumbling as he fended off Greg, who was was pestering him over photos that had surfaced of the trio leaving the restaurant. Henry was grateful Aubrey's face was shielded between himself and Peter, but Greg was doing his job: who was Henry with, and would he be seen with them again?

"Come on, Henry. Make my job easier, so I can make your life easier. You know how this goes…also, Christine is in my face this morning, demanding to know the story between yourself and Ms. Aubrey Stafford. I assume she is the woman between yourself and the man behind you? Would this be Peter Rivera? Details, Henry…and where are you? Please, please tell me I am not going to be inundated with pictures of you leaving someplace first thing this morning looking furtive…I stopped by your suite, and lo and behold, you weren't there…"

Aubrey was curled up with a soft blue throw, watching rain sheet down the windows. Henry paused to look at her. She was still in her pajamas, even though it was dinner time —that is, lunch. She had made soup and sandwiches for them, as well as put on a kettle for tea. It was only tea bags, he thought, hiding a smirk, but he could help her rise above... She could be a tiny mermaid, washed ashore. A fully grown siren, with sweet, lush curves and...

"Henry?"

He felt his face redden as it had not since his grandma Mairéad was alive to reprove him. Was she able to read his thoughts now?

Striving for an expression that wouldn't indict him, he deliberately kept his eyes locked on his phone ("Go away, Greg. Yes, Aubrey Stafford and Peter Rivera. Hands. Off. There will be no morning photos of any embarrassing promenades; I am taking today off to have a private life. In private. Which means GO AWAY.") as he hummed in response.

"Did you want to...talk about anything?"

He looked up sharply, seeing she was twisting her fingers. Without gloves, he was pleased to note.

"Yes." He tossed his phone on a tiny side table. "Will you sit closer to me?"

With a tight swallow, she did so, and he tucked her against his side. "Are you comfortable with this? It's your home, milady. I would be miserable if I thought I came into your safe place and made you ill at ease."

Aubrey nodded, bobbing her head like a puppet.

"I asked you when we first met if you had any talents that were out of the ordinary. You didn't wish to answer me then...will you now?"

She nodded again, but closed her eyes.

"Are you scared?"

Another mute nod. Even though she was wrapped up in his embrace, her mind was still stubbornly closed to his. How he wished Mairéad was still alive! He could use her advice, in more ways than one...

Of me? I would hope not, I would do anything to keep you safe, have you feel confident and secure...

Aloud, Aubrey answered, "What does it feel like, when I speak to your mind? You feel…warm. Like I imagine a warm, soft waterfall would, flowing over me, filling areas that are broken, and cracked. Soothing…healing. Almost like being tucked in. If you were angry with me, it would not be the same, I'm sure, but that's what it's been like…a hand brushing over something that was rough and jagged, smoothing it out…"

The images she used disturbed him, even as he was jubilant his mental contact was as caring as he would wish. "I cannot see where anything about your mind, your soul, would be broken or jagged…not when each time you have reached out to me, from the very first, I felt wrapped in compassion. Everything you are sings with genuine tenderness and a soft consideration of my feelings, an awareness of my sense of self…I was so frustrated when we first communicated, remember? As though I was little more than an a creature on a shelf to be exhibited, shown like a trick pony. You mentioned water, and I have that imagery as well: a gentle sensation of waves lapping against my heart, my mind and soul, just as if I was walking along the beach." He stroked her hair.

"I'm so glad!" The relief was evident in her expression, tone, and the way she sighed, leaning deeper into him.

"Why is that?" He continued to run his fingers through her curls.

My…quirk…gives me none of those feelings. It needs to be hidden away.

Ah, at last she had opened her mind to him, Henry rejoiced privately, and replied in the same manner.

I'm very sorry to hear this. What can you share with me? If I cannot help you, I may know someone who can…

Abruptly Aubrey reverted to using vocal speech. "I…hear things…sometimes see things…that aren't there. When I touch them. Like the man you spoke of, in the thrift store. It's called psychometry. But then you knew that already. It's why I wear gloves so often. I don't want to see or hear those things, Henry! I don't!"

There was a faint edge of rising hysteria in her voice. Henry did not hesitate to pull her completely into his lap. "There was no one to explain any of this to you, was there." He was stating a fact. Aubrey shook her head.

"No...when I was a very little girl, the stories were not so bad. I was home more often than not, with Mama, or the few people she knew. I assumed everyone had the same experiences. I thought...all stories began in the middle, with no beginnings and no ends. When I would talk about it, Mama and Daddy thought I had an overactive imagination. It was cute, a sign I was smarter than the average kid. But as I grew older, and got out into the world more, away from the house..."

"The stories weren't fun anymore, were they?" Henry's words stroked her ears as carefully as his large hand caressed her head and hair.

"No. They confused and scared me. People were always angry, or afraid of being caught doing things they weren't supposed to...or else they were just plain scared, period. I usually only heard voices. The worst ones had small movies attached, that I could see through even as I could see what was going on around me. The more intense, the less translucent, and I was terrified. I wasn't sure if there were ghosts trying to talk to me, or show me things...These days, I tend to wear gloves everywhere. I never know when these episodes will happen. I know now they are nothing more than echoes of things that have happened before. They can't hurt me. But I used to be petrified I was losing my mind. Before I met you, it was a constant fear I would someday get trapped in one of those places, and not be able to escape. As long as the voices never talked back to me though, I knew I was all right."

Henry was remorseful. "Ah, Aubrey...no wonder you

were running, horrified when I answered you, begging you to talk to me. I didn't know, darling, I didn't know I was scaring you so badly..."

Of course you didn't, Henry. I know that now. I also know, because I can sense when I touch you, you have no wish to hurt me. You don't want to.

He frowned down at her. "Why do you phrase it like that? 'I don't want to hurt you.' It sounds as though you believe I will, even though it isn't my intent."

Aubrey was biting on her lip. "I used to have a boyfriend, I use that word very loosely, mind you. His name was Paul. I thought we were becoming closer, even though I was traveling a great deal since I was still a new travel writer—I was quite junior, so was given all the crap assignments. I understood, you have to climb the ladder, right? I should have listened to my instincts, every time I touched him, I felt... vaguely sick to my stomach. Threatened, somehow. I thought it was because I was nervous, because I hadn't ever...done anything with anyone before."

Henry felt his insides turn to ice. If that...if this Paul...

He asked in a level tone of voice, "Did he hurt you?"

"Not like that. Besides, Peter would have killed him. No, it's the age-old story of the trusting, foolish girlfriend who busted her ass to get home early to surprise her man...but ended up being the one surprised when she found him banging someone else. Ugh, right?" She gave him a rueful, shaky smile. "As much as it hurt, and it did, I am glad I found out before the relationship went any further. I got my own back on the way out, never fear...hell hath no fury like a woman scorned, after all..."

"Tell me you crushed his balls," Henry begged, an encouraging smirk on his face even as his heart was coal, smoldering in his chest. He was furious anyone treated his One so poorly, jealous this Paul had caught her eye for even a moment, and shamefully delighted the fool never was able to touch his soul mate intimately. And angry all over again, because the wretch (and his paramour) had gouged his One's soul so deeply... how did this make Aubrey fear he would somehow wound her unintentionally?

"No, not quite...his flat screen television set took a hit, though. Literally. I would have taken the route of vandalizing his car, but this is New York City, so he didn't have one..." she sighed. Henry's laugh was maliciously pleased, before he sobered.

"Aubrey Stafford...do you have a middle name? I think this requires middle naming..."

She snickered. "Yes. It's Lillian. It was my grandmother's name."

"Aubrey Lillian Stafford. I solemnly swear to you, no matter what our future holds, I will never, ever, deceive you. I might make you so frustrated you rain all manner of vile curses on my luckless head, but I am not, nor will I ever be, a liar." He lifted her chin, ensuring he had her complete attention.

"I never thought you would be, and that is besides my point."

"Well then, what is your point?" Henry was confused, battling impatience, and not a small bit of anxiety. What was she holding him to task for, what sin had another committed for which he needed to atone?

No, Henry. It is nothing like that. I would never hold you responsible for someone else's sins. It is simply my deep-seated need to live simply. Will I be able to, and still remain by your side?

Henry felt the undertow of her apprehension dragging her away from him, faster than any riptide. He clutched her as representations of her fears filled her soul as nets, drowning her: flashbulbs popping in her face, bombs of blinding light. A vortex of voices swirled, screaming questions he could not decipher even while she shrank in a frozen panic. Paparazzi stalking her like predators. Being dragged, forced away from Peter.

"How could you think, for even a second, I would allow this?" The roughness of his voice did not match the manner he made a shield with his body and arms. "I would never permit anyone to raise a finger against you, let alone have you made the center of such a humiliating encounter with the press, media, anyone!"

"It's the only thing I ask, Henry. Please. I need to live as quietly, as privately as I possibly can. I am not ashamed of my feelings for you. Nor of yours for me. I recognize there will be times our photos will be taken, but I beg of you not to ask me to go out much." Her eyes were swollen, her pupils dilated. "As long as you can…live sometimes in my world, and I can live in yours. Together, but still allowing me my anonymity as much as possible…or at least my privacy. I need this. I can't breathe without it!"

She was fighting tears, choking on viciously restrained sobs while Henry unconsciously rocked her. He couldn't imagine what scarred her to this extent.

"Aubrey…have you ever seen things that came to pass later in your life?" It was his last stab in the dark. Was she also clairvoyant, and somehow failed to recognize it? Would she envision a future event so monstrous, it would haunt her until it manifested…? He was in over his head. He thought he carried a trident in his soul, perhaps she was the one with the trident, and all he had was a child's toy?

She shook her head wildly. "No, I just want to forget everything that happened before I came to New York. I was miserable. Everyone looking at me, always waiting for me to lose control, whispering I was a moment away from madness…I couldn't be trusted. Small town infamy. Can't you see how I need to leave that behind me? Can you imagine growing up, always being watched?"

"No, my darling. Not like that. I have you, Aubrey. I have

you." Henry soothed Aubrey, holding her close to his chest. "I will keep you safe. I promise."

"Oh, Grandma," he mourned in the most private recess of his heart. "I thought how tragic it was, your never being able to meet my One...but I was wrong. The real tragedy was she never was able to meet you."

THAT AFTERNOON, the pair of them sat down with their schedules. Henry gritted his teeth when he saw how slammed he was, from the very next day almost until the moment his flight departed for London after the curtain closed on *Gatsby*. Even then his time off was brief. Damn it, he had talked to Beatrice about this!

"We will make it work," Aubrey reassured Henry, handing him a large cup of tea. "We can take turns, perhaps. You can spend time in my world, and," she swallowed over the knot of fear lodged in her throat, forcing it into her chest, "I can spend time in yours. So we can see how compatible we are. I just have a project I need to finish by reviewing edits. I will be working at home. It will not take much of my time, and then I am free. Actually, you are lucky." She gave him a playful wink.

"This is the most free time I have had in...months, actually. If I had not met you, I might be going mad, having nowhere to go...usually I am going wild, trying to escape the holidays. Peter traditionally goes to visit one of his real siblings for Thanksgiving."

Henry winced at Aubrey's casual dismissal of her relationship with the man Henry knew loved her deeply. "Aubrey, I don't think that's fair," he protested, keeping his voice mild even as he stood up for Peter. Aubrey gave him an exasperated glance.

"Oh, don't be like that. Peter always invites me, and I always decline. There is enough tension and potential for drama, the last thing needed is his make-believe wanna-be sib tagging along, especially if his parents decide to surprise everyone with a visit, trust me!

"Getting back on topic, I don't have any travel scheduled at the moment. So I will have plenty of time to be with you... In any case, I expect I will hear from Voyager Publications soon, I believe the next stop planned for me was Africa. The continent is so huge, it's is easily a two or maybe a three month expedition, but the project would be quite the professional boost if I wish to stay with their publishing house. I would be listed as the lead author, but I wouldn't be leaving until after the New Year, and as it is..."

"Three months!" Henry repeated, in real pain. He could not bear the thought of being away from Aubrey for three days! He flipped through his planner, seeing with rising nausea if his schedule remained as projected, when she returned he would be preparing for an interminable film publicity tour, having him globetrotting like a madman. They'd be apart for another two months, if not longer...

"Peace, Henry, I beg you." She looked at him, a small blush turning the tips of her ears red. "The truth of the matter is, uh...well, I have a novel scheduled to be published in March. My editor is doing a Russian folk dance on my ass, because she wants me on a publicity tour as it is and I keep refusing. The last thing I want or need is my name and face splashed everywhere. I didn't plan on a marketing blitz when I sold my manuscript, believe me! I signed a contract agreeing to marketing, but there are enough loopholes to avoid hanging myself. I have no idea where I will be. My hope is I will be allowed to do interviews here in New York. I suppose I could fly to the West Coast, but..." she ran her hand through her hair.

"A novel...? Is there any end to how talented, how wonderful you are?" Henry praised her, and without stopping to think, kissed her enthusiastically.

Do You Hear What I Hear?

Both of them stopped as his lips pressed against hers. Neither moved.

Henry had been incredibly conservative, considering how fast some of his other relationships had moved. But this was Aubrey. His One, his future, his life…and he knew she was not used to being touched at all, let alone in any romantic or sexual fashion.

Aubrey…forgive me.

He felt a frisson of laughter.

I will not. To forgive you would mean I was offended.

You're not? Hope swelled in his breast, even as Aubrey's own heart extended its wings, an elegant skimmer reaching out to test its wingspan.

Do it again. I need to make sure.

Henry began by brushing his lips against hers, not seeking anything other than to nuzzle against her while cupping the back of her head. Aubrey became pliant and soft in his arms, her hands finding his thick hair. Her fingers luxuriated in his soft locks as his tongue came out, licking her lips, seeing entry. She smiled, and as Henry felt her grant what he sought, she sighed, a sweet little almost-moan that set his every nerve aflame.

Do it again, Henry. And again, and again, and again…

GREG LOOKED into Aubrey's cool, amused eyes over a conference table.

"I appreciate your agreeing to meet with me," he began, his voice cautious. "Henry has lambasted me in no uncertain terms about trespassing upon your desire for privacy."

"He's not wrong," she replied, leaning forward, grinning. "And yet, you've been pestering him night and day to see me. He's likened you to a mosquito, a rash, a pain in the…"

"I get the general idea," Greg cut in, wincing. "And yet, it is for both of your welfare I needed to get in touch with you.

You must understand, the longer the two of you are an item, the higher the certainty you will be accosted by some form of the media, whether it's reporters, photographers...I hate to think of you being beset without some idea of how to protect yourself."

"Doesn't 'No comment,' hold any weight these days?" Aubrey spun a pencil in her fingers like a miniature baton.

"No." Greg was brutally frank. "The lower the quality of the publication, and the less scrupulous the person, the less they will respect your requests to be left in peace. What's more, they will start to dig into your personal affairs. Your past, Ms. Stafford. The fact you are so adamant about not answering any of my perfectly reasonable questions gives me a great deal of concern. I am more than willing to treat you with the dignity and respect you deserve, not simply as a human being, but as someone close to Henry's heart. These locusts will grant you neither. If there is anything...less than favorable in your history...which I can completely understand, for who among us hasn't stumbled and made mistakes we would prefer not to see smeared across the internet, or some cheap magazine or tabloid show?...I can take care of it for you. If not make it disappear completely, at least make sure it is cast in a much more favorable light."

Aubrey simply continued to give Greg a polite smile, and remained quiet.

"Ms. Stafford..."

"Relax. You can call me Aubrey." Her posture was still relaxed, but her face remained blank.

"Aubrey. I am begging you. I have absolutely nothing against you, and trust me when I say I am the least judgmental person you will run across in your lifetime. I have been shepherding Henry for over a decade, after all." His attempt at humor fell flat.

"Really, Greg, there isn't anything to tell you you couldn't find out through a basic trawl through public records. I am a

Do You Hear What I Hear?

travel writer for Voyager Publications, and I am rather successful at it. I have a condo that I make regular payments on, I have a decent credit score, I'm a Scorpio…"

"That's not what I mean, and you know it. Aubrey, for God's sake. Do you have a criminal record, for starters? A drug habit, or a shoplifting arrest?"

Aubrey leaned back into her chair. "Seems to me you'd find that in the records at City Hall."

"Jesus!" This cat and mouse dance was making Greg more anxious by the second. "Have you ever *murdered* anybody?"

"I hurt a PR manager's feelings once…"

Greg groaned, and leaned over the desk, burying his face with his hands. "I cannot *believe* you said that."

Aubrey relented. "I promise you, on my word of honor, Greg. You will not find a single record of my having broken the law. Anywhere. At any point of my life, not even sealed juvenile records," She reached over, gently prying his hands away from his face. A wash of cool breezes stirred her soul, and she felt guilty for needling the man. Her heart was stirred with his sincere desire to serve as a bulwark against any who would rise up to disturb her peace of mind, and in turn rouse the formidable ire of his friend and client. "I grew up in an incredibly small, undisclosed town in a southern state. I was most unhappy, because I was a fish out of water for a variety of reasons I am unwilling to discuss. As soon as I could, I left. I can't see where that would be of interest to you, or anyone else. I was able to support myself legally, in a manner that will raise no eyebrows. No sex tapes, no salacious photos, no one coming forward with tales of my turning tricks in the bathroom or shooting up behind the school gym. Fair enough?"

"It's a start," he grudgingly admitted. "Although I would feel a lot better if I knew where you had come from, Aubrey. At least I could be prepared if someone with an axe to grind popped out of nowhere with a pack of lies, trying to make a fast buck by blackening your reputation, and potentially Henry's, by extension...because he will go after whomever dares hurt you, with no sense of perspective. Know this, Aubrey. He..."

The door flew open, and in the opening stood the man himself, smoldering with volcanic anger.

"Case in point," Greg sighed, covering his face again.

"Was there a meeting called, and I missed the memo? I guess so."

Body rigid, Henry strode in, placing himself beside Aubrey in a protective stance. "Aubrey, I had no idea Greg was going to contact you, I would have warned you, I would have never allowed you to be badgered thus, I *warned* him you were not to disturbed, I..."

Henry. Put trident down and breathe. I'm fine.

Greg looked at the pair with complete shock as Aubrey managed to disarm Henry without a single word spoken, just a wry smile and a small touch to his hand. The mountain of rage began to soften, although now Henry looked at him with betrayed, wounded eyes.

"Greg, I asked you not to do this. I only found out about this little...assignation via Christine. She thought I was on board. I was looking for you, because of this."

He tossed down a printout of an article from a gossip web site, bearing the title, "Who is Gatsby's Green Light?" There were grainy photos of Henry kissing Aubrey's forehead as he helped her out of the SUV, shielding her with his body as he hustled her into his hotel building, and another set of them walking arm in arm into the theater.

Greg sighed, a slow exhalation of breath. "Henry, it was bound to happen."

Aubrey looked at the photos, and something in her soul turned over. Her face was indistinct, and of course her name wasn't attached. She looked at the floor.

Henry immediately wrapped his arm around her. "Are

you all right, Aubrey? This isn't so bad, it's not obvious, and no one can pick you out of a line up," he teased.

She nodded, automatically. Greg tried not to be impatient.

"This is but the tip of the iceberg. Now it's public knowledge Henry has a romantic interest in someone, the sharks are going to circle. Henry, Aubrey, do you wish for our office to release a statement? The genie is out of the bottle, but we can…"

"No," the two spoke in unison.

"I am a private citizen," Aubrey spoke, her voice determined. "I will not have to have my name given out as a sop to keep the public pacified! I have rights…"

Greg slapped his hands down on the table in frustration, startling Aubrey. Henry growled, glaring at him. "Aubrey, you are being unreasonable. These photos? They are just beginning. They are going to get bigger, and clearer. It is simply a matter of time before your face will be easily identifiable, as Henry said, in a lineup. Your neighbors will be asking about you in the lifts, you will see yourself in the checkout lines in the grocery stores. These vultures have run *princesses* into the ground, Aubrey, you know this…!"

"I'm not royalty," she exclaimed, fire in her eyes and volume rising.

"You are rubbing elbows with an internationally recognized movie star, that's close enough for these leeches! Why are you being so difficult? *Let me help you.*" Greg matched her temper, unintimidated.

"And how are you going to do that?" Aubrey retorted. "Are you going to give me a hat and oversized sunglasses? A wig? A new name? A new background, a new identity every time I step outside? Somehow, I don't think so, Greg Knight… you are well named, sir, but even a knight in shining armor has limits."

"Tell me what you are hiding from and I will make it go away!"

"Why do I have to be hiding from anything?" Her plaintive cry tore at Henry's heart. "I simply wish to be left in peace, I don't want to be stared at, I want be like everyone else!" She stood so suddenly her chair tipped backwards, her arms wrapped tightly around herself. "I know the people I wish to know. And they know me. That is enough. I don't have social anxiety, or an inability to speak to people. I travel all over the world, talking to people from different cultures and walks of life. I'm good at it, and what's more, I love it! That isn't a life in hiding, Greg!"

"No," he agreed heavily, "it isn't...but it isn't a life in the public eye, either." He eyed her shrewdly. "And you know it, as well. You don't want the public seeing you. Looking at you, as you said. Why is that?"

Her lips thinned even as her eyes became red. Aubrey drew herself up to her tallest, posture proud with shoulders back and chin thrust out. "No comment."

Greg sighed again. "Aubrey. All I ask is you be reasonable. The ever-popular 'anonymous source' will release your name, sooner or later...does your building have good security?"

Her phone began to vibrate, buzzing in her pocket. Aubrey frowned. "I put this on 'do not disturb,' no one should be able to override that except...oh, God, Peter!" She blanched, and Henry placed his hand on her shoulder. "Take it, love. I'm sure everything is fine..."

Aubrey was already in motion, muttering, "Excuse me," to the two men as she fumbled with her cell phone, accepting the call as she walked out the door. "Yes, Peter, what is it, what's wrong..."

Greg looked at Henry, leaning back in his chair. "So, are you going to yell at me, fire me as your PR man, as your friend, or just kill me? Let me know so I know which plan to set in motion," he drawled.

Henry shook his head. "Leave it to you to be two steps

ahead of me, having a contingency plan for whatever I might do…why didn't you tell me you were going to do this, Greg?"

"And have you come down on me like the Neanderthal caveman who burst through the door earlier? No, thank you. You were all but ready to drag your woman out by the hair, club in hand. It's a free country, and she is a strong, independent woman, Henry. I phoned and asked her if she would agree to meet with me. She did, where she could have easily refused. I even hinted at having you present, and she chose to ignore it…but the fact remains, this is going to explode, Henry, and she is going to be at the center of ground zero. No matter what you promise her, you aren't going to be able to stop this. She isn't going to be able to have her private life. Not for much longer."

10

LIKE REAL PEOPLE DO

Peter reached across the table at Acoustics.

"I knew this would be a good place to meet, Hobbit," he greeted her with a kiss. "Lucy already has all of our favorites coming up."

"This sounds serious," Aubrey replied, uneasy. "You said you needed to meet with me right away, so here I am…if this is about Henry and that gossip website, it will be handled…"

"What gossip website?" Peter's eyes narrowed.

"Oh, shit." Aubrey grimaced. "How about you tell me what you had to tell me first, and I will backfill you…"

"Oh, no you don't, Aubrey." She knew he was serious when he didn't use any of his many casual nicknames for her. Trying to make as light of the situation as possible, Aubrey recounted the website's article and photo. When Peter pulled it up on his phone, he grunted.

"Tell that Greg person he needs to arrange for better security for you. Those photos are only going to get worse."

Aubrey rolled her eyes. "Enough already. Like I need security, when I have you and Henry in my corner. You're enough to make any photographer want to run home needing a clean pair of underwear…"

Do You Hear What I Hear?

They paused as Lucy began loading their table with all sorts of pub food and drinks. "Hey, Elf, that *is* your picture with Henry making its way across the web, isn't it?"

"What picture?" Peter demanded.

"This one," Lucy pulled her phone out, exhibiting a completely different shot from a different source. This one was much more defined, with Aubrey laughing as Henry was tweaking her hair. Unlike the last set of photos, this was taken in the daylight as they were walking around the city before Henry had to prepare for the evening show.

"Shit," sighed Aubrey again. She was relieved it wasn't around her home, but Greg was right. Damn the man. She could feel something inside of her cry out, seeking shelter. Her shoulders hunched as she looked around her furtively.

"It's okay," soothed Lucy, seeing Aubrey's distress. "No one's looking at you, hon."

Peter asked Lucy for the website so he could have the details, and pressed Aubrey to take a swallow of her drink as Lucy left. Then he leaned forward.

"Sis...I, uh, have to talk to you. About something important."

Aubrey lifted her eyebrow. "Ent. What are you up to? What have you done?"

Peter shifted, his expression a mixture of pride, happiness, and anxiousness. "Um. Well, you know, I've been working a lot. And I, um. Met someone. Special."

Aubrey's face brightened, and she leaned forward, grabbing Peter's hand. "Peter, that's marvelous! Tell me everything."

"His name is Seung Tam Moreno...he's a designer, and I've kinda had...a crush on him, for awhile now, but I didn't think he noticed me. He's wildly talented, and I wanted to give him my best work. He's a genius, but he's not really known yet. The presentations I gave, they were to his company, and I was determined to knock it out of the park, I want everyone to see what I see, so he can be on everyone's lips, he's just..." Peter was babbling, words tumbling over each other. "Not only did I want to impress him on a professional level, it was...personal. I needed to make sure the world would see how much potential he has, all he's missing is the right exposure, the correct...shit, I'm talking shop again..."

"I get it, he's amazing, but get to the good parts," Aubrey urged, stuffing a potato skin in her mouth, following it with another big swallow of her drink. She had a strong hunch she was going to need it.

Peter, her strong, unflappable big brother who took no crap, was...smitten? She'd seen him in lust before, going on about someone's physical attributes in such minute detail she would be screaming into a pillow or sofa cushion in laughter or embarrassment, begging him to stop. Never once had she heard him talk about someone's talent, or mind...

Now, his eyes shone. "Aubs...he thinks I'm just as talented. He wants me on his team. And...he's been watching me, just like I've been watching him...and he thinks we could be really good for each other. Together, I mean...And he's an outstanding kisser," he groaned.

Aubrey squealed. "Peter! I'm so happy for you! When do I get to meet him? I can't wait, we can hang out together, I can have another big brother, maybe...?"

The light faded from his eyes, and Peter seemed to deflate, and shrink. "Um. About that...there's a problem."

Aubrey sat back. "What? He doesn't like redheads?" She made her voice light, even as her heart and hands began to grow cold.

"He lives in Los Angeles."

Aubrey shook her head back and forth in denial. "So, you will have to travel to his studio...? That will be hard, but..."

"Aubrey...I'm going to move to LA. Not just to be with him, but...yeah. It's an opportunity I can't pass up," he pleaded with her to understand. "I'm going to be the lead graphic designer for him. The work I did knocked his socks off…and he wants me. Me! No one has ever valued my vision before like he does…and we could be together exclusively. To see if we could work, as a team, and as a couple, as well."

She looked at him, wordless.

"My sister and her family are there, as well…I'd be able to see them more, instead of maybe once a year," he added miserably. "But I'm sick at the thought of leaving you. I know you travel a lot, and damn it, you are gone as often as you are in that loft of yours, you know it's true…but you're the sister of my heart, as well as my best friend. The idea of moving away and leaving you alone, it's tearing me to pieces."

"Peter." Aubrey ruthlessly shoved her tears deeply into a well-used vault where she hid everything she refused to deal with, and locked it. "You are absolutely right. You cannot let this pass you by, and I would kick your ass from here to California should you try. This is not just the chance to move up the professional ladder, this is a chance for love. I have never heard you express so much admiration for someone's mind, for their soul and passion before…nor have you ever had someone appreciate the rare beauty of yours. Yes, I will miss you terribly. But you will still have me. I am forever your sister-from-another-mister, my aggravating brother-from-another-mother…"

He gave her a wobbly smile. "I knew you would say something like this. Seung predicted you would, too…I've told him all about you, you know…"

"Of course you did, I'm family," she teased. "Now don't worry about me. You get yourself together, and you fly, Peter Rivera. I expect calls, texts, and video chats, just like you get when I am traveling. I will hit you up for fashion advice just as often as I do now, Rainbow Ent."

Peter leapt up, grabbed Aubrey, and crushed her in a hug.

"I love you, Santa's Little Helper...and Henry said you dance like the kids in *A Charlie Brown Christmas*..."

"Henry said *what*...?"

HENRY RECEIVED a text from Aubrey that evening, simply saying she didn't feel well, and wouldn't be meeting him at the theater after his performance as had been her habit. She assured him it had nothing to do with the meeting they had with Greg earlier that day, or the photos that were continuing to sprout up on the internet like weeds. She hoped he had a good run that night, and she would speak to him the following day.

When Aubrey had all but disappeared from the meeting, only saying Peter needed to meet with her immediately, Henry already had a tight sensation in his chest. This text was now a rock, a sinking sensation making it difficult to breathe. The silence between the two of them felt like a gulf of fire, and he couldn't, wouldn't, let another hour go by without hearing her voice.

"Jon, please take me to Aubrey's for the evening. I won't be needing you afterwards."

Aubrey was wrapped up in a robe, wearing an oversized t-shirt and thick robe. After seeing Peter off with smiles and hugs, she made her way back to her home and downed half a bottle of wine in a bubble bath as she wept.

She knew she was being selfish, which was why she was doing this in secret, and bade Henry goodnight for the evening. She did not want to explain why she was being so mean-spirited, so egocentric she would cry when faced with her best friend's chances for happiness and success.

Aubrey had met Peter two weeks after she moved to New York City, and did not know anyone beyond those she met and spoke with at her new place of employment. While everyone was pleasant, the interactions were superficial and brief. It didn't matter, she told herself repeatedly. It was better this way. Aubrey Lillian Stafford did not need anyone in her life. She had her books, her imagination, and her music to fill her mind and heart. Real people were dangerous. Real people would hurt her in the end.

Real people would touch her, and she would find out things she did not want to know.

Peter Rivera burst into her life, knocking down the walls she was carefully building brick by brick, a wrecking ball made of sunshine, exuberance, and audacity. He found Aubrey in the break room, trying to get the snack machine to release a stuck bag of chips.

"Aw, hang on, Elf," he'd teased her, and gave the machine a punch in precisely the correct spot necessary to jar the mechanism into releasing the bag. Aubrey laughed with delight.

"Thank you, you great walking redwood," she'd replied. "That puts you back on the 'nice' list, I'm sure."

"No, I want to be back on the 'naughty' list," he'd whined, and promptly stole one of the chips from the bag she'd opened.

It was the beginning of a friendship that grew into a small family of two.

Aubrey was grateful for all the time they had together, but the grief of knowing it was over was pulling her under, and she was drowning.

She would be alone again. Just has Peter had broken down her walls, so had Henry, in even more significant ways. Eventually, she knew Henry would leave as well. This wasn't his home.

Irritated with her maudlin behavior, she wiped her face. The weep-fest in the tub made her face swollen and blotchy, and her eyes sore. Her head ached, her heart ached, and there was nothing for it. While her t-shirt proclaimed, "Adventure is calling and I must go" she decided bed was really the place that was calling her. She didn't have the energy for anything else.

Until she heard the knocking on her door.

Humble. Soft.

Aubrey. It's Henry. I know you said you weren't feeling well, but please, may I see you? Even if it is only for a moment? I need to know you're all right.

She could feel him reaching for her, although she did not have to acknowledge him. *Aubrey, sweetheart? Are you awake? I think you are, but I can't be sure...*

Henry was expecting recalcitrance. Frustration. Exasperation. After all, Aubrey had specifically told him she would speak with him in the morning, and he deliberately didn't listen to her. What the hell was wrong with him, that he didn't listen, he did not hear what she was saying...

He wasn't anticipating the wave of misery that responded to his plea. Wordless, not even aware of itself, a wail of sadness answering him before Aubrey opened the door.

"Aubrey?" His bewildered eyes took her in, the swollen face, the robe, all the hallmarks of a woman shattered by loss.

"Darling, what...?" She stepped aside, allowing him entrance, still mute. As soon as the door closed, he did not speak, but simply led her to the sofa.

"Please, what is it? Was it something I did, or said, was it Greg, is it the fucking photographs?" Henry was normally articulate under pressure, but he was barely able to keep from burbling like a fool.

Aubrey shook her head, wiping her cheeks angrily as she could feel tears escaping the confines of her eyelashes once more. Knowing speech was impossible past the knot in her throat, she stretched out her mind's reach:

Peter's leaving...moving to LA. He has a perfect job opportunity, and he's fallen in love. I'm happy for him. It's better for him that he goes...now so more than ever.

Henry brushed the hair that was sticking to her face,

tucking it behind her ear. *Now so...? You aren't making sense. Because of the holidays?* His heart ached for Aubrey, feeling how savagely the impending move was shredding her soul.

He sensed how her eyes were flickering aimlessly about her loft, seeking something to bring her solace, anything to make her pain lessen.

What can I give you? What can I do? Henry felt so helpless in the face of her pain. This was the person his world was set to revolve around, and yet he didn't know how to make her bleeding stop. He could hear the thoughts of everyone in the world, why could he not hear those of the One who mattered most to him?

I just wanted to be like...everyone else. Real people. Normal people. People that didn't have to be afraid, to live in the shadows, creeping about, not able to answer questions over where they came from...but I should have known better, Henry. It's one of the reasons I need to travel, I think. Not because I am one of the People of the Waves, like you call them. I'm not like you. I'm not your One. I might have this...cursed party trick some terrible demon laid upon me, but that's all. You should leave. Peter is escaping, and so should you.

The sadness was so heavy, he could feel her drowning in his arms, the briny water of her tears under his lips was filling his heart, his soul, his lungs.

My sweet Aubrey, I adore you. I love the way you sing, and dance as you walk, but look like a cartoon character on a dance floor. I am enthralled with the manner you stick your tongue out the side of your mouth when you're concentrating. I think the way you make sandwiches is endearing and I know, as surely as you are in my arms, you are my One. You are not cursed by any demon, and you are a descendent of the Lost Kingdom of the Sea, because my soul has never felt so at peace as it has since I have heard your voice answer my thoughts... and as far as real people are concerned, I have made my livelihood playing other people, shadowy characters on stage and film...but I have never felt as real as I did as when your lips touched mine.

Henry lifted her, and carried her to her bed. *I am not going to ask you any questions, my beloved...I already know everything I need to know about you, and will simply wait for you to reveal whatever it is you wish to uncover. All I ask* (he laid her down, and stretched out besides her) *is you allow me to keep kissing your sweet lips, tasting the nectar of your mouth, and resting in the softness of your embrace. Do not send me away, and say it is for my own good. It never could be. It never will be. I love you. I love you... you ground me. You keep me real.*

11

ARSONIST'S LULLABY

"Henry...I love you too."

He looked down upon her with joy. It was the first time she had told him what was in her heart, with words. He had felt the gentle warmth of her affection, the waves of her passion, the steadiness of her attachment to him...but ah, to hear her words declare them in those three simple words!

But the profession gave her no pleasure. He heard only mental anguish arising from her soul, as though she was betraying herself, and him, by confessing her heart. She made no sense, this woman of his...were all women so confusing?

"And why does this have you so unhappy," he demanded. "I know I am far from perfect, but I would think loving me isn't a reason for you to be so sad when you tell me so...!"

"It's because *I can't have you!*"

Aubrey was now naked in her agony, she pulled herself away from Henry's embrace. "I don't deserve you. Not your regard, your endless kindness, your love, your desire, *none of it!*"

Waves of her self-loathing were now pulsating from her, noxious, Henry was almost retching from what Aubrey was trying to keep contained within herself but was failing. The dam was buckling...

"Tell me," he implored. "It cannot be as bad as you have made it out to be in your memory. Whatever it is, I can help you, keep you safe. I can fix it, I can..."

"Have you ever killed a man, Henry?" Aubrey walked away from him, huddling on the floor by her windows. Her voice was flat, as her eyes were as still and as motionless as the lake outside his grandfather's farm...the one that seemingly had no bottom, and would claim lives of foolish swimmers that thought they could plumb the depths when they were bolstered with alcohol and bravado. "How do you cover that up? Do you have special makeup for it? A PR man who can force others to look away? I tell you, *I cannot be seen.* I ran away from home, as far and as fast as I could...I do not want others to look at me, to remember how Randall Tiller was found not far from the sad shack I lived in, and start thinking again...it is bad enough everyone in that town will see me and remember how I was taken away, institutionalized because I was 'not right in the head.' But what if they go beyond that, Henry?"

He couldn't breathe. "Darling...this Randall...what did he do to you? You would never hurt anyone unless they were threatening you. I know this, you are the most peaceful, loving soul I have ever encountered..."

Aubrey was silent, pulling herself into a tight stone of silence, pulling her knees to her chest as she wrapped her arms around them, closing her eyes. Her hair was a scarlet waterfall that shielded her face from him as she buried her face to her knees, and only the slightest shaking of her shoulders revealed how she was trembling with abject terror.

"Aubrey," Henry tried again, his voice thick with pain. "You do not even have to use your words, but can you...show me? Open your mind to me? Let me see why you are so frightened, even now."

Do You Hear What I Hear?

Without a word spoken, Aubrey breathed out the poison that was filling her, and had been for so long, warping her psyche:

She is ten years old. Summertime. A classmate of hers, Gayle Tiller, is dead. Reported lost, her body then found in the woods. The small town gripped with fear and suspicion. Only child of the mayor, lovely, intelligent, outgoing. Aubrey knew her only by name. All of the town at the funeral. Aubrey, hot and uncomfortable by the outpouring of adult grief and distrust, dress scratchy and tight. Awkwardly going to shake hands with the mayor at receiving line, to say "I am sorry for your loss," as drilled into her by her mother, standing in front of her, speaking in soft tones to Gayle's mother. Aubrey had seen her father buried in this very cemetery two years prior. Touching Randall's hand...and seeing...knowing...Randall killing his daughter by accident while molesting her...Aubrey seeing his guilt, tasting it, breathing it in through her pores, having it race through her very being. The shock and revulsion is too much, she drops his hand, looks at him, unable to hide her panic and fear. Randall does not understand how, but he knows intuitively this little girl, with scabbed knees and clothes that do not fit her skinny frame, sees his disgusting shame. Could expose him, somehow...and knows, as everyone in the small town, that her mother works the late shift, leaving her alone. Exposed. Vulnerable. And that Aubrey is known for wild fits of fancy...wasn't quite "right in the head." No one will think twice if she was to come to an...unfortunate accident. Different than his Gayle's, of course. At least on the surface... Aubrey almost fainting with terror, unable to inhale or exhale, as Randall gives her a small, flat smile.

Aubrey looking up, seeing Randall not very far from her, in the months that followed. School begins. Aubrey saying nothing. No one will believe her.

Dreaming of Gayle, of her last moments, the feelings of utter panic, betrayal, agony...waking believing it will be her. It is her.

Coming home and touching the back doorknob, gagging at the taste of Randall's greasy stress. Lock is forced open, now useless.

Plans made for that night, coming and taking her after dark. Nowhere to go. Who will have her? Who would help?

No one. No one.

Helpless. Cold out now.

Panic stricken. Then, very cold and clear, a plan forms...

Laying towels on wooden step, then doormat, and drenching the lot. Watering them on the hour to make sure they remained saturated...

Hooking the inside doorknob with clamps and dad's old electrical wire that he used for house repair to the generator that she was never, ever supposed to play with, but had watched Mama use when the power went out, as it sometimes did because they lived so far out...

Waiting.

Waiting...

Eight o'clock...Nine. Ten. Eleven...

Seven minutes past twelve, sounds coming up the back steps. Not Mama. Mama comes in front door. Aubrey hiding behind the sofa, clutching the sharpest knife, tears coming down her face. Not wanting anything more than to be left alone. Please go away... Please leave me alone...

Eight minutes past twelve. Grunting, muffled choking, the door vibrating in tandem with syncopated vibrations. Syrupy sounds. Thumping.

Nine minutes past twelve. Very bad smells.

Aubrey turning off the generator, looking out a side window.

The stinking, charred corpse of Randall Tiller...Aubrey putting away the generator. Then, with all her strength, dragging his dead weight back to his car. He was not a large man, and she is a tiny girl, but she possesses enormous will. Managing to get his form into his expensive, imported sedan. Dousing the interior with gasoline. Driving it to the woods, because what eleven year old (she had celebrated her birthday just two days before, there are still birthday cupcakes in pantry) did not understand the mechanics of driving? Stopping where Gayle's body was found, wrestling the disgusting, oozing body into the driver's seat, sticking a lit cigarette in between his lifeless, foul, lying lips. With vindictive, cold joy, lighting his crotch, his face on fire, leaving the engine running, sprinting away like a gazelle, red hair streaming behind her like the flames of the torch of an avenging fae.

A football field's distance away before the car erupts.

Back home. Showering until hot water runs out, shivering, crouched in corner. Never wearing those clothes again, even though she scrubbed them repeatedly, without mercy.

"You see, now, Henry. You hear what I heard. You see what I really am; what I've done."

Aubrey withdrew from Henry, unwilling to look at him or reach out for his presence.

"No one was able to trace his death to the visit he made to my house before…the woods. It rained later that night, it washed away any evidence that would have been left between my steps and his car…and any car tracks. There were noises about suicide but there was no note. There were a lot of whispers about his being found where Gayle was…but I was a kid, so the whispers dried up when I entered the room if it was being discussed…"

"Aubrey…Darling, let me hold you, please," Henry's voice was low, and had the appealing timbre and resonance in her ears as her father's had, when she was very young…it was that sensation in her ears that kept her talking, even though her body remained rigid.

"I began to fall apart afterwards…I couldn't relax. At first I wouldn't use the back door…even though Mama replaced the lock, I couldn't bear to stand upon those slats of wood, or touch the door…the smell, I…" A cold sweat filmed over her face and Aubrey shook her head physically to repel the ghost in her nostrils. "Then I wasn't able to be close to the door without hearing…I lost my appetite, the kitchen and table were right there, you see…and I couldn't take being where I had been hiding, waiting for Randall to arrive. The floor wept, the windows whispered…then I couldn't sleep. I did the best I could, trying to hide the fact my entire house was perpetually screaming at me, accusing me, warning and blaming me…"

Henry could not take listening to Aubrey's voice as it dwindled, smaller and closer to tears, without acting. He wanted nothing more than to scoop her body up into his, and cradle her. He had a strong hunch doing so would either propel her even deeper into herself, or she would fight back, as she was clearly locked in the memory.

He opted to seat himself around her on the floor. It was like a mountain range coming to settle around a smaller island, her side tucked into his chest, his arms gently around her, his legs were enfolded about her as well. "I have you now, though, Aubrey…What you endured was beyond terrifying. It must have been so difficult, being trapped in an environment where such horrors were imprinted, forced to relive them, but you were only a child, a victim that fought back, and won. You protected yourself from a vicious evil. The manner of it…it wounded you terribly…but…you were only seeking to save yourself from a terrible fate."

"Mama had me committed, Henry."

"What…?" It was so unexpected, Henry froze. He had been so wrapped up in caring for Aubrey physically, he had stopped listening to her mind to focus on her words. Had Aubrey said…

Aubrey being picked up from high school by her mother… "Mama, why are you taking me out of school early, I was told I had a doctor's appointment?"

Patti's lips thinned. "You're not right, Aubrey. You ain't been right for months now. Years."

"Mama, please, don't start." Aubrey rubbed her head, willing the pain back. "You know we don't have the money for this. I'm fine."

"Baby, listen to me." Patti's voice became softer. "I don't know

what to do for you no more. You don't eat, you don't sleep, you jump if so much as a mouse peeps. Your teachers at school, they say your grades are slipping and you fall asleep given half a chance but still you jump like you're expecting trouble. I love you, honey, and I want to help you, but there's nothing I can do for you. Nothing anyone can do for you, not here, anyway..."

"What do you mean by that, Mama, where are we going, where are you taking me...Mama?" Aubrey saw the signpost for the regional mental asylum, and she began to cry, and then to scream. "Mama, Mama, no! Don't do this, don't do this to me, Mama! Please! I'll do better, I'll eat more, I'll..."

"Honey, honey, listen to me!" Patti tried to speak over Aubrey's terrified wails. "I am doing this because I love you! I can't think of nothing else to do to help you, I want you better, like you used to be, this ain't you, this ain't my girl, you're better than this! You're a smart girl, a good girl! This ain't a punishment because you did something bad, you ain't done nothing wrong, it ain't like you hurt or killed nobody! You ain't like them kids on the news!"

Aubrey became silent so fast is was as though a switch had been flipped.

"You're not punishing me, because...I didn't hurt or kill anybody?"

"Well, 'course not, sugar...I just want you better, and you need help. You're not right in the head, baby, you know you ain't. And nobody at home can help you, but everybody can see it..." Shame stained Patti's face.

"I'm sorry, Mama. Didn't mean to make things harder on you."

Henry could feel the way her heart was leaden, her muscles sluggish. Inwardly, her mind was screaming denials, urging her to leap out of the traveling car, to run...but she remained still. Docile.

By the time the beat up car made it to the front gate, Aubrey was shutting down. Henry was horrified when he sensed how remote she was becoming, beyond terrified when he felt how truly lost she was as she exited the car.

He rocked her without knowledge of his motion, or of the

tears that flowed from his eyes. Was this all because she did not know of her abilities, and there was no one to believe in her…? Partially. What she also needed was protection, deliverance from evil, something that he took for granted as a banal statement when he was her age, buffered with loftiness of privilege granted by his family's love and stability, having nothing to do with his gifts.

Once again Aubrey closed her mind and emotions to him, seemingly without effort.

"I remained in the asylum for four weeks. It was covered by the public health system, so at least I did not exhaust Mama's resources. I was quiet for the first few days, but it was expected, and I was never dangerous to anyone, or myself. I was diagnosed as having an eating disorder, as well as having auditory hallucinations. All attributed to depression and stress, delayed reactions to my father's death. No one noticed the link to Gayle's death, or God forbid, Randall's, because I never mentioned it. My mother never noticed, I hid as long as I could," Aubrey repeated.

Henry continued to rock and cuddle her in his arms.

"It was there I learned, as I had time to do nothing but think, the Voices, or even Scenes, could neither help nor hurt me. All they could do was repeat, endlessly. I couldn't engage with anyone. Nor could I extend my consciousness to witness anything in greater detail. It was simply a tease on an endless loop…all I had to do was tune them out. I admit, I have gotten some great ideas from bits and pieces of them along the way. I decided I wasn't going to try to muffle my demons with the pharmaceuticals the asylum was all too happy to provide, but I was going to keep them on a tight leash." Aubrey chuckled, her body becoming more soft under Henry's. "My lead psychiatrist was the first one to encourage my creative writing, everyone in school was sweating bricks over what I might produce, as everyone knew 'I wasn't right in the head.' He thought I should write about whatever I wanted to...under his supervision of course. In case I was harboring violent delusions. Once he saw I wasn't, he tried to find all sorts of books to motivate me, anything to give me something to strive for, to keep me inspired and not fall into depression again...he knew I was desperate not to return home. Too embarrassed. Nothing to return to, you understand? No jobs, no prospects...my grades had slipped, and who was going to write me a recommendation for university now? And how would I ever afford it? Don't talk about scholarships and financial aid packages, those things didn't happen for kids like me, and that was before I got carted off to the local loony bin."

Aubrey concluded by showing Henry snippets once more, how she could sense Dr. Twiddy could be trusted (*smells like warm tea and cream*). He found funds for her to take her GED. She managed to pass, even though she was hampered by not having taken all of the math classes. She was now seventeen, old enough to be emancipated and get a job. Once she was released, Aubrey found a position in her hometown, working in a warehouse doing clerical support. She saved all of her salary, except for the amount she gave to Patti for utilities and food. Patti was devastated, having dreamed Aubrey would return to her happy, healthy, and like the rest of the girls in town her age, not this quiet, determined young woman. Not this Aubrey, who had no interest in going back to high school for proms, dances, and high school graduation, and had in fact completed her formal education as far as Patti could envision. Her daughter was now working, insisting on giving money for "her fair share," had no desire to go shopping for clothes, even! No interest in anything "fun." Patti's life was fairly bleak, and she had hoped once Aubrey was an adult, they would be able to enjoy some simple pleasures together, such as going to movies, or bargain shopping. But Aubrey had little interest in going to the small Main Street shops or cinema. She couldn't bear the gaping, the whispers that stopped once she entered a room, and began once she left it.

When Patti came home from work the morning after Aubrey's eighteenth birthday, all she found was a note, and an envelope stuffed with cash. Aubrey explained she needed to leave the town where everyone knew "she wasn't right in the head." She had given the warehouse appropriate notice. She was giving Patti all the notice she herself had been given before she had been taken to the asylum, perhaps, but it was the only way. Aubrey was leaving her with a good portion of the salary she had saved, to cushion the blow.

"I love you, Mama...but I can't be here any more. I need to make a fresh start. I hope you understand."

Aubrey kept lines of communication open with her mother, and returned to her side when Patti became ill two years later with an extremely malignant cancer. Aubrey cared for her mother from the initial diagnosis until she died two months afterwards. The contents of the house were swiftly disposed of, and the house razed. The land itself she sold to a developer. It was worth so much more without the dilapidated cabin sitting listlessly upon it...and Aubrey was more than half-afraid it might haunted beyond what could sense.

Aubrey started work in a travel agency, and as part of her job, traveled often. This suited her, as she had little possessions, wanted few, and became restless quickly if she stayed overlong in one place. (Henry nodded wisely as she disclosed this facet of her personality. It was further evidence of her Atlantean heritage: wanderlust, and ultimately, the hiraeth tendency that would only intensify with time and no bond to ground her.) However, Aubrey took personal care to write reviews at every place she did business: no matter how large or intimate, she would refrain from filling out the preprinted reply cards but opted to handwrite them on personal stationery, as well as submit them online on any and all websites she could find.

Do You Hear What I Hear?

In the earliest days of her career, she did this as a way to thank smaller businesses for giving exceptional service. As she was able to give them future customers, she wanted to do everything she could to give them as much foot traffic as possible, and it was such a small thing to do. It grew into a habit, for even as her words were sincere, the action itself became rote. No matter how many venues she visited in a day, Aubrey would write letters, thanks, reviews.

Her reviews became noticed by several publishers as her traveling had her crossing all about the country. She was invited to write columns for local newspapers. She squeezed in classes from her local community college, making sure she could handle professional writing demands, and took enough courses she felt satisfied she was competent. Aubrey was then dumbfounded when she became approached by several groups, asking her if she would consider writing for them exclusively: Condé Nash. Lonely Planet. Fodors. Frommers. Voyager Publications.

All because she started with writing personal thank you letters on plain pieces of stationery.

Once she secured a contract that threw her heart into paroxysms of amazement, it was as though fortune smiled on her once more: two of her short stories she had submitted (under a nom de plume, of course) had been accepted in two different publications. Did she have anything else they could look at...? *Did she*...?! You *bet* she did...! It was how she whiled away the hours during long layovers, longer nights alone: recording the stories that appeared to her via Voices, and her curious imagination filling in gaps, as playful as a kitten batting around a ball of yarn, asking her, "What if...? And then what?"

Aubrey was now writing professionally as a respected travel reviewer, and also beginning to have her creative writing career gain a toehold.

"Aubrey, I am so proud of you, and so happy! But I can't see how any of this is an obstacle to our…"

"Henry, I can't be seen…I can't be your 'One'! The press would tear me to pieces, your fans would riot…you, this stunning, talented actor of stage and screen, carrying on with someone 'who ain't right in the head'…?! And what if… Emmie Tiller vanished after her husband died, she went back to her family, but if she…no, no! I can't, Henry, I will ruin you! And I will be ruined! It will come out, I'm not the person I seem to be. I've never once lied to anyone, never falsified any papers or applications…but my image isn't of someone who didn't go to college, or finish high school like most people. I'm someone who hears, sees things that aren't there, I…"

"Stop! Aubrey, you need to stop…"

"No, Henry, you need to hear me!" Agitated, Aubrey yanked herself out of his embrace and stumbled away from him. "I cannot protect you from my past, I will destroy you… and there is no way I can escape. I am a PR nightmare. Just call your man, ask him! And everywhere you go, there are cameras, I will not be able to maintain my privacy much longer…everyone will know. Everyone. And then what? We will not be these…fated lovers you speak so tenderly about, we will be enemies, you will loathe me, cursing my name until you cease to be, I will be the one that destroyed your career, and you will be the reason I was outed and seen as a charlatan…everything we will have worked for, our entire lives, ruined…"

Henry also had sprang to his feet. "Aubrey, a life apart will leave *everything* feeling like ashes, no more than sand slipping through our fingers. Please, if you would just give us, give *me*, a chance. We will be so incredibly right for each other, fear will have no place in your heart, ever again."

Aubrey looked at Henry, her heart in her eyes. "I want to

believe you, I want to, so much," she moaned. "But if I'm wrong, I've ruined everything we've worked so hard for…"

"Let me take that risk," Henry replied firmly. "I love you…I want you…I cannot imagine life without you. Please don't shut me out, don't turn me away."

Aubrey's mind was churning, everything at war with itself: her desire to remain safely tucked away in anonymity, her burning desire to throw caution to the four winds and give herself over to the masterful portrait Henry was painting with his words and emotions.

"I hope we both do not regret it…because I think I might die if I hurt you, Henry," she whispered, coming back into his arms. "I really do…I cannot take on any more guilt in my life."

"No guilt," he murmured, raining kisses down upon her face, her neck, and daring to move further down her body, aware of how little she was wearing. "Let me show you how much I adore you, my precious, and trust me? Do you? Trust me, that is?"

Aubrey's eyes looked up into Henry's loving gaze, and she bit her lip. "God help us both, Henry…what is your middle name? I feel this is a middle name situation," she breathed. The enormity of what she was about to offer both exhilarated and shook her to her center.

"Declan," he grinned at her, his face split with the enormity of his smile.

"Henry Declan Rhys, I do trust you. More than my better sense is comfortable with, I trust you with my heart, my body, and my soul. May the fates see it as a blessing, and not a curse."

Henry took her face in his hands, and kissed her with all the love he had in his heart.

"My beautiful, sweet, strong Aubrey," he murmured, "as long as *you* see it as a blessing, that is all that matters…I know exactly what you are, and forever will be, for me…"

He nuzzled her gently, took her hand, and brought her back to bed, where he revealed to her what she was to him, multiple times:

Delight. Elation. Satiation.

Love.

12

ORDINARYISH PEOPLE

Henry hung up his cell phone, bemused.

"Whassamatta?" Aubrey's voice was muffled, issuing from under a thick blanket and a sheet of hair as she poked her head from the duvet. Dawn had only just made its way through the sky when Henry's phone began ringing, causing his arm to lash out blindly.

"That was Andrew," he replied, still preoccupied, but wide awake as the ramifications trickled through his thoughts.

"Andrew? As in Andrew Cooper, *Gatsby's* director? That Andrew?" Aubrey sat up in alarm, holding the blankets to her breasts in alarm. "Why is he calling you at this hour? What's wrong?"

"A water and sewer main ruptured. The whole street is shut down, and with it, all of the theaters. For at least the next three days," Henry answered. "That means the playhouses will be dark for at least four, because most of them won't be ready for a day afterwards…what a mess. We won't be able to reschedule the lost days, as the next productions will be hard on the heels of ours closing, for the holiday run will begin…it can't be helped, though."

"That's...wow," Aubrey replied, rubbing her eyes. "I'm sorry, Henry."

"I'm not!" He gave her a cheeky grin. "It's like a snow day, but better, as we aren't hemmed in by bad weather!" He texted rapidly. "I am giving strict orders I am not to be scheduled for a thing, not one interview, photo shoot, or publicity event!"

"So, what do you have in mind, you naughty boy?" Aubrey teased, lifting her eyebrow.

"You and I are going to run away. Go on holiday. Like ordinary people, love. Quick, throw some clothes in a bag, so we can escape before Greg catches wind of this and tries to overrule me…!"

"Where are we going?"

"Does it matter? Just pack, quickly!"

As it turned out, Henry and Aubrey did not go far. Henry quickly found a luxurious place for the two of them on Long Beach Island, New Jersey, a long barrier island extending out into the Atlantic Ocean. Henry was ecstatic at the prospect of spoiling Aubrey as much as possible, and he located a beautiful home out by Barnegat Light. Aubrey surprised him when she bashfully revealed she had a car of her own, although she did not have opportunity to drive it often.

"A Mini Cooper?"

Henry couldn't stop laughing when she pulled the protective tarpaulin from the vehicle. "I came all the way to the United States of America to get into a Mini Cooper? I want to get in an American muscle car, like a Mustang, a Thunderbird, a Corvette!"

"Shut up, Gatsby, and get in," she retorted, "or you can walk your Welsh ass all the way to New Jersey…"

He was still laughing when they crossed the Hudson.

The day they arrived began perfectly. The skies were bright blue, with warmer than average temperatures.

Aubrey secretly thought they could have been on their

honeymoon. Henry had arranged for the kitchen to be stocked with all manner of foodstuffs, including a magnum of champagne, chocolate covered strawberries, cheeses, crackers, and assorted fruits and dips he hand-fed her by the fireplace that was already laid for them in the master suite. They both drank from each other's glasses, made love in the moonlight, and enjoyed the oversized tub that could easily fit even Henry's frame, as well as Aubrey as she snuggled in his embrace.

"This is wretched excess, Henry," she chided him sleepily, sated and still buzzed from the gifts of the vineyards of France.

"Nonsense, my One…this is simply Gatsby doting upon his darling," he replied, nuzzling her ear with his nose.

"You're not Gatsby, there are no wild parties, and no green light across the bay," Aubrey hummed in return.

"I thank God for it," Henry's response was serious. "I never want any body of water between us, not a bay, not a river, not even a tub. God forbid an ocean…when the curtain comes down, will you want to live in the London residence? It's closest to my family, and I know they will be so happy to meet you…but Mairéad left me the Welsh property, and I cannot wait to share it with you. I haven't interfered with the sheep farm, when Grandpa passed, she turned it over to another family to run until I came into my majority. I didn't want to deprive them of their livelihood, and had no desire to raise sheep…Nor could I bear the thought of losing the land I grew up on…I had so many fond memories of spending time with Mairéad, so I had a snug home built on the edge, away from the woolly blighters…"

"Hang on, what now?" Aubrey sat up so she could look at Henry in dismay.

"When *Gatsby* closes in the second week of December," Henry patiently repeated. "Since Peter has left, there's nothing to keep you in the city any longer, is there? I thought…"

"You thought? You thought! Did it ever occur to you to *ask*?" Upset, Aubrey pulled away from him, getting out of the tub.

Was it his words that caused her to shiver? His presumption? Had the water become cold?

"Aubrey? What's wrong? I…you are coming home with me, aren't you?"

She looked at him, her face a mix of shock and more than the beginnings of anger.

"Were you ever going to ask me, Henry? Or were you going to wonder why I didn't have my bags packed, suitcase in one hand, plane ticket and visa in the other?"

"Aubrey!"

She was gone, robe clinging to her wet skin and already in the other room, drying her hair with far more vigor than necessary. Henry wrapped a towel around his waist, feeling as if he had been harpooned.

"I have said time and again, we are for each other, and how can we be together, with the Atlantic Ocean between us?"

Aubrey threw her hands in the air, her face distressed.

"Yes, Henry, *you* have said this, time and again. You say many things…but I wonder, do you ever ask me what *I* think? No, because you are so certain you can hear my every thought…but I wonder, Henry, do you ever *listen*? I never said a word about leaving New York! It's true, I travel often, and I miss Peter's presence sorely. He was my best, my only true friend in a city of millions…but did ever I say I was going to abandon my loft? Did I even think it?"

Henry stood mute in the face of her red-headed temper. Well, he had been warned…

"I…I waited, so long, hoping and dreaming of finding you," he whispered.

"I have no doubt you did," she replied, the frustration in her expression fading, only to be replaced with weary resignation. Aubrey disliked seeing the woebegone, panicky look in Henry's eyes. He resembled a small boy in a man's body, and she hated her words putting fear in his face. "But I am not...some trophy, or award the fates have seen fit to hand to you, to be picked up and moved about at your whim..."

"That's not fair," he flared back. "I want to give you... everything. Anything I can bestow upon you, Aubrey, beginning with my heart, and...don't you like this house? It's just the beginning, darling! I can give you so much, I..."

"Henry, all I have ever wanted is to be able to live a private life, doing the things I loved, which was traveling and writing! I was happy, I thought, living my life. Peter. Going to Acoustics, and having our musical Sundays when we could. I realized I was still...unsettled, when I allowed myself to think about it. I tried hard not to be, life is never perfect...I blamed my spells of pining for something I couldn't define on being worn down, the Voices, or worse than that, fearing Scenes I wouldn't escape. I thought I had almost everything, until I met you." She gave him a lopsided smile. "I don't need anything you can buy me, Henry, although I know you have a generous heart. I grew up having very little, and it doesn't take much to content me...I still don't know if I will ever understand matters as clearly as you do. You talk of having this shared legacy, all I know is when I am with you, I feel more complete than when I am not."

"Then what is the problem?" Henry fought to keep his tone even.

"The problem is you take assumptions where I am concerned. It hurts me, Henry."

He actually had to take a physical step back as the breath was knocked out of his lungs. Dazed, he shook his head like a dog shaking water from its fur. "I've never wished to hurt you, I love you more than I've ever loved anyone, Aubrey."

"I know you've never wished to hurt me, Henry. You're a good man." She sighed. "I'm tired, and we should be curling up next to each other, rather than beginning discussions I'm uncertain of where the middles are, or where they will end…I would much rather us enjoy our time here. We ran away from everything so we could be free and happy. I want nothing less for us both."

Chastened, Henry opened his arms. "I'm a fool of a man. Forgive me? I will do better, and not take such decisions for granted. I promise, I will. We'll discuss December later…"

Aubrey knelt up on top of the bed before she entered his embrace, impish smile on her face. "I need the extra height, you giant forgiven fool of a man, if I am to kiss you and make you happy again."

After Aubrey was fast asleep, Henry was still wide awake.

It was true, he did take shortcuts in his logic when it came to his plans for the future with Aubrey. After all, he couldn't see where the difficulties lay…why would she want to remain in New York alone? It made no sense to him. Yes, he should not have taken this for granted, but…

He shifted, and turned over. He needed to assuage his guilty conscience.

The bubblings of self-reproach were novel sensations for him. Henry was singularly unused to setting a foot wrong… anywhere. His ability to know what people wanted, and expected, made it very easy for him to provide whatever was anticipated, or avoid a situation where he would be found lacking.

"This is terrible," he said to the sound of the tide, audible even through the closed doors to the balcony overlooking the beach. "How do ordinary people *do* this?"

Henry sent a text to Christine:

```
Help me, I opened my mouth and fell
into it, big time. It wasn't atro-
```

```
cious, just stupid…Would you please
get a lovely 'I-fucked-up-and-I-am-
sorry-please-forgive-me?' present for
Aubrey? If I buy it in front of her,
she will balk.

—Kicking myself, Henry.
```

He wasn't surprised to get a response almost immediately:

> Oh, Boss. Well, at least you're trying. Not a problem, just tell me what you want and I'll take care of it.

"Oh, bollocks," he grunted, and texted his assistant back.

```
I don't know, whatever the usual is
for something like this…Flowers? If I
go overboard she'll have even more
reason to give me THAT FACE. I don't
want to see THAT FACE again. Ever.
```

Christine's answer hit his screen so quickly, he could almost swear it sizzled:

> Oh, no you don't. You want to make it up with the lady, you need to come up with it yourself. I am not getting in the middle of mommy and daddy fighting…

Henry all but choked at the mental image.

```
THAT. IS. REVOLTING. CHRISTINE YOU'RE
FIRED DON'T SAY THAT TO ME EVER AGAIN…
of course, you're not fired but now I
need brain bleach. And given my
propensity for screwing up this
evening, I do not trust myself. I am
bound to make a hash out of this HELP
ME PLEASE I AM BEGGING YOU…!
```

Back in New York, Christine shook her head.

> Nice try, Boss…but no. Look, if she knows it came from your heart, you can't screw up. Even if she hates it*, that alone will take you far.

> —*You are in love with the woman. Certainly you must have some idea of what she would like…? One woman's flower is another woman's allergic reaction. Use your head! And I am refraining from making filthy jokes because I respect you. And I happen to like my job. You're welcome.

> —Going to sleep now, Christine.

Henry made a terrible face at the ceiling. "All you women stick together," he complained.

He turned over and looked at Aubrey, pondering what she

had, what she treasured, until he was inspired. After some searching, he discovered what he was certain was the perfect gift. Relief made his heart lighter and his eyelids heavier. Henry wrapped himself about Aubrey, and fell asleep.

The next day found them taking a long, lovely stroll along the water's edge. Aubrey delighted in the privacy of the deserted beach, and her joy flowed, unfiltered, into Henry's mind. Hands were held, with many soft, gentle kisses shared as they walked along the surf. Henry picked Aubrey up and swung her around whenever he felt a wave was encroaching too close to her ankles, which never failed to make her squeal with giggles. This in turn set off his rich, boisterous laugh. They spoke of many things, such as Henry's love for horseback riding and sailing. Aubrey confessed she had never tried either activities, but dreamed of learning to sail. She had seen horses when she was growing up, but they were attached to farms, and not meant to be enjoyed. They were like cows, and goats, she said innocently. Henry kissed the top of her head, and promised to take her riding someday.

"Considering how you drive, once you learn how to gallop, nothing else will satisfy you," he mocked her with a grin. "The wind in your hair, and nothing but open fields around you...I will never get you indoors again!"

"Laugh if you must, but I didn't hear you complaining when I got us here in record time!"

"I couldn't complain, you never would have never heard me! Peter was right, you aren't happy unless you can feel the music in your sternum when you drive...! You'll miss your hearing someday, milady Aubrey..."

"Oh, you!" Aubrey laughed enough for both of them as she kicked icy cold water up the back of Henry's legs, and he yelped in shock. Sensing immediate reprisals, she bolted, running in a random pattern, making it difficult for Henry to catch her as she ducked and dodged.

She was quick. Agile. But as she'd suspected, Aubrey was

no match for his long legs and incredible reach, even though they were well paired with a runner's stamina. Within minutes, she was squirming in his grasp as he held her over his shoulder in a fireman's carry, spinning her just as he would his sisters.

"No! No! Henry, stop, I'm gonna barf!" Her pleas for mercy were diluted by her helpless peals of laughter.

"You do the crime, you do the time…!" Henry was the most cheerful, unremitting gaoler Aubrey could have ever imagined.

"I'm gonna do it all down the back of your shirt…!"

"You're lucky I am feeling benevolent," he rumbled, his eyes twinkling. Henry gently set Aubrey down, keeping her against his chest as she regained her equilibrium.

"*You're* lucky I love you…and ready for lunch," Aubrey replied, the half-smile curling her lips taking the acerbic sting from her words.

While they ate, Aubrey diffidently asked Henry if he would like to enjoy a traditional Thanksgiving meal with her. "It's been years since I roasted a turkey," she warned him, "but I am fairly confident I can manage. God knows there are enough cooking shows to walk me through anything." Henry's eyes grew wide, and he all but began drooling at the prospect. "They are going to need to let all my costumes out," he prophesied with glee. "Are you certain it won't be too much work?"

Aubrey sniffed, pretending to be insulted. "Just for that, no pie," she replied haughtily, and Henry got down on his knees, dramatically begging her pardon. The sight was so absurd, Aubrey could only maintain her demeanor for a few minutes before she dissolved into giggles, ordering him, "Up, get up, you silly man! Let's enjoy the top deck as our food settles and I get over that display. I think I will cherish that memory forever! I'm looking forward to Thanksgiving for the first time in…oh, I can't remember when!"

Do You Hear What I Hear?

They were there an hour before Henry's phone began ringing, signaling Greg was calling. With an eye roll, he silenced it as they stretched out, relaxing with the sounds of the surf. Aubrey was catching up on her reading, and Henry was playing a video game on his tablet, a time-consuming pastime he hadn't allowed himself in months.

His phone went off again. This time it was a text, still from Greg, imploring him to pick up the phone. Henry gave a cheeky reply:

```
I'm on vacation, you git. For at least
one more day. Feck off.
```

He had just sent his snarky response when Aubrey's phone rang. "Oh, it's Peter," she chirped happily. "How are you, my Ent? Have you become one with the redwoods?... Slow down, I can't...There are what? No, that's not..." She looked at Henry with confusion. "No, I mean yes...we were on the beach this morning, but no one else...! Not another soul!" Book forgotten, she fled inside.

Henry's stomach turned over as he read Greg's return text:

> *I KNOW IT IS YOUR VACATION. THE TROUBLE IS, SO DOES AT LEAST ONE PHOTOGRAPHER WITH A LONG-RANGE LENS, AND THE FUCKER SOLD A HUGE BATCH OF PHOTOS TO THE HIGHEST PAYING BIDDER. I CAN'T SCRUB THESE, HEN. I WOULD SAY I AM SORRY—AND I AM—BUT I TRIED WARNING YOU. NO NAME ATTACHED TO AUBREY YET WHICH IS A **BLOODY FUCKING MIRACLE**. THE CLOCK IS TICKING, FRIENDO. YOU NEED TO LET AUBREY KNOW, BUT BE GENTLE. SHE WILL NOT HAVE SEEN THIS COMING, AND IT WILL UNDOUBTEDLY BE A SHOCK...FOR WHAT IT IS WORTH, AND I KNOW IT ISN'T MUCH, I HAVE*

NEVER SEEN YOU LOOK SO GENUINELY HAPPY. AND YOUR LADY LOOKS SIMPLY RADIANT. NOT THAT SHE WILL CARE.

Henry did not need to search for Aubrey. He could find her by the soft sounds of her weeping, as she sat hunched over her tablet, following the links Peter sent her revealing their private moments, stolen and spread out for anyone to see.

"Aubrey…love…I'm sorry…"

Aubrey scrubbed her face with a napkin. "Do these things happen to you all the time, Henry? Photos taken without your knowledge? Without you even being able to see…?"

Henry was rubbing her back, distraught at her pain. "Yes. I'm afraid so, it's gotten so I don't notice, or think much about it…"

Aubrey drew in a shuddering breath. "Okay then…I can see now…I understand…"

"See, understand what?"

"It doesn't matter. We had a good run, didn't we? Of pretending to be like everyone else…I hate to pack up, but I guess it's time to go, isn't it?"

"No, Aubrey, we haven't done anything wrong, we don't have to leave! The theaters are still dark, I still have time off…" He tried to catch her eyes, helpless as Aubrey avoided his face altogether.

"But can we have fun, knowing we are living under a microscope…or in this case, in someone's viewfinder? Because I *can't*, Henry. I told you this, from the beginning. I can't live like this."

Her arms wrapped around her torso, hugging herself, knuckles white. "We can stay. This is a lovely place. I want to be here with you, and I know you love being close to the water. I find it peaceful…or I did…I just won't go outside."

"Aubrey…"

"I have a headache, Henry." As she finally looked up, her eyes were burning holes into her face as color leached itself from her skin. Only her hair and eyes retained vibrancy, Aubrey could feel her vitality seeping away through the bare soles of her feet. "Please excuse me."

Defeated, Henry watched his castles in the sky crumbling as she slipped away from him, in more ways than one.

13

ZERO TOLERANCE

Henry requested to make a special stop on their return home.

Aubrey smiled at him, her expression tolerant compared to his Cheshire Cat grin. After the emotional outbursts she'd been subjecting Henry to since they'd arrived, she wanted to be more patient with his foibles. She had yielded to his entreaties, and ventured out of doors, but only once the sun was down. The moon became their sun, and only then would she frolic by the waves with him, once more dashing along the lapping surf. Henry's heart ached in a way he hadn't thought possible, but he was grateful for what she gave him. During the daylight, Aubrey shut herself up fast within the large house, abjuring even the top exposed deck. She would only risk the enclosed balconies to read, or lounge with him.

"Just plug it into the GPS," she agreed, patting his cheek affectionately as they pulled away from the luxury rental.

"Is there any chance I could tempt you with some Christmas music?" Henry schooled both his tone and expression into giving nothing away.

As he expected, Aubrey grimaced. "Oh, Henry, no...it's not even Thanksgiving yet!"

"Please…" he dragged the word out, whining. "I have a playlist even you will love, my precious Tiny Tim…"

"Never call me that again," she capitulated. Henry chortled, usurping her musical selections.

Seconds later, Henry roared in mirth as she began screaming in frustration, helplessly gripped by a temper tantrum she couldn't stem. "No! *No no no*! Turn that off *right this moment*! I heard what you said about me…!"

"You don't like *A Charlie Brown Christmas*?" His face was innocent, for all he could barely speak through his guffaws. "I was certain you did, for all you danced just like so many of the characters on the stage…"

The string of blue comments she hurled at him in reply left him truly impressed.

"Whoa, Aubrey…you would in fit very well with sailors at sea, indeed…!"

She simply screamed, a wordless retort of fury as she strangled the steering wheel.

Henry couldn't remember the last time he laughed so hard. He only wished there was some way he could have shared this moment with Peter.

Aubrey then lapsed into a sulky silence, occasionally giving Henry a baleful glare. It occurred to him this was most likely not the best way to get back into her good graces, even though teasing her had been great fun.

Oh, all right, darling…I am sorry. I couldn't resist teasing you. I love the way you dance, because you take so much joy in it… You're so free, all of your limbs moving like a limbs of birch swaying in the wind…as the spirit of Rhythm guides. I laughed, because it was so unexpected, to see you so fluid, when all I had seen before was your rigid control in all you said and did…it was a revelation, an entirely new facet of you. But when you move, I'm the one who is moved…my heart pounds as fiercely as if I was there beside you… You are a spellcaster, luring Motion, itself, to you. I was captivated, caught under the spell you threw out like a net…You have me,

Siren, Songstress, Nymph...I will watch you dance around the fires as long as you will. And beg you dance with me, as well.

Aubrey's temper began to subside. How could it not, when Henry touched her heart with words like these?

Smooth talker...you must be able to ease you way out of trouble with every woman you meet.

Henry gently tugged one of her hands from the wheel, and placed it on his heart.

Can you feel this? Can you hear how it is thudding? This is for you, only you, and it has been waiting for you.

Her eyes flickered towards him briefly, as it was all she could afford him, her lips curved into a genuine, pleased smile.

Henry...what on earth am I going to do with you...

Love me, Aubrey.

You foolish pirate. I already do...now, listen to your Christmas music.

Henry laughed, cheering as Aubrey appeared more content. Watching her creep about the beautiful mansion he'd rented made him feel he'd taken a beautiful wild creature and clapped it into a cage. Now, driving with the top down, hair pulled back in a ponytail, sporting a ball cap and sunglasses to protect her eyes, Aubrey seemed more herself. Her car ate up the miles, music filling the cabin and their ears.

Despite herself, Aubrey was soon lost in the music, singing along with the pieces Henry had selected. He had to half-yell as Aubrey sang at the top of her lungs. "You've already enchanted me to your side with your seductive wiles and voice...but would you please spare my hearing, and lower the volume...?"

"You're as bad as Peter...!"

They continued to banter until they reached Henry's mystery destination: a large suburban shopping mall. Aubrey frowned. "Henry, are you sure this is it?"

"Quite sure," he replied, looking insufferably smug. He

was also wearing a ball cap and sunglasses, and hadn't shaved since they left for their little jaunt. Even Aubrey had to admit being away from New York City proper, it would take the average passerby a double, or triple take to recognize him as the polished celebrity they saw in magazines. The paparazzi photos from two days ago showed him bareheaded, his face unobscured.

"Relax, sweetheart. Who would think we would come to a place like this? A big, important star such as myself would only patronize the grandest, most expensive venues in Manhattan," he whispered in her ear, adopting the pretentious accent of Jay Gatsby. "Don't you agree, old sport?"

"Don't call me old," she winked. "Now what on earth are you looking for, Jay?"

He wrapped his arm around her, heading straight for his goal. Henry was determined to make this stop joyful and perfect for his love, so had studied the mall's directory beforehand.

As they walked, he spoke with a voice that wavered between confidence and hesitance. "Aubrey…I've been thinking about what you said, the first night we were at the beach. I am very sorry if you felt I have been taking your presence in my life for granted. You aren't some…thing that's been dropped in my path, but you *are* very much a gift. I wanted to give you a present, as a way to let you know I am sorry…but I didn't know what the perfect thing to give you might be."

Aubrey opened her mouth to protest as they approached a jewelry store, and Henry shook his head. "Ah, ah, ah…I thought hard about what you love, and treasure the most." They stopped in front the window, filled with pieces that gleamed with stones of cold white fire, blues as vibrant as the ocean, greens as mysterious as the fabled green flash of tropical waters. "I thought of bedecking you with rings of gold, diamonds, sapphires, emeralds…but realized, I don't think this is you. While I hope to treat you with things like this in time…that time is not now." He led her away from the shop.

"No, I know what you *love*…and I thought I might give you something to go along with it. Perhaps something…to give it a mate." Hope and uncertainty wavered in his eyes as he brought her to another store, one filled with all sorts of plush animals that could be made on the spot to a child's wishes and specifications. "Look…"

He brought her to a display that stocked dragons very similar to the plush toy Peter had given her years ago, but different enough not to be duplicates. "I'm sorry I pushed you, Aubrey. May I give your dragon a mate? As a way to say, 'I'm sorry I was an ass, please forgive me…?' See, you can insert a disc with the sounds of a heartbeat, and…*oof*…"

Aubrey had thrown her entire self against him, not just her arms, but all of her being. "You amazing…wonderful… how I love you, I love you…you could not have picked out a better present if you tried…but I already forgave you, Henry Declan, you idiot…!"

"Hey, I'm an idiot now?" He was laughing in his relief. "I am just so thrilled it is making you this happy. Come, pick one out, you can have whatever you want. Anything at all…"

Aubrey was shaking, she was so overwhelmed and touched by Henry's thoughtfulness. When they paused by the jewelry store window, her heart sank like a foundering ship. She was crushed by the thought the man she had fallen so hopelessly in love with did not understand her at all. While Aubrey loved looking at all things beautiful, she did not want jewelry as tokens of apology. She dreamed of such things given to her pulsing with exuberance, as gifts laden with joy.

Peter had teased her, but he knew she craved soft things to hold when she was alone. Aubrey had been inexplicably fascinated with dragons as a little girl, and Peter discovered a cache of children's films about them. Henry had learned there was an animated movie about dragons coming out for the holidays, so there was a corresponding blitz of merchandise. This shop offered a large variety of other dragons for her to choose from...Having grown up in rather stark surroundings, being able to immerse herself in such playful, rich fantasy was like putting Aubrey in a candy store. Henry was already planning to take Aubrey to see the show when it opened, but he wasn't willing to wait that long for this moment!

Peter had simply given her the dragon, wrapped in a box "just because." Now, given choices...her head was spinning.

"Whoa, there...we have time, no rush," Henry calmed her.

It was the middle of a weekday, so there were not many customers in the store. The retail workers were happy to let the couple browse, completely unaware of Henry's identity. There was a young mother, a little overwhelmed with a pair of twin boys in a side-by-side stroller, and their older sister, all of whom had definite ideas about what they wanted, and one older man who was browsing as well.

Aubrey made her choices with care, a dragon similar to the one Peter gave her. A heartbeat sound to go inside its chest. Henry could even make a voice recording if she wished, but she blushed, refusing.

"Are you sure," he purred suggestively in her ear. "I could go off to the side, and leave you a personal message meant only for your ears, my love..."

"Henry!" Aubrey was now the color of her hair. "There are *children* here...!"

"And don't I know it," he groaned as one of the twins began to screech. "I said I would find a private area!"

"No, thank you," Aubrey replied, her eyes dancing. "Knowing you, you will leave something so provocative I would never be able to fall asleep!"

"That's the idea," he whispered as the other toddler began to cry. Aubrey put her head down, smirking.

"Once more, no, thank you...let's just put my order in, but let the mother go ahead of us. She has her hands full. I wish I had something in my bag to help distract her little ones. They sound like they need a bottle and a nap..."

"How do you know that?" Henry looked at her in surprise.

"From traveling. I always have little trinkets and small toys that can't hurt anyone, but could distract little ones... sometimes parents are so overwhelmed and never get any support. It's sad." She looked around and said quietly, "I know because...well, damn it Henry, you *know* how I know."

His eyes widened with understanding. "I said it the first time we met, and I will say it again. You are so incredibly kind...let me see if I can be of some help. You are a good influence on me, milady Aubrey..."

Henry ambled over to where the boys were miserably sobbing. "Hey there, little men. What's all this fuss about?" He squatted down, making himself much smaller. The mother's eyes grew large, and Henry heard her surprise and even a touch of alarm at first, being approached by a stranger. She saw her daughter *Jenny don't go too far!* sadly looking at toys off to the side as she tried to get her purchases created and paid for *I should have known it was too close to lunch to get all this done, Timmy and Tommy are exhausted, Jenny is bored, never again...* Henry couldn't hear exact thoughts from the boys, as they were so young, but he sensed their frustration, restlessness, hunger, and weariness. He would neatly counter and distract them with silly faces and voices as their discomfort would spike.

It only took about ten minutes for everything to be created, rung up, and paid for...

Ten minutes. Fifteen, at the most.

He would swear to it, in a court of law.

Everything then seemed to happen at once:

Mrs. Margaret (*Molly*) Harlowe looked up, and called out, "Jenny? Jenny, where are you?"

The employee who worked closet to the store entrance

asked a coworker, "Hey, where's the hanger that belongs right here...? You know, the heavy one to grab merch hanging on the higher hooks...?"

Henry said aloud, "Aubrey? Aubs, love, where did you go?" He opened his mind away from the little boys who were happily grasping their new bears, and heard Aubrey...*screaming for him...*

Henry please please he's going to take her hurt her you need to call security I don't know if I can stop him in time!

Henry dropped Aubrey's selection and ran as Molly began to shriek.

Jenny was gone.

AUBREY HAD BEEN LINGERING by some of the toys and accessories by the entrance to the mall, when she noticed some scattered all over the floor. With a sigh, she bent over to pick them up.

She had fallen out of her habit of wearing gloves while she was with Henry. She trusted him to keep her grounded should she stumble across any Voices or Scenes, and she rarely touched anything besides him when they were in public.

Therefore she was completely unprepared for the assault, the Scene, overwhelming her when she picked up a blue plush unicorn:

Greasy, oily lust...washing over her, fire...Aubrey could see herself, on the periphery, but the focus was on the tiny little girl... overwhelming lust...lust for her body, her blood, her life...fighting it, panting...gripping the toy, sweating... "Do you like that, sweetheart?"

"Uh huh...but I like the pink one more better. The store says they're all gone. Mommy says we gotta wait until they get more."

"No, no, honey, I have one. I'll let you have it, if you want it.

It's okay. Come with me, and I'll give it to you. It won't take a minute."

"I...should tell my Mommy..."

"Oh, she's so busy, and it won't take a second. She won't even notice you're gone, she's so busy with your brothers. See? Everyone's paying attention to them. Just come with me, so I can give it to you..."

The toy, on the ground. The girl, gone. The man, gone. Where did they go? Where? Where?

Aubrey did not stop to think. She just grabbed the heavy metal hanger by the entrance, and bolted.

Mentally, she was wailing, screaming for Henry. She needed his gift, she needed him to sift through all the mental voices she couldn't hear, to locate this *beast* before he could hurt the little girl... Instinctively Aubrey turned towards the darkened corner marked "Employees Only."

Her mind was racing, jabbering at her, "He will want to hide, a private exit, away from the public, CCTVs are everywhere, he will need a quick way out..."

Henry where are you? Why aren't you hearing me? I need you!

Her intuition paid off: she heard a little voice plaintively crying out, "I changed my mind, I don't want it anymore, I wanna go back, I want my Mommy! You're scaring me!"

A male voice, thick with emotion oozing in reply, "No, just another few steps, shh..."

"No! No, I don't..."

The sound of a slap, echoing through the concrete hallway. "Shut up! Shut up or you're going to get worse, do you hear me?"

Aubrey had always enjoyed running, just for the freedom it gave her. It wasn't about competition, fitness, or anything more than the joy of putting her headphones on and having the beat of her music fuel her feet. But now she was so grateful she was able to pour every bit of will into muscles used to flying across the ground as her soul screamed out:

Henry please please he's going to take her hurt her you need to call security I don't know if I can stop him in time!

Henry's reply, black with rage, filled her being just as she laid eyes on the little girl, being held fast in the arms of an older man as he was heading for an exit.

Darling where are you?

Employee...only...hallway...I see them! Oh no...not going to...!

Henry's head was swiveling, almost like an owl's. He could hear security rushing to the store, but he was already running towards the area he sensed his One was.

Aubrey's voice always touched his mind with the softness of a butterfly's wing. Her soul was gentle, and peaceful. When he thought of his beloved, he thought of a songbird in flight. Even when she was sad, or angry, he sensed compassion, a tender warmth.

But now...all he felt was implacable ice.

Aubrey?

He didn't need to hear her in his soul. Not when her voice echoed through the hall.

"Let. Her. Go."

While he stopped at a corner, trying to decide if he should go left or right, Aubrey was walking slowly but steadily to the man clutching the terrified child. She was holding a pole like a baseball bat. "You are never going to get away. Security has been notified, and are right outside this door. You can walk out or be carried out, I don't care. But put her down."

The man sneered, "Oh, and another little girl is gonna stop me?" He pulled a gun from his pocket, aiming it at Aubrey, who kept walking, shaking her head.

"I can tell you how this is going to end. You think you can push me around like you're doing to this little girl?" Aubrey kept her voice conversational, but firm. As though she was addressing an errant child...or a slavering animal. "It's not fair, what you've just done to her...and you would do worse.

I have zero tolerance for guys like you…I'm not gonna have another little girl live in fear. Look at me, make your choice: how are you going to leave this hallway? You have no idea what I am capable of…I don't want to hurt you, but I will, if you don't put the gun away, and let this little girl go."

*Gun? Jesus Christ, Aubrey, he has a fucking **gun**?!*

Her mind was silent. She was utterly present in this moment. Prepared to act, as she had been before, once upon a time…except today, she wasn't afraid.

Henry ran faster, praying he took the correct turn.

Eugene Hodges was sweating. Who was this bitch, that having a gun aimed at her face didn't stop her? "I swear I will, I'll blow your fucking head off!"

Henry came around the corner…

Aubrey looked at the would-be rapist, the man who had already ruined this little girl's dreams for years to come, and dropped her pole. "Okay. Fine. You win…"

Aubrey! No!!!

Henry was paralyzed.

Aubrey exploded into five sharp movements: ducking below the line of fire, grabbing the gunman's wrist, kicking his groin with all of the strength in her runner's leg. As he doubled over, he released both the child and gun. She kicked the weapon away, swooped up the pole…and smashed it into his skull like a hammer…or the fist of an avenging fae.

Eugene Hodges dropped the floor, a noticeable dent in his head. Aubrey then kicked his ribs for good measure, a thick, meaty sound echoing in the hallway.

Jenny was slumped into a ball, trembling. Afraid to move, cry, or breathe.

Aubrey knew that sensation intimately. She picked up the gun with distaste, touching it only through the fabric of her sweater, placing it in the pocket of her coat.

"Hey there, little one," she cooed. She moved slowly towards the cowering child. "I know you are very scared right now, but it's over. That nasty, evil man can't hurt you anymore. You're safe. Pinky promise. I'm going to get you back to your Mama now. Okay? Okay."

Aubrey.

Aubrey looked up, and saw Henry still standing at the junction of the hallway. Pasty white, and covered in sweat. He looked ill.

Henry, you need to leave.

What?!

Now!

It was a percussive blast that echoed through his skull, as deafening as any gunshot. He jerked, looking at her as his pupils dilated until scarcely any blue was left

The police are going to be all over here in a matter of moments. You do not need this kind of publicity, especially if they start asking questions about how I was able to figure out how that fucker had her…get out of here, Henry! There are no CCTVs back here, that's why the bastard took this exit…! Run!

No, Aubrey, I'm not leaving you…

Henry, you are.

The cold finality in her words, and the manner she would not even look at him as she cradled the weeping child convinced him how serious she was.

Like a rat deserting a sinking ship, Henry disappeared.

THE NEWS WAS EVERYWHERE. Not local. Not state, nor regional.

National…

With a sickening jolt, Henry saw it had been picked up by the BBC.

International, now…

"Rumored love interest of international star of stage and screen Henry Rhys seen leaving under police escort after wanted child molester and suspected murderer Eugene

Hodges rushed away by ambulance at New York suburban shopping mall..." breathlessly reported a local newscaster.

"Woman seen with Henry Rhys identified as Aubrey Stafford..." blasted an internet fan site.

"What is the connection between Henry Rhys' constant companion, Aubrey Stafford, and Eugene Hodges? Hodges has been on the run for months after escaping arrest for aggravated sexual assault on a minor..."

"Aubrey Stafford, travel writer for Voyager Publications, would have ample opportunity to act as a lookout or even procure victims for Hodges," speculated one writer who had been dissecting Aubrey's appearance since the first set of photographs had appeared weeks ago, and no one knew her identity.

"In photos taken just days before the dramatic rescue of four year old Alice (name changed to protect her privacy), Aubrey Stafford is obviously very intimate with actor Henry Rhys...(photos displayed of Aubrey kissing Henry, holding his hand, smiling at him) but is shown here being escorted into the police department under heavy guard..."

Henry threw his television remote across the room, cracking it in half. "What about Aubrey's privacy?" He was bellowing, enraged.

Greg sent him a terse message: "Do not go anywhere, make any statements. Remain silent and DO. NOT. MOVE."

Peter has sent him three blistering texts and a voicemail that should have melted his phone into its component parts: "What *the absolute fuck* is going on over there? Where is her protection, did you give her *nothing*? You *promised*, dude, you *promised* me you'd look out for her...!"

Henry, not knowing what to do after Aubrey banished him, drove back to his suite in New York City. He vanished, as she ordered him to do...and because he was the lowest of the low, never completed purchasing her dragon...the mate for her beloved plush...the gift he wanted to present her, to let her know how sorry he was.

He was sorry, all right...the sorriest excuse of a soul mate to ever walk the face of the earth.

How was he going to fix this? He tore at his hair, his clothes, moaning in agony.

Henry was relieved Aubrey had been at the right place at precisely the right time. The thought of that tiny little girl being mauled by...his gorge rose.

He never should have listened to Aubrey, never left her. Damn the career. Fuck the photographers, his reputation, all of it. Today, Aubrey proved she was more of a man, no, more of a human being than he ever could be.

I know I don't deserve anything, Aubrey, but I am begging, if you can spare a crumb from your very big heart, from what you feel for me...please let me know you are all right? I never should have left you to weather this alone...

Just as before, silence was the only answer to what he flung out into the universe.

GREG WAS WORKING FEVERISHLY, ever since he received an impassioned phone call from Aubrey.

"Greg, I need your help. I'm going to have trouble, big trouble. I haven't done anything wrong, but Henry will be implicated by my actions..."

Greg was beyond stunned. "Slow down, Aubrey. Start from the beginning," he urged her, picking up his tablet and his laptop with a frantic grab, startling Christine. They had just finished going over Henry's revised schedule when Aubrey's call came through.

Tersely, Aubrey recounted the events, along with the slight alteration she had given to the police: how Henry had taken her to a shop to choose a gift, but she noticed the little girl wander away. Concerned, she followed, and by the time she realized she was witnessing an abduction in progress, her phone had poor signal, and Aubrey was too scared to wait to notify authorities. Henry followed her once he realized she had left, but by then the situation had escalated...by the time he located her, she had subdued Hodges, and begged Henry to leave before his name was linked to the publicity storm that was certain to erupt. "Greg, I'm sure I did the right thing...the last thing he needs is to have his name attached to a serial child-killer, which is what this man is, I am sure of it...and I confess, I uh...took that creature down with everything I had. I may have killed him," she whispered, barely audible. "I just didn't want him to get up again, Greg, I...he had a gun, he was going to murder that little girl, I know he was..."

"Shh, Aubrey, shh..." he soothed her. Christine's eyes were huge and swollen as she was pulling open her laptop and tablet as well. She felt so helpless.

"There are going to be photos, and my name is going to..." Aubrey's voice choked, and Greg's eyes prickled. Aubrey was going to lose her privacy, not due to her heroism, but because of her link to Henry. Otherwise, it would be buried in the local news and lost...she could plead to remain anonymous; if she wasn't someone the media vultures were already circling it might have been possible. Improbable, but now...

"It doesn't matter," she continued, having regained her composure. "Protect Henry. I sent him home. I have no idea what state of mind he is in, or even where he is right now...! He has my car, that's all I know. I'm begging you, Greg, take care of Henry, I'm not even mentioning he was with me. No one recognized him, as far as the world knows, he went straight back to New York City..."

"I've got his back, and *yours*," Greg replied firmly. "Just make sure you have representation, Aubrey!"

"I'm fine, Greg," she replied, her voice barely a sigh. "I

have to go. Thank you, for everything. Truly. Goodbye, Greg…goodbye."

He was left holding a dead line.

Christine was shaking. "Greg…she sounded so…final…"

"Not if I have anything to say about it," he snapped. "That lumbering *git* has never been happier than he has been with that stubborn redhead. Be *damned* if I let it fall apart on my watch. Not for something like this…! What's more, I don't believe she followed anyone…she's protecting him. I think she was *abducted*, and she's protecting him…I *told* Henry she needed personal security, and he blew me off!"

Greg was masterful. While he could not put the genie back in the bottle—Aubrey's name was now out in the wild, forever matched to her face, Christine was invaluable in pulling up site after site—he was filing cease-and-desists, threatening libel suits against any publication slandering Aubrey by linking her with the sex offender without proof or just cause. He made certain Henry was not going off the deep end, as he feared he would. He expected a raving madman, taking on all comers. The mental image of Henry, sitting meekly in a room, waiting for news, made his blood run cold.

What in the name of God was going on between those two…?

Fan sites, as could be predicted, went feral. The vitriol against Aubrey was thick and toxic, doing everything but claiming she had gone out hand-selecting victims for this Hodges slime. It took every contact he had to begin to stem, and then turn the tide, showing how Aubrey was not only blameless, but actually the heroine of the hour. She was escorted into the police station as a material witness, not even remotely linked as a potential accomplice. Evidence was clear: Aubrey Lillian Stafford saved the preschooler from a terrible assault, and most likely a terribly violent end.

Greg picked up his phone, and prepared to make a call to his *client* he would not soon forget.

Christine's phone rang.

"Christine? It's Henry...I need you to do something for me. It's most urgent."

Aubrey wasn't looking at anything online. She already knew her name was everywhere, because she could see the local news on the television screens at the precinct.

She was treated with deference and respect there, offered countless cups of coffee, and baked goods that proliferated throughout the station. She recounted her story as often as requested, spoke to the counsel she was offered. Rested her head on the table, took the aspirin the police detectives gave her. She never attempted to be obstructive about her background, speaking briefly about her place of birth, when she left, where she moved to, where she lived currently.

Nothing came up as being remotely suspicious. Even her ruthless swing at Hodges was dismissed as self-defense. A uniformed detective brought her a freshly-baked cupcake, mentioning casually her strike against the "perp" was so profound he might not survive it, adding briefly, "Good job. The man is shit on the bottom of humanity's shoe. He isn't worth a bullet, let alone a trial...but that's my personal opinion. I have a little girl, just that age..." He wandered off, and Aubrey never saw him again.

The local PD was more than happy to arrange for her to be brought back to her residence in an unmarked squad car. It was very early the following morning when Aubrey limped into her front door.

Every bone, every muscle, every nerve she had was screaming with pain. Her neck muscles were in agony, as though they had been stretched on the infamous rack, her head pounding as she had been dancing around a migraine for hours.

"Will you speak to me now?"

14

MAD ABOUT YOU

Aubrey's shredded composure gave way. She startled, releasing a small scream.

Henry was sitting in the darkness, holding something in his lap. He jumped up, his hands in a supplicating gesture. "Aubrey, it's me! Henry!"

Gasping, Aubrey collapsed, falling to her knees. Henry flew to her, but she pushed him away as he tried to pick her up, slapping at his hands. "Stop it, stop, stop, stop," she wheezed.

Defeated, Henry once again did as she ordered.

In the dim light, they sat on the floor, close, but not touching.

"What can I do, Aubrey? I heard you, you told me to leave, and I did...but by God, I wish I did not," Henry rasped, his voice thick with tears. "I should have stood besides you, and not run like someone ashamed of being seen with you, of being yours. Because I'm not, I..."

"Enough, Henry."

Her voice sliced through his stumbling, a knife through his heart, "I am not embarrassed or ashamed of what I did. I am profoundly grateful I was there...but at the same time, today proved what I was always afraid of, deep in my heart. Henry, I am not what you think I am."

No, no, Aubrey, don't say this, don't think this...

Aubrey continued, her voice exhausted.

"I am pretty sure I killed another man today, Henry. What does that make me? In truth, tell me, what? The first time, I deliberately booby-trapped my home, when I was just a girl. Knowing full well if Randall came, what would happen the instant he touched the back doorknob...and I was right. I then carted off his corpse, and arranged it so it looked like he committed suicide...

"When we were at the shop today, I touched something without gloves, Henry, and was thrown into a Scene. I didn't have a choice. I was locked in his head...I knew what that fiend was thinking, feeling...I was trapped, watching as he lured her away..." Aubrey shuddered. "I knew what he was going to do, and I didn't stop to think. I just...acted. Like I did with Randall. Because there was no time. I know how to make split second decisions. I learned in my self-defense classes. You practice and train because you won't have time to think. All you can do...is act." Aubrey was shaking so violently, Henry reached for her blue throw, and gently draped it over her shoulders. It only slid off as she continued. "I stopped him...by striking him so violently, he will die from it. I don't even feel remorse...because he murdered that little girl's sense of security, her happy dreams, her love of pink stuffed unicorns..." her voice broke, the rising pitch revealing a crack in her stoic façade. "She is going to see his face in every dark corner, behind every closed door. And only I know what he really planned, how he was going to hurt her, over and over, before her body would finally give out.

"So I've killed again, and Henry, I can honestly say I don't even care. What does that make me, I wonder...?"

Henry knew he wasn't supposed to answer.

"Now, everyone in the country knows who I am. Where I

am. I moved to New York so I could have the anonymity I so richly deserve, and...while I am thrilled I was able to stop that monster...my nightmare has come true. Everyone will be looking. Staring. How will I be able to work, to...did you know I have been fighting with my editor, Joelle, for months...she wanted to put my photo on the jacket, and I wouldn't agree? She argued since I was using a nom de plume, what difference did it make? Now, I wonder if she will push the point. Everyone will know my face now..."

"I'm sorry," he whispered, uselessly.

"I'm sorry, too, Henry. The woman you are waiting for shouldn't be a powder keg. I can only imagine what is going on with your fan sites right now, as everyone already made the link between my face and you, but now my name? And this? At least I was able to contact Greg and beg him to keep you well out of it..."

"Now it's my turn, please," Henry spoke fiercely. "You need to hear what *I* heard, and listen to me! Knowing you contacted Greg, things make a little more sense. Only a little, mind you...he was more than half-convinced you were abducted, and were lying to him to cover my back. I talked myself breathless to clear that up! He is *enraged* with me, saying I haven't protected you! But Greg's done so much, threatening the worst offenders against your reputation with lawsuits, and they've retreated, the insinuations you were somehow tangled up with this Hodges have vanished...I am as clean as can be, and..."

"Stop."

Aubrey was so tired.

"I can't do this anymore. I love you, but I can't. I'm not this...gift, this soul mate that will make your life perfect, and better. I'm nothing but a loose cannon making things complicated, over and over...Now, everything is just...worse. You promised me, repeatedly, things would be okay. But nothing is okay. The photos, they just kept happening. Nothing got better. You made no changes to your life at all, but want me to make all these changes to mine...You aren't someone that is going to make my life better. If those photos hadn't appeared, today's events would not have blasted my name and face all over national news...But they did. I can't breathe, I can't...

"Please forgive me, but I need to disappear for awhile... and I need you to leave."

HENRY COULDN'T REMEMBER how he got back to his suite.

Or how he managed to get through the next few performances, as the theater reopened.

He went through the motions, smiling, laughing, shaking hands, going to stage doors. Signing autographs and smiling. Interviews, photo sessions. Smiling.

When asked about Aubrey, he would smile, shaking his head. "I am tremendously proud of Aubrey and her role in saving the little girl from that horrible predator. Other than that, I have no comment."

"But where is she?" Reporters with more bravery than sense would continue to badger Henry until his smile grew closer to a snarl, baring his teeth if Greg wasn't close enough to stop the interrogation before a bloodletting ensued.

"Where is she? If you were an adequate journalist, you would see she is clearly not here. Perhaps she is seeking respite from what was obviously a traumatic experience for her, compounded by having her own reputation smeared by incompetent reporters to such an extent lawsuits were lodged...shall we continue?"

This was the mildest of his replies. They rapidly devolved into more savage verbal attacks. Word on the street quickly spread—Rhys could flay the skin from your bones in five sentences or less.

Greg had his stage door events curtailed. It was safer.

The week after the shopping mall event, Henry learned

Do You Hear What I Hear?

his presence was obligated at the annual Macy's Thanksgiving Day Parade, a spectacle he was completely oblivious of, cared nothing for, and he was apoplectic.

"No! Absolutely not!"

Greg was forced to require Beatrice to video conference with himself and Henry, because Henry was refusing to participate. "I have plans! With Aubrey! I am not going to stand outside with a microphone, talking with strangers about this event I know nothing about, for a holiday that isn't even mine…" he was ranting, pulling at his hair, pacing as he bellowed. "This is *my life* and I am *not having* this…*constant interference* without so much as a by-your-leave…!"

It took half an hour for the pair to calm Henry down sufficiently for him examine his contract. Buried in fine print was a clause stating he would participate in extra publicity for the play should there be any unexpected closures due to acts of God, facility issues, etc. Henry was not the only one who would be engaged in this event, the entire cast would be televised doing similar "person on the street" interviews (with heavy security, obviously). Henry seethed.

"Is there *anything else* you have planned for me?" He grabbed the schedule. "It looks as though this…*spectacle*…is only a few hours…"

Beatrice shook her head, saying, "I'm out," as she terminated her feed.

"Sure, I'm the sacrifice," Greg sighed. "Henry…it was decided to open Thanksgiving night, in an effort to recoup the losses incurred when the house went dark from the water main debacle. You will need to go straight to the theater afterwards, there will be two shows, similar as a Saturday. Special matinee and evening showtimes…"

Henry turned a shade of red Greg had never witnessed before. "I see…what times, exactly…"

When Greg slid the notice towards him, Henry hissed, "Why is it I am so spectacularly uninformed?"

"This was released when you were in New Jersey. I'm sorry, Henry. I thought you knew."

Henry shook his head. There had been a spate of notices he had willfully ignored while he was soaking up time with Aubrey. He had not wanted to think about *Gatsby*. This was his fault.

Thanksgiving had been doomed even as they had been making their plans…

Henry squeezed his eyes tightly shut. He did not want Greg to see the tears threatening to escape.

"Henry…"

"Go away, Greg."

"I'm sure if you explain…"

"Greg, so help me…not another word. Leave."

Henry knew it was useless to reach out to Aubrey mentally, or try to call her. So he did the only thing he could, which was send her a text. The written word was like catnip for his One. At least he knew she would read it.

```
My dearest Aubrey: I have just been
informed that I have no choice in this
matter. Even should you still desire
my presence on Thanksgiving Day, I
will be unable to be by your side.
Apparently I am being forced into some
"man on the street" interviewing
during the Thanksgiving Day Parade as
a part of publicity for Gatsby. To
compound that, the theater will be
open for not one but two shows, a
special matinee and evening perfor-
mance. The theater is trying to recoup
the lost income for the days it was
closed due to the water main issue.
```

Do You Hear What I Hear?

```
I do not even know if you were still
planning on having my sorry self with
you, I confess I was very much holding
out hope you were. We had made so many
plans, and I have been dreaming of
being with you once more. Are you
ready to speak with me again?
```

Aubrey read the texts, her heart even heavier than before. She had been unable to leave her building without being beset by photographers.

> Dear Henry: I regret the day was taken from us, but don't you see how it was meant to be? Even as we made our plans, they were nothing more than pretty sandcastles to be washed away by the tide. We were fated to spend it apart, because of who you are, and what I am.

> In the end, it is the best we remain apart. I am sorry, Henry. I can't see where continuing to be together will be good for either of us. The same problems will arise, over and over. I am me, and you are you. I love you for who you are, and I believe that you love me, despite for what I am...but oil and water will never be able to mix.

> I am sorrier that I can say. Everything hurts.

Henry read her return text, and his heart split. He did not need to read Aubrey's thoughts to hear the implacable tone in her words. Nor did he need her gift to feel the anguish radiating from them.

Henry began trying to call her, desperate to find a way to make Aubrey understand their relationship did not need to end.

The first attempt ended with him leaving an impassioned

voicemail after the phone rang an interminable time, stripping his nerves.

Afterwards, he found his calls did not even ring, but went straight to voicemail.

Thanksgiving came.

He did his job as required, public mask nailed in place, feeling little more than a court jester, a fool, or dancing bear for a hurdy-gurdy…

Aubrey huddled on her bed, watching the parade broadcast so she could catch Henry's few televised appearances. She smiled with dry eyes, even as she saw past his false smiles and empty hearty laughter. Later that day she had a turkey sandwich, a handful of potato chips, and tried to work on a short story as a way to get through the many silent hours.

Thanksgiving went.

Henry felt as though each day was flying past him, days slipping through his fingers. The cast and crew decorated the house front and backstage for holiday gaiety, but he begged off. The joy of the season was sandpaper against his soul. He threw himself into his performances, they were all he had left.

After removing his makeup, Henry would make his way to Jonathan and the vehicle awaiting him. Jonathan would simply ask, "Where to, sir?" Each night, Henry would reply with increasing listlessness, "The hotel, please." There was no camaraderie, no banter. Just Henry, looking out the window, at nothing.

The bleakness of Henry's disposition grew worse with holiday lights appearing, and the world around him growing more festive. The play was drawing to a close.

"Green lights, they're everywhere," Henry mumbled as he

dozed off in the back of the SUV. "Will I be seeing them the rest of my life?

PETER THREW his phone across the room in despair.

"My heart, what is it?" Seung reached across the bed, his arms around Peter's waist. "You wake up like this, it worries me. Aren't you happy here? You say you are, but then you wake like this, three days in a row…"

"It's Aubrey. She won't return my calls, the little shit! She sends me brief texts that say absolutely *nothing*. She hasn't been right since the whole New Jersey thing…I swear, if I ever get my hands on Rhys, I'm gonna tear him apart. It's his fault, I know it is…"

"It isn't his fault, my love. Look at this photo." Seung pulled up a photo of Henry getting into his car. "You know I loathe the paps as much as you, but in this case, they are proving slightly useful. Look at him, closely…does he seem like a content, satisfied man to you?"

Peter scrutinized Henry's profile as he avoided the photographer. He had his professional veneer on. Blank, revealing nothing.

"I don't see jack shit, Seung."

Seung gently thumped Peter on the side of his head. "Stop looking at his face, moron. Look at his body. The way he is carrying himself. Is that confident Henry Rhys? The same man you went out with and didn't stop talking about, for weeks?"

Peter peered at the photo, and noticed what Peter was referring to: the slumped shoulders. Scuffed shoes hinting at feet that were barely more than dragged evidence, rumpled shirt, and…was that a *stain* on his trousers? Where the hell was his PA?

"Jesus, the man's coming apart," Peter muttered in disbelief.

"Exactly my point. If your sister is hurting, she is not alone in her pain."

Aubrey woke up choking again. Gasping, gagging, unable to drag in the air her lungs were burning for, her throat having closed on itself again.

When Henry had left her apartment, she had gone to bed without turning on any of her lights. It wasn't until the next day she found he had somehow managed to get the toy dragon, after all. How, she had no idea, but when she hugged it, there was a comforting heartbeat emanating from its chest...and when she held one of its paws, Henry's voice spoke, simply saying, "Sleep well, milady Aubrey. I love you."

His tone was husky. Poignant, as if he knew when recording, it might be the last time he would tell her goodnight. The first time Aubrey heard it, a wail escaped her lips, one that might have grown into something like his name had she not stoppered her mouth with a fist. Clutching the soft toy to her breast, she tried to see if direct pressure would soothe the ache of her heart struggling to beat.

The stabbing pains continued, even as she managed to pull herself together. Peter would not stop ringing her, for all she would not answer. It wasn't cruelty or indifference on her part. Aubrey did not trust herself. Her throat closed into tight knots at the most inopportune moments: in the lift when greeted by neighbors, all eager to ask about what had really happened in the concrete cinder block lined hallway. At the grocery store, when she saw her face in the checkout line on the cover of a cheap gossip magazine. When she was accosted by a group of paparazzi, all calling her to "Look this way, Aubrey...give us a smile, sweetheart!...What do you have to say about Hodges's death in the hospital, did you really have to hit him that hard? What were you thinking when you did?"

It was better she reply to Peter with texts. "I am doing well, Peter, and hoping you are enjoying the sun on the West Coast, love you!"

Considering how she was being hounded every time she left her loft, Aubrey decided it was best to seldom venture out. And bearing in mind the...uncomfortable, sometimes prurient amount of interest her neighbors had about Henry, Aubrey withdrew her permission for him to be allowed into the building. A simple email to the security desk took care of that issue. The last thing Henry needed was to be trapped in the excruciatingly slow lift with a bunch of magpies, all intent on tearing him apart...subjecting him to the same coarse, vulgar questions...stares that made her skin crawl...

She had meals and groceries delivered. Not that she was looking for much, these days. Her appetite had fled.

Aubrey's work on the text of her novel, *Sea and Sky*, was complete. A bound galley copy was now in her hands. Henry had been so eager to read it, but Aubrey had demurred, refusing to allow him access to her book until she was satisfied all the errors were gone.

She had wanted to give him something of herself that was perfect.

Aubrey tossed the book on the small side table, the end product of two long, hard years' work, as though it was nothing. Once upon a time, she anticipated celebrating this moment with Korean barbecue, wine, and Peter. Yet she would just as soon use it to balance an unstable piece of furniture now it had arrived.

Everything felt like nothing...and nothing felt like anything, at all.

Aubrey was never one to celebrate the holidays in the interim between moving out from her childhood home, and meeting Peter. It was he who nagged her into obtaining some lights and greenery for her loft, but she didn't much care for it, as he would sometimes disappear to spend Christmas Day with his siblings if they were up for guests that were *not* their parents...he would always urge Aubrey to join him, but she would refuse. Holidays were stressful enough, she'd explain, without a sister-from-another-mister.

Now she knew the hole in her heart was permanent for the foreseeable future. Each heartbeat was a pain she could not escape, and each breath was not enough to fill her lungs.

It was understandable, she argued with herself as she would run on the treadmills in the exercise room, running until she was drenched with thick perspiration, hair sticking to her scalp. Of course, she missed Peter, and now Henry, who had woven himself into her soul. It was inevitable the tear into the fabric of her being would hurt. She would have to get used to it.

She ran, and ran, and ran...morning. Noon. Nighttime. All hours.

Because no matter how hard, how long, or how fast her feet flew, she could not escape the chasm she was facing.

HENRY WALKED to Aubrey's building, ticket in his hand for the final performance for *Gatsby*. To his horror and humiliation, he was turned away at the door.

"I am sorry, Mr. Rhys, but Ms. Stafford has revoked permission for your entry," the doorman informed him discreetly. "If you wish, I can contact her..."

Henry closed his eyes for a second. "No. That will not be necessary." His fist clenched the envelope. Aubrey no longer responded to his texts, or voicemails. Nor had she ever replied to the times he had reached out to her mentally.

"I see you have something, would you like for me to leave it at the front desk, sir?"

Do You Hear What I Hear?

"That won't be necessary," Henry repeated, his voice a monotone.

"Is there anything else I can do to be of service?"

Henry could hear pity in the man's mind, and it was more than he could bear.

"No, thank you." He was turning away, then swallowed his pride one last time. "Does she…is she well? Ms. Stafford? I am concerned about her."

Aloud, the doorman replied gravely, "I am not at liberty to comment on our residents, sir," but Henry got what he was looking for, the man's floating mental stream *…haven't seen her in ages…hasn't left since she was jumped by those fuggin' photographers last week…can't go anywhere without vultures circling…she does something good and this is what she gets… asshole paparazzi should be rounded up and thrown in the river…*

Henry nodded. "I understand. Thank you. I will be returning to London soon, so I would like to thank you for continuing to take care of Ms. Stafford, as…I won't be here, or the one to do so." His smile was twisted, and he fought to keep the bitterness at bay.

"Rest assured it is my privilege, sir. I wish you continued success with your career. I've heard great things about your performances, if I may say so, even mentions of nominations for Tony awards…"

Henry had heard the rumors, as had the rest of the company: Best Play. Best Performance by Leading Actor… Actress…Featured Actor…Actress…Direction…all manner of technical awards. The potential to sweep everything. It was heady stuff, the cast and crew giddy with anticipation, the "what if" of it all.

Henry was numb.

"You are kind, and thank you," he replied, trying to keep his professional face on, a modest smile. "It was a team effort, though. The company worked together from the very beginning. We will have to wait and see..." his voice trailed off, as he was unable to maintain the façade.

"Merry Christmas, and Happy New Year, sir."

"To you, as well."

Henry walked away, heading back to his hotel.

He kept walking.

He had nowhere else to be, it was the last free day he had...he'd thought, he hoped he could somehow entice Aubrey with a ticket to the final show to see him, one last time. She had enjoyed the performances so much, she had told him so...

What a fool he was.

Everywhere he looked, there were holiday decorations and couples walking about holding hands or arm in arm.

It was cold, December bringing the kiss of seasonal chill with it. Henry tried not to think about the some of the gifts he had already purchased for Aubrey, including a thick sweater and muffler. He also purchased exactly the same jumper for himself, and a muffler almost the same, but in a different color (so they would know whose was whose)...he'd dreamed they would wear them when he introduced her to his family...of standing in front of the Christmas tree there, drinking champagne...smiling into each other's eyes...

He found himself standing at The Rink at Rockefeller Center. Bloody hell, he really wasn't paying much attention to where he was wandering, was he...? Just following the crowds.

He wondered if Aubrey could ice skate. He wondered why he didn't know.

He sat on the perimeter, and put his head in his hands as music played, listening the happy laughter of children too young to be in school, or were maybe homeschooled, he thought vaguely.

Henry wanted a family. He had gingerly brought up the topic with Aubrey, and was touched by the longing he saw tucked away in her eyes...but then, any woman who got onto airplanes with toys for children would hope for her own, someday. "Henry, you massive *wanker*," he addressed himself savagely.

Mairéad's voice rose up in his heart, rebuking him.

"What's ailing you, boy?"

"Grandma, everything's gone wrong..."

"Well, what is it?"

In his mind's eye, his grandmother sat next to him on the bench.

"I lost her...Grandma, I met my soul mate, but I screwed everything up. I lost her."

Mairéad leaned over and cuffed his ear.

"Ow!"

Even in his imagination, Mairéad still had a way of finding just the most tender place...!

"What kind of a numpty are you, Henry Declan? Did I teach you nothing? What do you mean, 'you lost her'? Were you careless? Reckless? Did you set her down where another will find her, like a toy, Henry?"

Henry was silent, not sure how to answer.

"Have you tried mending the hurt?"

"She won't answer my calls, she's banned me from her home, she..."

"If you've turned into such a coward, or so lazy, it's glad I am to be six feet under!" She glared at him. *"What will be the value of your life when you are living it without your soul mate? Are you foolish enough to believe the adulation of the world will suffice? Have you gone mad?"*

"Grandma, you don't understand...I promised her myself, everything...it wasn't enough!"

"You promised her everything, did you?"

"Yes!"

"Did you deliver?" Her eyes were remarkably sharp, and so was her tone. *"Did you honor your word, so she knew she could rely on*

you? Did you conduct yourself as a man of honor, one she could trust with her heart, her life, her soul, no matter how rough life's seas become? Or did you give her nothing but words?"

Henry became very still.

He promised Aubrey, countless times, he would take care of her. She had asked of him one thing, the right to privacy. How many times had she told him it was necessary for her happiness, her peace of mind...for her to *breathe*...?

And yet, he did...nothing.

He couldn't change the world around him, of course. Couldn't make paparazzi vanish, or intrusive reporters leave her alone.

But he could have given her more protection. Talked with her about any of a million potential ways to shield her from the press...but did nothing, cock-sure because he said everything would be well...it would be. He had spoken!

She, on the other hand, had also spoken...but he had never internalized what she had to say.

"You hear my thoughts, but you don't *listen*!" echoed in his head.

Mairéad's shade leaned forward. "Are you going to listen now? She told you to leave, twice, and you listened then...but you never heard what she asked from you. What's a woman to believe? Am I doomed to become some modern ghost of Christmases past, present, and future, haunting you for the rest of your existence? I refuse to be reduced to some derivative Dickensian character in your memory for my afterlife! Are you prepared for her to become another's bride, someday? To know she will lie beneath him? Grow round with his children?" Mairéad sighed as she began to fade away from his imagination. "I will warn you only once more, Henry: you will have everything, or you will have nothing. There is no middle ground... Your life will be glorious, or everything a mockery of what you have lost."

Passersby saw a man, sitting alone, pale as winter's snow, shaking with the cold.

Do You Hear What I Hear?

Henry had fallen into the abyss.

Greg's biting words chased him, "Henry, I can't say I'm surprised Aubrey has broken things off with you. I have no doubt you care for her, very much, but there is no depth to it. I *warned* you but you were so lost in your own little bubble, so confident everything would work out as you wished. Welcome to the real world, Henry. I still do not know what Aubrey is hiding from, but now the world knows the face of Aubrey Lillian Stafford, your once close companion, who lives in New York City, and is...or was, a writer for Voyager Publications. I have no idea if she is still employed there, she seems to work contract to contract. Regardless, whatever she fears, there's a giant target on her back, just in time for the holidays while you are blithely returning to your life in London and the rest of it. 'Happy Christmas to all, and to all a good-night.'"

Henry sat, blind as the sky darkened. Bright Christmas carols filled the air, along with the laughter and cries of the children skating.

Lyrics of an old carol began to punch through his fog of despair, a song Mairéad would sing when he was but a wee lad, rocking him in her lap by the fire, a song that kept asking him, "Do You Hear What I Hear?" He leaned forward, head in his hands. It contained evocative imagery of dancing stars, music above treetops...he knew the message being related, but all that filled his soul was Aubrey. Aubrey. Aubrey.

Would he ever be able to hear music without being brought to his knees, mourning the loss of her? Remembering her joyful singing at Acoustics, in the shower, the car? Dancing without form or care, free from fear?

Aubrey...free. Free from him.

His heart broke wide open as he imagined a life without her. He could not breathe, there was no air. Nothing but darkness, and drowning.

This is what Mairéad was trying to tell him: having tasted

the exquisite bliss of having his soul mate by his side, nothing else would bring him a modicum of satisfaction or contentment for the rest of his life. He would only exist. And it was all due to his complacency. His inability to hear her not with his gift, but with his heart.

His career had been the driving force in his life for over ten years. It had been lucrative, successful by any parameter of the field. His star was still rising...as he continued donning the faces of others, speaking their words, aping their lives. Whereas his life, his words, became increasingly meaningless to himself.

The higher his star climbed, he farther he had to plummet into the sea. He was no better than deaf Icarus, who was also warned but chose not to hear.

No more.

He could give Aubrey what she desired: a private life, and her freedom...and, if she will let him, keep her close to him, his One, his soul mate.

All he needed to do is man up, and be the one to disappear.

15

THE SKYE BOAT SONG

Aubrey was sitting by the windows of her corner loft unit, wrapped in her thick blue throw.

Still, she shook.

She was trapped, staring at the sunrise above her, the water below.

Her head was reeling from not having eaten well for the last two days, her pantry was almost empty, she couldn't stand the thought of cooking, nor ordering another meal to be delivered. The notion of eating alone was enough to kill her appetite.

"You'd better get used to it," she grimly told herself, "or you'll die like a rat in a trap up here. A beautiful, expensive trap, between sea and sky."

The last three words had her laughing hysterically…it was the title of her novel, and it had meant so much to her.

Exhausted, she rested her head against the glass as her mind wandered. She was only brought back to reality by her cell phone, with Joelle's insistent, recognizable ringtone. Aubrey knew if she did not take the call, Joelle wouldn't leave a message, but keep calling. Without ceasing. Aubrey had learned this bitter lesson early in their relationship, when she was churning out manuscript pages. Joelle wanted replies to queries, but Aubrey was deep in the writing zone. It was a case of the unstoppable force versus the immovable object. It ended with Joelle banging on her door after Aubrey turned off her phone in desperation, as it had been ringing for over three hours straight.

"What is it, Joelle?" Aubrey did not waste time with niceties. "I received the galley, thank you. Am I done?"

"Merry Christmas and all that rot to you, too, Scrooge," was Joelle's snappy rejoinder. "No, you aren't done, not by a long shot. Marketing, my dear reclusive author. But before I plunge into the shop talk, how are you? This is the first time I've managed to track you down since you made national headlines. You are my hero, darling...I never would have thought you had it in you, the way you're always so quiet and controlled. You went straight savage on that piece of shit, and I for one could not be more proud. Well done!"

"I don't want to talk about it, Joelle. In fact, I don't want to talk about anything, at the moment, so if you can let me go, I'd appreciate it."

Joelle heard the deep fatigue in her author's voice, and her hackles raised. "I most certainly will not. I asked how are you doing, and you haven't answered. I hear you are spending time with Henry Rhys, the same man who was at the restaurant the day we had lunch and you took off, claiming a headache...He tore through the dining room like a bull through Pamplona. Spill, pet. I know you hadn't met before, you said you didn't know the man that day and you can't lie worth a damn. So when did you meet? I hope like hell he is taking good care of you, because you sound like you aren't eating, or sleeping, or something...or is it he's the reason you're not sleeping? In a good way, I hope?" For all of her pushy and often abrasive ways, Joelle cared about her little author, and was concerned: was Aubrey was having difficulty processing the events in the shopping mall? She began looking through her lists of therapists as she awaited Aubrey's reply.

"I will only say Henry and I...are not people to be mentioned in the same sentence at present."

Joelle paused for a fraction of a second before bursting out, "He left you? After what you did?! Did the fucker think you were bad for his image or something? Son of a bitch! If anything, he's bad for *your* image, that cowardly..."

"*Enough.*"

The icy rage in Aubrey's voice jumped through the editor's phone like a slap in the face. Joelle physically recoiled. "Whoa, Aubrey...slow your roll, girlie..."

"*You* need to retract everything you said, and thought, about Henry. This second. Nothing could be further from the truth. I was the one who said I needed to disappear for awhile. Am I quite clear on this, Joelle? I need to be absolutely sure before we proceed in any capacity. Henry Declan Rhys is blameless, and has conducted himself in a manner unbefitting any of the..."

"I'm sorry, I'm sorry!" Joelle was shocked at the heat and lethal precision of Aubrey's tongue, slicing through her with implacable speed. "Guess who is still carrying a torch for tall, dark, and gorgeous," she mused. Aloud, she stated with her most professional diction, "I fully retract my former statements, they were incorrect, fallacious, and wholly without merit. I apologize fully, and regret any distress it caused you."

"All right, then." Energy left Aubrey, as air would escape a balloon with a slow leak.

"So, we are going to conduct business before you disappear any farther. You were most insistent you publish *Sea and Sky* under a nom de plume, because you wished to retain your privacy. You used the same logic against my strongest arguments for using an author photo on the jacket, and all of my plans for marketing this novel, which I am confident is going to be worthy of all the buzz it has generated thus far.

Your reasoning is now invalid, my dear. On both counts. Your face has been tied to your name, and splashed about the country. While I have no idea if people will still remember in a few months, the possibility is very real. I need you to spend serious thought on this, Aubrey…you have an amazing piece of work I am proud to have worked with, and I am very pleased and proud to have worked with *you*…for all you are as stubborn as a mule at times," she ended with a snort. "I am not going to waste either of our time clashing with you, but I am putting you on your honor, Aubrey. Think about this, and get back to me. And for Christ's sake, have something to eat!"

"Joelle, I will, but I have to check and see if I am obligated to Voyager for a stint down in Africa," Aubrey evaded. "I will call you back soon. Goodbye." Aubrey ended the call by hanging up and tossing the phone away from her, as though it was a poisonous snake.

"Why did I say that," she asked herself wildly. "I didn't sign anything for that excursion…" Aubrey pulled herself over towards her tablet, and reread the contract. Henry had been so appalled, not wishing them to be apart…Aubrey had also been conflicted over the timing, as it ran against the release date.

The venture was slated to take two, possibly three months. Aubrey would have to turn the loft over to the professional management company, Peter wouldn't be available to check on the property, air it out when she returned, and she could forget about having fresh food stocked. She didn't have anyone she would feel close enough to impose on…Peter had spoiled her dreadfully…

A sly voice of her own devising whispered no one would be staring at her in Africa. Any photos taken, any questions asked, would not be about her. Aubrey would be in her element, enjoying pleasant conversations, engaging with people about places to visit, eat, relax. Her heart clenched when she realized she would have no reason to purchase as many silly souvenirs, as no one would pounce on her demanding presents, she would still have her trinkets for fussy children (and why did *that* give her such pain?) along with a gift to send Peter once she returned…and by that time, certainly everyone would have forgotten, wouldn't they?

Forgotten her face. Her name.

Forgotten about her, altogether.

Aubrey's eyes ached from looking at the screen. Restless, she cast them about, searching for something to give her ease. She flickered her focus from one thing to the next, unable to rest on any one item in her uncluttered home, until her eyes fell upon the dragon Henry had given her, where she had placed it carefully on the sofa.

She signed her name to the contract.

HOURS LATER, Aubrey was still hungry. The pounding in her head had gotten so intolerable she went digging in her almost empty freezer, discovering a dinner Peter had stashed and forgotten. She paired it with two ibuprofen. It felt early in the day for carbonara, but needs must.

She picked up the copy of her novel again, tracing her finger over the title while the microwave hummed.

Sea and Sky.

Aubrey found her mind drifting to her father, a merchant sailor who died at sea when she was only eight years old. When he was not away, Lewis Stafford did odd jobs around the house, singing the sea shanties that would not get him in trouble if his daughter picked up new vocabulary words.

While Lewis worked on vessels powered by all the latest technology, he had the heart of a sailor of old. He would often take his little girl out on clear nights, showing her the constellations. He did not have a strong traditional education, but Lewis always knew where he was by looking at the night sky. He loathed light pollution, and was proud the piece of land his grandfather and father handed down to him was still remote from civilization, free from the stain of man's light stealing from the stars, he would tell the tiny Aubrey, whose eyes were as round as the moon. He would chuckle, and whisper in her ear, "Oh, Aubrey...you're just like me, aren't you? Daddy's little girl..."

When Patti would patiently remind Lewis it was past Aubrey's bedtime, he'd waltz the sleepy child inside, singing "The Skye Boat Song" to her. He didn't know the history of the folk song's lyrics, nor did he care. To him, it was about a lad gone to sea. As he sung his beloved little daughter to dreamland, he'd adapt the words to croon in his warm tenor, "Sing me a song, of a lass that is gone...over the sea to Skye..."

Aubrey jumped as the microwave beeped. Another memory had floated to the surface of her mind, this one of her mother and father bickering. Her grandfather had worked the land, as had her great-grandfather. But Lewis had no intention of doing so, and never had... "Patti, I told you I was no farmer. I make more money a few months at sea than I would all year behind a plow. Told you that from the get-go. Something inside me would wither and die...nothing I'd plant would thrive. I was meant for the sea from the day I was born." Her daddy's voice was even, but with the slow rumble warning he was losing his patience. Aubrey had stuck her head under the pillow, not wanting to hear any more.

Patti's voice would become tight when Lewis would sing his lays to her as she grew older, romanticizing the call of the sea. "Stop distracting her, Lewis, she's doing her homework." When he would call Aubrey his little mermaid, Patti would snap, "She's already got a wild imagination, stop encouraging her." The last time Aubrey saw Lewis, he'd patted her cheek. "Don't cry, wee Siren. I'm off for a little adventure, but I'll come back for you. Someday we'll go off and sail together, to the sea and sky...I will come back with a special gift from the ocean, just for my beautiful sprite...Give Daddy a kiss, now."

He'd never come back, with a present or otherwise.

But now, Aubrey had made the connection:

Her daddy was like Henry—he carried a trident in his soul.

She dropped her fork in shock.

His deep-seated, lifelong passion for the sea...Henry's tales of people being linked by their need to keep exploring. Constantly being drawn back to the water...

Henry was not simply caught up in a sweet set of stories his grandmother told him to help accept his unusual talent... and what he told her was not a coincidental link of his ability, and her curse.

Her daddy was a descendant of the People of the Waves. If he had a quirk, or a talent...she would never know about it now, but as she was transfixed in thought, pieces of herself were flying into place. All the tiny fragments, seemingly random shards she thought were evidence of how broken, how unfixable she was, came flying together, creating a harmonious whole.

Her daddy's honest love for being on the open sea...it mirrored her need to travel, explore, and be close to water. She carried his love for looking at the stars with her constant habit of sitting on the floor by her windows, looking up to the sky. Aubrey was her father's daughter, through and through.

Aubrey realized being "not right in the head" was never an issue, and even the two worst moments of her life upheld this.

What she had done to Tiller, and Hodges...they were not acts of incipient madness, cruelty, or weakness. They were acts of strength, utilizing tools she had available. Each time, she gave no quarter because she knew none would be given: the first time acting to protecting herself, the second time defending a child smaller than she had been, when she and her classmate Gayle faced evil in the eye.

However, she had allowed herself to be crippled by fear. Fear of losing her mind. Fear of being caught for perceived sins of the past. Fear of being seen as mad; "less than;" a burden; a liability for those she loved.

Fear of herself.

As all of these epiphanies burst upon her, she was panting, gripping the small table she'd shared countless meals with Peter, and then a precious few with Henry. A blur of Scenes erupted: she saw herself, afraid, even as she was always surrounded by love and acceptance. Gloves on, whether physical or metaphorical, to shield her from any true intimacies…

"Oh, Henry…" she mourned wordlessly. How she had kept him at arm's length…! Her heart felt like a ship tossed against a reef, the tide pounding against it so relentlessly it did not have a chance to right itself as wave after wave of truth crashed over her.

Aubrey was stunned to her core when she realized her greatest fear, losing her anonymity, had occurred.

And absolutely nothing came of it.

Yes, the paparazzi had been as terrible as Greg had warned. But no one had arrived from her hometown, pointing and jeering in the media, demanding to know more about that terrible night with Randall Tiller.

Maybe…No. It was very likely she was finally free from that terror.

She could lay it down, and walk away.

She wasn't cursed.

She did not have to live with crushing anxiety.

And as that was real, and true…she…could allow herself the freedom, the joy, the privilege of being with Henry…

With that thought, she was able to take in a great, whooping breath of air.

For a moment, she could swear she heard Lewis's voice once more, singing faintly, "…All that was good, all that was fair, All that was me is gone…Sing me a song, of a lass that is gone, Say could that lass be I?"

"Daddy," she spoke aloud, "I'm looking back at that lass that is gone…and while I might not know the one who remains, I think you would like her. I'm free: I know what I need, what I want to do, and I won't put a foot wrong, because I'm not frightened any more. I don't know where the tides will take me, but oh, the stories I will be able to tell while I am on my way!"

Aubrey leapt up, jumping and clapping her hands with glee as she had not done for weeks. (Months? Longer?) Looking about her wildly, she knew what would be, as surely as the moon directed the tides: she would find her way to Henry immediately. She wanted to admit to him her sea-change, tell him how she did not need to hide from the world any longer. Even as she would never be a publicity addict, in the see-and-be-scene crowd (it wasn't her nature), she would hold her head up high and stand besides her love in daylight, oblivious of cameras or spectators. She would be proud of herself, and visibly proud to stand besides the man she loves…The one who made everything feel like life was more colorful, music more vibrant, and the air more wild and free.

Her One.

But this kind of announcement…after the way she had cut him so completely! Again, Aubrey's eyes were bouncing around her loft frantically. She could not do this without a visible sign of what lay under the surface, a heartfelt gesture to make sure he heard all she could not say. Henry deserved no less, after the way he had been so patient, so tender with her from the beginning…

After dashing around the small apartment, looking for this elusive token, Aubrey came up with the perfect representation. She wrapped it with care, a Christmas gift for her beloved soul mate…the first gift of many, she thought as she tied the bow with a flourish. She seized her laptop, grateful she still had Henry's schedule shared with her calendar.

Upon opening it, she froze.

Sitting there, blinking up in accusation, was the signed contract to Voyager Publications, committing her to the two (maybe three) month's jaunt to Africa.

Her phone then buzzed discreetly, fracturing her focus. "Excuse me, Ms. Stafford? This is Scott, with front door security. Are you available to come down for a moment?"

Numb. Chest unable to expand for a deep breath. Aubrey croaked, "I am. Is there a problem?"

"I cannot say. I am most sorry to disturb you, but there is woman here who is most desperate to speak with you. I would have turned her away, but she isn't like the others. She is older, for one thing, and does not have the same look about her, at all. She says it is about a personal matter, and insists it is most urgent. She has given me identification, and it all checks out…her name is Emmie Tiller."

16

UNDER PRESSURE

Henry paced the floor of his suite, agitation etched on his face even as his voice remained pleasant and firm.

He had been on pins and needles, waiting for his agent to ring him back. He knew he was being a bit of a shit, all but demanding she telephone him on a Sunday, but he needed to get his course of action moving immediately. He had very little time left before he was scheduled to fly back to the UK, and he had to show Aubrey he was serious about his intention to change his life for her, and her needs.

To prove he did hear what she heard.

As his long legs pounded the pavement from Rockefeller Plaza to his hotel, his mind was whirling as he made plans, contingency plans for those plans, and backup plans for those in turn. He was determined to have a clear show of good faith, he would...

"Beatrice. Thank you for talking my call on a Sunday morning."

"Sunday afternoon, you berk," his agent sniped. "I still have not quite forgiven you for the stunts you pulled lately: back at the restaurant months ago, and then that video conference! If someone had told me you could be such a diva...! Have you pulled your head out of your ass yet? Greg did his magical best to smooth everything over, saying you've found love at last. So I am almost ready to forgive you. Almost. It sounds like your lady is a bit of a heroine, having rid the world of an absolute monster, so I suppose I will give you a pass. Now that you've taken me from my family and saved me from Christmas shopping, which I loathe, but watching the kiddies see Father Christmas, which I adore, what is it?"

Henry's voice was rich and warm as he replied, "I quit."

He took a deep breath as he counted silently, "One-one-thousand, two-one-thousand..."

"I'm sorry, the line must not be that clear," Beatrice replied slowly. "It sounded like you just told me..."

"I quit," Henry reiterated pleasantly. "I mentioned it at the luncheon, but no one took me very seriously. And then life, you know...I was never able to ring you back to discuss it in more detail. But as I have a little extra time in my calendar at the moment, I thought I would bend your ear to make my position perfectly clear. I'm taking a holiday. An extended holiday that may prove to be permanent. Once the curtain closes on *Gatsby*, I will not be taking on any new contracts for the foreseeable. Please make that happen. Ta ever so."

"You...you can't be serious," she wheezed. Beatrice weakly lunged for her cigarettes and the cup of tea with whiskey she had prepared (calls from Henry always had the potential for being contentious, but if she had known this was in the cards, she would have skipped the tea and just kept the bottle). "Christ you make me wish for smelling salts! Are you drunk? Where's Greg!"

"I am not drunk and I have no idea where Greg is, that's irrelevant. In any case I am insulted you would think I am drunk, tonight is the closing performance of *Gatsby*. I've never done a show impaired in my entire career," Henry replied, stung. He took a steadying breath, reminding himself to remain focused, thinking, "Keep your eye on the prize, friendo..." It was curious, how much his mental voice sounded like Greg's.

He continued speaking in a milder tone, "I did try to let you know. It's not my fault no one was listening."

"No. No. Don't you dare take that approach with me," Beatrice snapped, having taken a deep drag of her cig and a gulp of her tea. She was pulling Henry's calendar open for the next year, and screeched in pain. "Do you have any *idea* who you'd be blowing off...? You will never work again, besides the fact you will get your ever-so-sexy ass sued clean off for breach of contract...!"

"I am certain there are loopholes," Henry replied. "There always are, people drop out of projects all the time. Find them, set legal on the contracts. It isn't as though work has begun on anything yet. And if I have to pay off some damage suits, so be it, I won't starve. The worst thing I might have to do is liquidate some assets, it won't kill me. I have more than enough." He remained serene. As he had power-walked back from the ice rink the night before, planning for just this phone call, he had been deciding what he needed to have, what he wanted to keep, and what he could let go of with a smile. The answers were very simple: Aubrey, Aubrey and his holdings in Wales, and everything else.

"I know I need to do the publicity tour," he added, a touch of magnanimity in his voice. "I'm not unprofessional, Beatrice, I simply do not wish to take on any new projects. I need a break. I've been working nonstop for how long? Something has to give, before I break. I am willing to consider voice work, *only*, based out of London in the latter part of the year. No photo shoots of any kind."

"Henry, you'll be lucky to get a spot at a children's panto when this blows up in your face," Beatrice mourned.

"Bea, you're making such heavy weather here, it will all be fine, I assure you." He winced, his nonchalant assertion reminiscent of the countless times he had given Aubrey the same empty promises, bringing him to this point. The difference now was his commitment, and knowing he had the muscle to ensure his words would have weight and meaning this time.

"You've lost your mind," Beatrice whispered as she pulled up contract after contract. "That's what it is. It's the pressure, isn't it? Tell me what's gone wrong...is it the woman, whatshername? Oh God, is she knocked up? That's it, isn't it? Have you told Greg?"

"Beatrice, have you always been this disrespectful, sexist, and rude, and I failed to see it?" Henry's voice shifted from genial to glacial without missing a beat. "Perhaps we have come to an impasse? We seem to be talking past each other as a rule as of late. A frightening habit I cannot allow to continue. I will not countenance such impolite talk about Ms. Stafford, ever again, nor will I allow my personal life to be a topic of conversation, as it seems you are unable to speak in a courteous manner. Do I make myself clear?"

Beatrice was flabbergasted. Never had Henry upbraided her caustic, and yes, hectoring manner of speech. She had always regarded Henry as she would a little brother, someone she needed to keep under her thumb or else he would go rogue, running wild in the street. He might balk, shooting her truculent glares, but he would knuckle under eventually. It was for his own good! He was the master of his acting career, she couldn't, and wouldn't, dictate otherwise: the man was a stubborn pillock, but an amazingly talented pillock with a fantastic sense of what roles would best suit him and would be worth his time. But she still bullied him into other jobs to keep his profile high, his name on everyone's lips, and his face ever-present. She was indifferent if he hated the modeling shoots, he had a face and a body that could make cameras (and panties) melt. It would be a sin not to take advantage of it. He grumbled, whined, and generally was a pain in the ass, but he was not her problem once he signed on the dotted line—then he became Greg's cross to bear.

Who was this man, taking her to task for being flip and tyrannical?

"Crystal clear," she blurted. "Okay, um…I can't do a single thing until tomorrow morning, Henry. It's Sunday, for God's sake, and I can't call in staff unless it's an emergency, and your wishing to break contracts to break your neck doesn't fall into that category. I will bring in legal first thing tomorrow and begin contacting producers in chronological order…? If that meets with your approval?"

Henry released the breath he didn't know he was holding.

"That is lovely, thank you," he replied, his voice gracious once more. "Thank you for taking time out of your weekend to listen to my concerns and give me your plan of action. Give my best to your family. I am sure we will be speaking again soon. Goodbye, Beatrice."

"Break a leg tonight, Henry, I've heard great things about your work…"

Henry simply hummed his thanks, and disconnected the call. He began counting again.

"One-one-thousand, two-one-thousand…"

He managed to get to "eight-one-thousand" before Greg was pounding on his door.

"Henry Declan Rhys!"

He opened the door with a smile. "Good morning, Greg, how are…"

"Quit the shit, you know I just got a text from Beatrice. What the absolute hell is going on, cancelling all of your work for the next year? Have you lost it all?"

Henry's shoulders drooped. "Not yet. Perilously close, perhaps. But I still have a chance."

Greg closed his eyes. It was too early for this headache. "In Queen's English, if you please."

"Greg...I looked into the mirror, and didn't care for whom I saw," Henry replied quietly. "You were right. I treated Aubrey abominably. I promised her repeatedly everything would be fine, simply because I said it would be...and disregarded every sign of her world sinking beneath the waves. 'The loneliest moment in someone's life is when they are watching their whole life fall apart, and all they can do is stare blankly.'" Henry paused. "People think Fitzgerald wrote that, but he didn't. I learned that when I was studying for *Gatsby*. It's still all over the internet, quite a popular misattribution." Henry looked at his feet, then into his friend's eyes. "That's the insidious power of the web, what can happen when someone doesn't have a 'Greg' looking out for them...and it's a part of what terrified Aubrey on some level, I am certain of it. Why she's been so frantic to retain her rightful privacy."

His PR manager took a deep breath. "Be that as it may... throwing your career away isn't going to go back and rewrite the past."

Henry tried to grin, but it morphed into a rictus. "And well I know it, didn't I just complete an entire play revolving around that very theme?" Greg rubbed his forehead, and was opening his mouth to reply but Henry forestalled him with a gesture.

"I love her," Henry continued simply. "I know you said it wasn't deep enough to matter, or make a difference, but I do."

"Henry..."

"Fitzgerald did say 'There are all kinds of love in the world, but never the same love twice.'" Henry's eyes were naked, stripped of all artifice, burning with raw emotion. He stumbled over his words, desperate to find the best ones. "Love is strange, isn't it? Old fashioned to some, radical to others...It forces you to...change the way we look at ourselves. And protect those we cherish. I am going to give Aubrey what she needs, more than anything else: a quiet, private, safe place. And that means no spotlights. I am shutting them off, Greg. It is my duty, my honor, and my privilege to care for that woman, any way I can." He paused. "It's my last chance."

Greg spoke heavily. "What if she doesn't agree with you, if she's moved on?"

Henry shook his head. "She hasn't...in my heart, I know she has not."

Henry might not have heard a single word from Aubrey, but the burning sorrow in his chest was so heavy. If Aubrey had found peace, he was certain there would be some surcease of his pain. Even Mairéad said one day she simply "woke up." If somehow Aubrey managed to move past the pull of their mutual soul mate tie that bound them, he would have a slight lessening of his own agony.

Greg persisted. "You leave in a handful of days. What if you cannot convince her in time? Your visa..."

Henry exploded, "I will apply for an extension. I will return the next day. I will come back and try, over and over, until I get it right! Understand this, Greg: you cannot dissuade me from this path, or stop me from my decision. I will go onstage tonight for *Gatsby* and breathe not a word of this to anyone. The contracts must be examined by legal so I can begin to get myself out as quietly and painlessly as possible. I understand the pressure I'm putting myself under. But she is worth it, because she is worth everything to me." He extended his hand. "If you feel we need to part ways professionally, I hope you will remain my friend."

His hand was batted aside in favor of a strong hug. "You ass," Greg replied, his throat curiously tight. "As if you have a chance of getting rid of me...I will be working by your side until you fire me."

"And then?" Henry chuckled, his voice also struggling with the same issue.

"Ah, I'll run fan clubs, or something similar. I know where bodies are buried…"

"You would expose me?" Henry was aghast.

"No, I mean the fan clubs's bodies, I have moles placed in a half-dozen of the more organized ones, and a handful of the lesser ones. Ass."

17

GLORIOUS

Henry was almost ready to leave for the theater.

His heart was heavy as he picked up his jacket. The pocket crinkled with the ticket he had saved for Aubrey. He was not going to return it to the box office. If Aubrey was not going to be in that seat, he did not want anyone else to be there, either. But as the house was expected to be sold out, he might face some push back on the issue, so he was keeping the paper copy to prove he had reserved it, and would pay face value if necessary.

A quiet knock on the door disturbed his train of thought. He frowned, the rhythm did not have the stridency of Greg's pounding, or the bossiness of Christine's rapping. This was confident, but still respectful…

He opened it, revealing Aubrey's smiling, hopeful countenance.

"Greetings, fellow trident holder," she addressed him gravely, her eyes twinkling. "I have come to wish you well on your final voyage as Jay Gatsby. May I come in?"

To say Henry was nonplussed would be comparing a hurricane to a gentle spring rain: he was rooted to the ground, his jaw unhinged. Aubrey waited, a gift bag in her hands.

A moment later, Henry visibly shook himself. "Yes, oh God, I'm sorry!" He stepped aside.

Aubrey did not venture far into Henry's suite. She was never very comfortable there, for all he tried to make her feel at home. It was richly appointed, and was filled with breakable objets d'art. She would have downgraded the facility for this if she was reviewing it in one of her travel guides. The thought made her laugh now, recognizing what made her feel so ill at ease from the first.

"Care to share the joke?" Henry prodded. He was at a loss, having no idea why Aubrey had chosen now to arrive. She had to be aware he was about to leave soon. He checked his watch against his will.

"I was just thinking about the decor in your suite, it is lovely but has such an air of sharp corners and fragility…it doesn't lend itself towards a feeling of comfort. I would have to mark the space down for it," she commented demurely, mirth still in her eyes. Henry could swear he saw the trace of the fabled green flash in their edges as he broke into his own laughter.

"You are so right! When I first moved in, it was worse! I had housekeeping take out at least five pieces straightaway. It was a given I would knock them over in the first three days…"

He scrutinized her appearance, trying not to be obvious in his appreciation. Aubrey had a simple wool coat over her shoulders, covering a lovely dress and boots. "You look…I have no words for how breathtakingly lovely you are, Aubrey," he sighed, longing heavy in his face and tone. He hesitated, unsure how to proceed. As much as he wanted to tell he everything, he was loath to begin right before the show if she wasn't ready to hear him out, and run the risk of distressing her. He wasn't prepared to begin discussing his plans until after the curtain fell! He only had thirty minutes before Jonathan was expecting him.

Do You Hear What I Hear?

"I have a gift for you. No strings attached if you don't want it," she began, her confidence beginning to waver, extending a small gift bag with tissue paper inside.

"Aubrey, I will happily accept anything you wish to give me," Henry firmly stated, taking the bag from her hands. "May I open it now?"

She nodded, her head doing the funny little bob he often likened to a marionette.

He took the bag from her hands, noting she wasn't wearing her usual pair of gloves, despite the temperature. "Odd," he thought, distracted, and hoped she had not lost one, knowing it would distress her.

He pushed past the tissue paper to reveal...the very pair of gloves he'd expected to see her wearing. He looked at her in confusion.

"They are yours...along with myself...should you still want..."

Aubrey could not get any further in her explanation of the bag's contents, as she was being crushed by Henry's arms, and very thoroughly kissed.

Not that she minded. It was much easier than trying to explain herself without words at the moment, anyway.

Darling...you mean it? You've forgiven me...?

Henry, there was nothing to forgive, as much as I needed to figure some things out on my own. The most important thing was, I needed to realize I love you so much more than I was ever afraid. And just so you are aware...I was very, very afraid. Of a lot of things. Mostly of myself. But I love you even more. I need to be with you, have you in my life. I am your One...as you are my One. Without you, nothing else in the world matters.

He drew back, overwhelmed by all the love he felt flowing from her. Complete acceptance of her place in his heart. No more doubts, lingering confusion, holding bits of herself back.

I...I can't believe it! You accept what I told you, about Mairéad and...

Her mind was so light, so unfettered by the anxiety he was used to finding obscuring her mental landscape that he could barely keep up with her. Aubrey's soul was spilling over his as waves from the sea, soothing him even as there were bursts of flickering sunlight dancing over the crests of the breakers, shimmering with the hushed sounds of the surf. She shared with him how she had been feeling trapped. Joelle's call pushing her into a panicked flight mode, to the point of signing the contract for the trip to Africa, convinced it was the only way she could escape the stares scorching her...Then, as she looked at the cover of her book, whether it was due to being tired, hungry, panicked, or something more, having revelations about her father, and coming to the conclusion she did not want to live in fear another moment.

I finally felt it, Henry...this effervescent knowing, at last, where I am meant to be. It's right beside you, wherever that takes me. You are my home...my heart finds its place in you. I was able to take a deep breath for the first time in my entire adult life. And I swear, I heard my dad singing to me, and the music was everywhere, like a symphony of life in the air, and I know I will hear it, as long as I have ears to hear. In the water. Your arms. Everywhere...It was the most glorious awakening...Mairéad told you she woke up one day, and felt she needed to begin living? I woke up, Henry. I want to continue waking up, every day of my life, with you at my side...

If Henry did not have a play opening for the final show in a few short hours, he would be bearing Aubrey off to bed, so he could show her how the rest of their life would begin, starting right away...

Aubrey then gave a rueful laugh. "Just as I was thinking I had faced my demons without any consequences, I received a call from front door security. Someone was trying to get in touch with me, very urgently...a woman by the name of Emmie Tiller."

Henry had already grown tense with the mention of the signed contract for Voyager Publications, but the mention of

Do You Hear What I Hear?

Tiller threw him into a burst into activity. The ups and downs of this conversation were making his stomach churn. "Tell me what you need. An attorney? A safe place? You can have the farmhouse in Wales, no one knows about it except for family, I can put you on a plane tonight…"

Henry. Peace, my love. Let me show you…

Aware of Henry's narrowing window of time, Aubrey unraveled the woman's visit as quickly as possible: Emmie, shattered by the shock of her husband's death, so shortly after her daughter's, had the entire estate packed into storage. She fled to the familiar safety of her family, several states away, and it was years before she felt able to go through her husband's personal papers. Then she was thrown into another nightmare, as she uncovered the depths of his depravity: the man had kept a journal on his personal laptop, unaware his wife had his password. The trauma of discovering the man she loved and mourned was responsible for their beloved child's death—the nature of her passing, as well as the coverup he had engineered, ensuring he would not be held accountable for the blood on his hands—almost sent her into another decline. In his arrogance, Randall narrated his obsession for stalking "the little Stafford girl" and his plans for stoppering her mouth with clay, sealing away any insights she had concerning blame for Gayle's death. Emmie knew Aubrey was alive when Randall died, and only hoped he had never hurt the girl that Emmie dimly recalled as being labeled by townsfolk as "not all there" with "a vivid imagination." Sickened at the thought Aubrey could well be exhibiting signs of a child who was stalked, harassed, and sexually abused with no one to believe her, she found courage and flew back to the small town she had left years ago…only to learn Aubrey Stafford had vanished. There were many rumors of her having been taken to the county mental asylum, addiction to drugs, and more. The only thing that was known for sure was Patti had withdrawn Aubrey from class one day, and the girl never returned to the local high school. Patti told her friends (who told their friends, and so on) that Aubrey was suffering from an eating disorder and a nervous condition from still grieving her daddy, got her GED, and left town for a better paying job as soon as she was eighteen…and Patti herself died shortly thereafter. Aubrey had returned like a good daughter to take care of her Mama, but then sold up and out, never to be seen again.

Emmie always worried about "the little Stafford girl." Once she learned of Aubrey's whereabouts from the news, once again she dropped everything, this time to fly to New York City. Even though it seemed impossible, she worked tirelessly until she found Aubrey. Emmie was desperate to tell Aubrey she had learned of Randall's true nature, to see if Aubrey needed any help, therapy, adding if Aubrey needed money for treatment, or anything else, she, Emmie, would help pay for it. Aubrey had taken Emmie's hands in hers and promised that while yes, Randall had followed her around and frightened her, he never touched her. Emmie could return home and put it all behind her, as Aubrey herself had done. Emmie was tearful but relieved, and left after reassuring Aubrey that these days, everyone "back home" was "ever so proud" of Aubrey, saying "they knew her when" and there wasn't a word said about her lack of mental capacity. Aubrey's photos were everywhere, she was praised for her "fine looks" and "book smarts." The city council even allocated funds for the library to purchase a copy of any Voyager Publications title having her name attached to it, showcasing them as written by their "local author."

Henry could see that last had Aubrey not knowing whether to laugh or cry. "I sent Emmie back home with peace in her heart, and that's what counts," she concluded.

"I suppose they will be getting a book about Africa to add to their collection at some point soon, then," he replied, trying to smile. He was weak in the knees. If Aubrey was going to

Africa, then he was going to Africa with her. His place was by her side. If she heard symphonies in air and water, then he would be there to watch her dance like whichever *Charlie Brown Christmas* dance scene character she was channeling at the time. He would be there to sing her to sleep, teach her how to dance with him, and listen to her voice soar as she sang, playing her music so loudly he could feel the notes build and reverberate in his bones. That would be his place in the universe, and as she said, it would be glorious.

Aubrey leaned forward and kissed his lips, a butterfly-kiss as she shook her head. "Henry...as soon as I came back upstairs, I turned my laptop back on, because I knew the signed contract would be there. I wanted to see if I had a 'back-out' clause...and as it turns out, I had what Peter might say was a 'Santa clause,' it was such an unexpected gift..."

Laughter burbled in her voice as she added, "I signed it, but never sent the damned thing."

Henry's eyes grew large before he picked her up and swung her in an exuberant circle. "Santa's Little Helper is off the hook!"

Aubrey groaned, then squealed in laughter, but soon her mirth morphed to moans. "Nooo...gonna get sick! And you need to get to Jonathan...! I can meet you after the production, though, if you like..."

Henry rained hot kisses over her face. "Are you joking? I tried to give you this..." he felt about for his jacket, but only succeeded in knocking it off the back of the sofa as his phone beeped, letting him know it was time to leave. "Come with me. I have my own story to tell you..."

He hastily donned the coat, then a heavier overcoat. "Aubrey, there will be photographers everywhere tonight..."

"I don't care." Her smile was serene. "I have you beside me. You will keep me safe from anyone who steps over the line."

"Damn right I will..." Once they were in the express

elevator, Henry's hands were once again pressing her close to him, his mouth exploring hers, until the split second before the doors opened. Aubrey giggled like a schoolgirl, glad her bag contained everything necessary to repair any damages to her face and hair.

Jonathan was overjoyed to see both Aubrey and the liveliness that had returned to Henry's demeanor as they both entered the vehicle. He did not mind a bit when Henry winked as he raised the privacy panel so they could continue their conversation...Henry could continue caressing her, making sure he was in fact awake, and not dreaming.

When Aubrey learned how Henry attempted to deliver the very ticket in his breast pocket, she flushed, ashamed. "I am sorry. I knew how impetuous and stubborn you can be, and I couldn't be sure you wouldn't press the issue, and keep visiting when I was positive your reputation would suffer by association," she began.

Henry stopped her apologies with yet another kiss, and now his hands did not play with her thick hair, but roamed over her body, hungry for her. His own was clamoring to feel every inch of her skin against him, to claim her...Now with Aubrey openly accepting his suit and proclamation of her as his soul mate, his One...and declaring him as hers, as well... he didn't have time, damn it! He wanted to worship at the temple of her body, to declare himself repeatedly...restless and impatient, he tugged at the front of his slacks, now painfully tight.

Aubrey pulled away with a moan and a gasp. "Henry, this isn't the time or the place. I don't want you arriving like this, so uncomfortable and with no way to...not even for a quick..." she licked her lips, unconsciously telegraphing her desire. Henry groaned, checking his watch and looking out the window. She was right! Where was a traffic jam when you needed one?

"I am *so glad* this is the last call on my time," he growled.

"After this, the only person I have to please is you…over, and over…"

"What?" Aubrey pulled away from him in confusion. "Hang on. What on earth do you mean?"

Haltingly, Henry explained. The SUV was just pulling up in front of theater when he finished, explaining, "You will have all the privacy you need, milady Aubrey. All the spotlights will turn off. It will be just you, and me. We can live as peacefully, and privately, as you desire."

"Oh, my beloved." Aubrey shook her head. "No. You love what you do, and I want for you to do what you love…you shouldn't have to give up your heart, to keep your soul." She pressed a kiss to his palm.

Your soul is waiting for you, this time. Go.

Jonathan opened the door, so Henry could alight from the vehicle.

"No more beating against the current, then?" Henry's eyes looked into Aubrey's green ones, and saw his forever.

"No, this Jay Gatsby will get his happily ever after…go."

Once he slipped inside the doors of the theater, Jonathan looked at Aubrey, with a wide grin. "I am so pleased to see him happy once more…I think his dressing room would be soaked in sadness if he left tonight without the two of you being together again."

Aubrey looked down, making a noncommittal hum. "What play is slated to follow?"

"*A Christmas Carol*," the driver replied readily. "I expect Scrooge himself will have his dressing room."

She looked out the window, a dreamy smile on her face. "I think I will walk about until it's closer to curtain," she said. "I want to dream of all the Christmases yet to come. Lots of Christmas carols, but no ghosts, for a change."

. . .

It was the strongest, most poignant, most powerful performance the company had given.

The applause was deafening, the curtain calls endless… Henry was unashamed of the tears on his cheeks, but they were contagious, everyone was sporting them.

Aubrey had a box seat this time, and she agreed with the assessment Christine had made so many weeks ago…they had prestige, but not always the best vantage point. Still, she enjoyed the entire show. She knew Henry would not be able to focus on her, but when Jay Gatsby said, "I knew that when I kissed this girl I would be forever wed to her," his eyes left Nick's to find hers, with his voice purring in her mind:

I adore you, my One.

She answered in kind, when he stopped speaking:

I wish I'd done everything on Earth with you.

In retrospect, it was an error in judgment, for Henry was so moved, he struggled to restrain his tears…but Jay was an emotional character, and it was a fraught scene, so no one noticed anything amiss.

The after-party was, as all parties were, filled with exuberance and relief, hugs and laughter, and promises to keep in touch. To a person, everyone was thrilled to see Aubrey in attendance, many telling her so, as Henry was filled with so much joie de vivre it was as though they were being treated to Henry at his best and brightest.

Greg was so amazed to see the difference in Henry, he could hardly believe he was speaking with the same man as he had conversed with earlier in the day. Pulling Henry aside, he murmured, "Have you had an opportunity to speak with Aubrey about your career decision yet?"

Aubrey popped around Henry and impudently replied, "There will be no need for any career changes…"

Stubbornly, Henry shot back, "I still want a break, Tiny Tim."

"Oh! Oh! You did *not* just go there…!"

"I most certainly did, Elf," Henry replied, a big grin on his face. "I won't need to refuse all of the work, perhaps…but definitely for the first part of the year. Someone has a tour of her own to go on, and I want to accompany her. It will be a fantastic opportunity, to go with someone as part of their support team…and I won't be budged…"

"Coal in your stocking," Aubrey threatened.

"Stick it in your candy cane, Santa's Little Helper!"

Aubrey's face became white then red as Henry laughed, his voice brimming with holiday spirit.

"It's a bloody Christmas miracle," Greg whispered, confused and delighted. He walked away, texting Beatrice all he had witnessed, lest she awaken everyone early and create havoc where none was needed. If Henry wanted a holiday for the first few months of the year, Greg would make sure it happened. Anything was better than his initial proposal.

He also had a special Christmas gift planned for Henry: he was not going to be flying back sitting next to him in a few days as planned, which left his seat available…and he had a pretty good idea who was going to be occupying it: a tiny little redheaded Elf, who even now was laughing merrily as Henry hoisted her under the mistletoe, kissing her to deafening cheers and applause.

"I think he will be happy about going home, this time," Greg smiled, taking photos with his phone. "And 'God bless us, every one!'"

EPILOGUE

BELIEVE

Ten years have passed since *Gatsby* closed on Broadway. Nothing, and everything have changed for Aubrey and Henry. They look a little older, the years sit lightly upon them…

When the curtain rises, the pair are in their shared study in a farmhouse in Wales. There are wall-to-wall bookcases, and a pair of matching desks. One side of shelves contains a vast collection of books, everything you would expect of an award-winning author. *Sea and Sky* was awarded the coveted Booker Prize, and the author proceeded to publish several other novels, collections of short stories, and recently books for small children. There is an eclectic mix of all sorts of works, but not her own, for those are relegated to the bookcase on the other side of the room.

There, on a shelf of honor, rest the works of Aubrey Stafford, and Aubrey Stafford-Rhys.

Above and below are a hodgepodge of awards, lovingly polished by Aubrey but largely overlooked by the recipient. Tony Awards for *Gatsby*, BAFTAs for plays performed in

London's West End. An Academy Award for Best Supporting Actor.

But what are truly loved, and often looked at with great joy and pride, are the photos of their wedding day. Pictures of Aubrey, as she grew round carrying their children, his proud, tearful face as he held his son, then his daughter, for the first time. Countless snapshots of their family as they grow.

Photos of Greg and Christine's wedding, and Peter and Seung's. Family reunion pictures with his parents, sisters and their spouses and children. Goofy pictures, serious pictures, candid pictures, posed pictures.

All filled with love, and laughter.

All proof this is not a showplace of architecture, but a home.

On the floor is a dog bed, covered in fur, because Aubrey hasn't had time to run the vacuum, and Henry doesn't allow maid services into their private sanctum. There are times Aubrey has hired the children from the nearby farm as "Mother's helpers" for an afternoon when she is on a deadline and Henry is either away, learning lines, or otherwise preoccupied…but no one but family is ever allowed in their study. It is too personal. Just as Henry still carries his own luggage (and now organizes the bags for his family when they travel, whether on trains across the continent, planes carrying them anywhere, or even ships crossing the seas), he doesn't want anyone else in what he thinks of as the heart of his home (along with the bedroom he shares with his bride… and the kitchen…and the family room, and the children's rooms, and…).

Well, Aubrey does still crave her privacy.

And Henry is fiercely proud about providing whatever his One desires.

They travel, as Henry's job requires, although he is chary about accepting any role taking him away from his family for long. Aubrey no longer works for Voyager Publications, she is too busy with her own writing and taking care of the two children.

Excuse me, three children and one dog, as she likes to quip in her interviews.

Aubrey is more relaxed these days with regards to answering questions about her life, especially after Henry accompanied her for the publicity tour for *Sea and Sky*. He stuck to her like proverbial glue, always using his ability to ensure she was never taken aback by questions not vetted by Greg, who was more than happy to take a leave of absence from Henry's personal retinue to work for Aubrey in a professional capacity.

The fact he was privately courting Christine at the time had some bearing on this arrangement, but no one minded.

AUBREY'S CONFIDENCE was boosted after one incident with a popular talk show host, Mae Hill, who decided to go off-script in the hopes of gaining an exclusive. She was convinced Aubrey was inexperienced and could be browbeaten into answering any question posed to her. In her smug egotism, Mae mistook Aubrey's soft-spoken manners for insecurity, and on the spot came to the conclusion she would be able to shake Aubrey's composure by asking questions listed "not acceptable" while interviewing her in front of a live studio audience. However, Mae was the one with her equilibrium shattered when Henry strode onto the stage just as the incendiary questions were raised. He had been sitting in the green room, then had suddenly risen, and rapidly begun striding towards the soundstage. Greg had watched him with eyebrow raised, but not challenged him. He had learned there was an uncanny link between the two lovers, and it was not wise to get between Henry and Aubrey when his friend had that look in his eye.

Ever.

Do You Hear What I Hear?

There were some who tried to slow Henry's approach, but upon seeing the look on his face, decided discretion was the better part of valor, stepping aside. Mae's personal security attempted to block him, only to be told by Greg in a low voice, "Just don't, son."

When Aubrey was asked point blank about the events in the New York shopping mall, at first Mae was pleased by the gasps she elicited...until she realized they were due not to her question, but Henry's sudden appearance onstage behind her.

There was sudden riotous applause. She leapt up, seeing even larger ratings for this episode, but noticed how he wasn't smiling at her, walking over to greet her by kissing the cheek she had already proffered, or even shaking her hand, but was approaching Aubrey.

He kissed her Aubrey's cheek instead.

All right, love? I heard her plans, and got here as fast as I could...I knew we couldn't trust her, I am so sorry...

Henry, I am fine, but I beg you, put the trident down. Don't lose your temper. She's not worth it...

Henry's eyes were blue flames as he turned to face the host, his smile more of a baring of teeth as he gave her the barest of nods before he turned to acknowledge the audience, with a more genuine appreciation for their enthusiastic greeting.

"Thank you, but please, I am only here for the ride!" Someone hastened to give him a mic that he attached expertly to his casual sweater. "Truly, I thank you one and all, but I ask you take your seats."

Eagerly, the studio audience did so.

"Henry Rhys, ladies and gentlemen!" Mae gushed, as though she had planned the entire surprise.

"I think they know me," Henry riposted, a shit-eating grin on his face. He turned back to face the audience once more. "I am here because I am proud to say I am Aubrey's first, and biggest fan." He picked up Aubrey's hand, and kissed it gently. The sound of "awww's" and applause filled the room. Mae began to speak, but Henry overrode her by lifting his hand, and continued talking.

"I apologize if you think I am stealing your thunder, my love." His voice and expression was humble, and as contrite as a little boy's as he faced Aubrey. She leaned forward, covering her face with her hands, complexion resembling a beet. Somewhere, Peter was howling: with rage, at Mae's question, with glee, at Henry swooping in, and laughter, at Aubrey's discomfiture. Peter was in charge of selecting Aubrey's outfits for all on-camera events, as Seung was her designer...seeing Aubrey turn so red was not what they anticipated when they chose today's clothing, but as Seung would shrug, "The cat's in with the pigeons now, so you might as well enjoy the buffet."

Seung was full of sayings like that.

Mae leaned towards Henry with a fatuous smile, thrusting her new and improved figure into Henry's direct line of sight. "We're so glad you're here! What brings you to my sofa?"

Henry gave her his most pointed, lethal smile. "I simply need to hear why you decided to ask the top question from the list of topics not to be discussed...Aubrey's public relations manager, Greg Knight, is also my PR man, so I am certain you were briefed how Aubrey finds this a very painful subject, even today. And of course it has absolutely nothing to do with *Sea and Sky,* her novel that is enjoying public and critical acclaim. I am sure you have an interesting explanation. I, for one, am all ears."

The dead air from the silence following his inquiry lasted a full five seconds before the show abruptly cut to a commercial break.

Aubrey never worried about interviews afterwards. She knew Henry was always going to be there for her.

. . .

Do You Hear What I Hear?

It is Christmas Eve, and Henry is grumbling softly about how early their offspring will be waking them the following morning.

"Henry, it is one morning out of the year. I think you can handle waking early one morning," Aubrey teases as she attempts to straighten Henry's desk, even as he gently slaps her hands away.

"Do I try to mess with your desk? Do I? I do *not*," he scolds her. "You would come after me with everything you have, if I was to touch your stacks of papers when you are writing…your chapter print outs, your plot-lines, outlines, timelines…" he raised a mischievous eyebrow, "Waist lines…"

Aubrey looks pointedly at her neat desk, then at Henry's, which is covered in scripts, correspondence, drawings from the children, and so many other things that stacks of paper are listing to one side and threatening an avalanche at any moment.

"I'm busy," he replies with dignity, and Aubrey tucks her chin down, fighting to hide her smile. It's true, Henry is often busy, but with his habit of shoving everything aside as soon as Mairéad (who is three) and Lewis (who is seven) come looking for their Daddy, gravity is often put to the test.

Gatsby, their very large dog of uncertain parentage has also learned Henry will toss a hank of rope for a long period of time, and Henry will gleefully put off tidying his desk in favor of "exercising" Gatsby whenever he comes bearing the toy, eyes hopeful and tail wagging. Aubrey would despair, if she wasn't the one who brought a tiny pup inside, shivering and pathetic, five winters ago. "Serves me right," she sighs whimsically whenever the dog (decreed by the vet to be most likely a Welsh sheepdog cross, "Crossed with a Welsh Cob!" Henry often snorts) climbs into her lap, giving Henry a smug canine grin as he gets between them. Gatsby often lies on the floor in a position Aubrey has affectionately named "Dead

Cockroach," and even the children have been overheard complaining, "Gatsby, get off! Stop roachin' on my bed…!"

"Have I ever told you about the time I met Carrie Fisher and her dog?" Henry asks.

"Only five or six times…a million," Aubrey snickers.

"Elf, I think Gatsby is really a lost reindeer," Henry teases her in response. "Santa is still searching for his lost Little Helper…"

(Aubrey usually has very colorful suggestions about what Henry can do with those comments, hissed in his ear if the children might possibly overhear…Henry habitually follows up with what he would like to do with his Elf, instead, resulting in said Elf turning the color of Rudolph's nose, with one or the other parents looking around calling out, "Bedtime!")

But now, it is dark, both children have been fed and bathed, with biscuits left out for the jolliest elf of them all, and there are the sounds of little covered feet hastening to find their mummy and daddy, with the padding of four feet alongside them. Gatsby might have shepherding of sheep in his soul, but he adapted quickly to the Rhys livestock. They are smaller, much more entertaining, and tasty food dispensers in the bargain.

"Mummy! MUMMMYYYYYY….!!"

Aubrey throws Henry a look of alarm, which only becomes deeper when she sees her husband hiding a smirk behind his hand, turning away from the door quickly. "Oh, no you don't, oh, no you *don't*," she hisses in alarm. "You are *not* leaving me alone to put them to bed by myself…!"

"Wouldn't dream of it, my One," he assures her, stifling laughter by means of sticking his nose in a book, as if absorbed in its contents.

Both of their offspring fight their way through the doorway for supremacy, each bearing an expression of woe and righteous indignation. Gatsby (wise creature) watches from the cheap seats in the hall...

"Now, now, what is it?" Aubrey takes care to speak softly. Henry bends over to pick up Mairéad, giving Lewis a tolerant, rueful smile. He knows better than to automatically blame their oldest as the source for Mairéad's distress. His little daughter has an uncanny knack for getting into trouble all by herself.

"Lewis...! He's gonna eat alla the Christmas candy if Sanna brings any...!"

The look on the little boy's face is priceless. "I never said that, Mummy, Daddy, I never...!" Aubrey bends over to pick up their son. He is still small enough she can lift him in her arms, but not for much longer.

"No, but you *thought* it! I *heard you!*"

Aubrey and Henry exchanged shocked glances. No. Surely not...Not *yet*, anyway!

Lewis has a grumpy expression on his face. "Well, it's not nearly as bad as what *you're gonna* do...!"

Henry is no longer laughing as Aubrey looks at him over Lewis's head.

HENRY? Has clairvoyance ever been a talent spoken about as a gift of the People of the Waves...?

Henry's answer is enough:

...oh, SHIT.

A pair of disapproving little faces turns to face him as Mairéad's voice primly scolds him, "Thassa bad word, Daddy," and Lewis adds, "We heard that!"

"Okay!" Aubrey manages to chirp. "Time for bed!"

Aubrey singing Christmas carols, Henry dancing with his tiny daughter in his arms, they slowly process their family up to their bedrooms.

Aubrey doesn't wear gloves in this home of theirs. Any Voices, any Scenes, are all joy-filled. And although holidays are always celebrated now, she doesn't need to wait for them, because she feels like celebrating every day of the year.

Henry looks down at the face of his daughter...his son...his soul mate, and his heart swells with so much bliss, he wonders how he got so lucky. The dreams he thought would never set sail are all right before him, as he tucks the wee Mairéad with his coloring into her bed...kisses his son with Aubrey's eyes and hair good night...and draws Aubrey into his arms, hearing what she hears:

Sleigh bells.

Melodies in the breathing of their children at rest, symphonies in their laughter.

They hear what the other hears, every single day.

She cast away her fears, and found her strength...he learned to listen.

They believe in each other. In themselves.

In magic, and love. Family, and soul mates.

They learned to listen...to hear...and believe.

The End

ACKNOWLEDGMENTS

Writing is a solitary pursuit, but even still, music can accompany us anywhere we go.

Bearing that in mind, I would like to thank the following musical artists for providing me with inspiration, company, energy to get out of my chair and dance, and songs that provided me with titles for chapters in *Do You Hear What I Hear:*

Glass Pear, Roxette, Billy Joel, Bruce Springsteen, Joel Cory X MNEK, U2, Elvis Presley, AJR, Hozier, Tommee Profitt, Sting, Bing Crosby, Queen with David Bowie, David Archuleta (covered by the enchanting Stephanie Mabey), Josh Groban…and The Piano Guys.

I would like to add my love and gratitude to my father, who died as I completed the edits for this novel. I wish you could have seen this project to its completion, Daddy…I know you carried your version of a trident in your soul. I'm very proud to say I am your daughter.

With all my love,
Claire Hamilton
November 2021

CHRISTMAS ON THE SIDE BOOKS

Dawn Ibanez - Christmas Remix (A K-Pop Romance)

T.B. Bond - I Gave You My Heart (A Paranormal Romance)

Jenna Jaxon - The Present (A Contemporary Romance)

Carly Brooks - The Christmas Fix-it (A Contemporary Romance)

Obelia Akanke - A Holiday with Finesse (A Contemporary Romance)

Nan O'Berry - Old Acquaintance Be Forgot (A Historical Romance)

Hannah Carey - Hunting for Love (A Contemporary Romance)

Claire Hamilton - Do You Hear What I Hear? (A Paranormal Romance)

https://www.facebook.com/Christmasonthesideseries

Made in the USA
Columbia, SC
06 June 2025